A DARK DUCHESS

The Dark Dukes
Book 3

J.M. Diedrich

ARE YOU SIGNED UP FOR DRAGONBLADE'S BLOG?

You'll get the latest news and information on exclusive giveaways, exclusive excerpts, coming releases, sales, free books, cover reveals and more.

Check out our complete list of authors, too!

No spam, no junk. That's a promise!

Sign Up Here

www.dragonbladepublishing.com

Dearest Reader;

Thank you for your support of a small press. At Dragonblade Publishing, we strive to bring you the highest quality Historical Romance from some of the best authors in the business. Without your support, there is no 'us', so we sincerely hope you adore these stories and find some new favorite authors along the way.

Happy Reading!

CEO, Dragonblade Publishing

Additional Dragonblade books by Author J.M. Diedrich

The Dark Dukes Series
A Lady's Duke (Book 1)
A Duke's Keeper (Book 2)
A Dark Duchess (Book 3)

Dedication

You would've loved Lord Bromley, dad.
You are kindred spirits. I miss you.

Acknowledgements

Amy McNulty is a boss and the best editor. Thank you for helping me grow as a writer. (And answering all my annoying questions.)

Gwyn Jordan, thank you for always responding to my texts, emails, calls . . . and loving Percy as much as I do. Cheers to a long partnership with many more heroes to tame!

Kathryn Le Veque, Shawn Morrison, Mary Ellen Sexton, Evelyn Adams, and the rest of my Dragonblade family: three books out in a year. We did it!

To my mom: even as I write this you are wrangling my boys so I can meet my deadline. Your support is helping me achieve my dream. You are appreciated.

Readers. I've been privileged to connect with so many people since I started my writing journey at age sixteen. Readers of every genre from suspense to fantasy and back, but romance readers continue to be the most welcoming and hopelessly wonderful people I know.

Writing this series has been a privilege and a joy, an experience I hope to repeat many times over.

Co-workers, co-conspirators, family, and friends: Thank you.

CHAPTER ONE

London 1892

Percy Cole had to give Lord and Lady Leishire their due; this was the least pompous, mind-numbing ball he'd been to . . . this week.

He took a sip of watery lemonade and resisted scratching at where his wig hid evidence of midnight curls. He accepted the less desirable aspects of his job with sport—the prosthetics, the ridiculous fashion, the itchy head pieces—the only way of rubbing elbows with the elite to don a façade as paper-thin and fictitious as those of the rest of the liars of the *ton*.

The place was a jungle. Vines, thick as his forearm, draped across parapets of marble and coiled around pillars capped in ancient Grecian scrolls. Giant, red flowers hung above, greedily demanding attention—alive, as far as his untrained eye observed. No doubt the reason for the six fireplaces in the grand ballroom to be lit despite the warm night—keeping the plants alive while the rest of the hosts' guests suffered for air. At least they'd all perish in style.

Percy pulled at his collar under the guise of taking another sip of lemonade. He'd never understand the eccentricities of the upper classes: vines on walls; flirting glances over laced fans and calling it wanton behavior; candled chandeliers dripping wax onto esteemed guests in gilded ensembles that could feed an entire family for weeks. He'd like to see these dressed-up peacocks survive a week in the rookeries: no heat, no water, no hope for rescue.

The lady on his right made an off-hand comment about vegetables that had him wishing to stick any of the four knives on his person through the ear and into the brain, preferably his.

His attention strayed to the commotion at the edge of the dance floor, where Hamish and Charlotte Hurstfield, the Duke and Duchess of Camine, had made their first move—a poorly acted heat spell and fainting that would lead them to find a quiet room. The perfect place for a killer to slip in and finish his business.

There was no way Nic Brandt would resist going after them. Not Percy's former partner. The man who would go to any lengths to finish a mission. The same man who'd once sat shoulder to shoulder in the trenches with Percy when they'd been but children—no food, only rust-colored water to drink—all with a smile on his face as the screams of war had echoed around them.

Percy's hand went to the knife hidden in his coat pocket.

Silently working to tear apart Hamish's negotiations in Dockside, going after Charlotte in the woods . . . Percy hadn't seen his former partner in eight years, but it seemed Nic hadn't lost an ounce of skill or his love of machinations.

A shiver of anticipation drew the heat of the packed room away.

Finally, he'd extricate himself from these insipid people and do something worthwhile. The information he'd kept about his history with Nic from Hamish had been unfair to the duke, a man he considered a friend, but his past was a sorted one, one that would reveal too much, for all parties present.

The lady at his side turned to him, her fuchsia dress looking like wilted petals under yards of lace. "What do you think, sir? Aren't artichokes the finest vegetable?"

Percy's lips jerked upwards in semblance of an interested

smile while he racked his brain to remember the woman's name. Between the yards of lace, the feathers adorning coifs, and the overabundance of bustles, it was hard to tell faces from tails, let alone faces from faces.

Memory clicking, he said, "Potatoes, Lady Blanchett. You'll find no finer vegetable on or off the field." *No finer to stomp under foot and feed to the pigs.*

The greying gentleman beside Lady Blanchett—her husband or lover; it was hard to tell by the way she kept brushing against the man's leg, *by accident, of course*—animated. "Potatoes are scarce even now after the trouble in Scotland. Do you grow them on your land, Mr. Seymour?"

Seymour? Ah, right. He'd decided to play one of his less-used aliases as an up-and-coming American merchant here with an invitation from his *personal* friend, the Duke of Lux.

Renard would be livid when he found out.

Percy's smile grew in sincerity. "Potatoes don't grow well in Virginia, I'm afraid, but I've a fine coconut grove imported all the way from the southern islands." Each lie rolled off his tongue more inaccurate than the last.

Lady Blanchett's maybe-husband-probably-lover exclaimed, "Astounding."

The others in their small party nodded in agreement.

Percy smiled at each of them in turn, sure he could tell the fools he spun gold and they'd keep nodding like chickens picking corn from the fields.

"Palm trees don't grow outside the tropics," someone said.

Percy's smile didn't falter. There was always a risk of discovery when spewing falsehoods like sins confessed on Sunday, but talking himself out of trouble remained his best skill.

Noting the naysayer's tone as distinctly feminine, he turned on the newcomer with his most charming smirk.

And startled.

The lady was a goddess made flesh. Tanned skin, as if the lady didn't care a wink for staying out unprotected in the sun. The dark tone set off the amber of her eyes and complemented the lovely, walnut-colored hair pinned on top of her head. She wore no ornaments anywhere except for a velvet reticule that matched that dress . . . Percy had never seen a gown so perfectly tailored to showcase a woman's body as she moved.

His mouth went dry as she popped out a hip, the navy-colored satin going taut across the curve.

She looked him over with a hard set to her jaw, her expression hiding nothing of her suspicion of him. Without a stitch of lace or bustle in sight—and the crafted brilliance of her form-highlighting dress—she was the epitome of real.

And Percy couldn't stop staring.

He shook himself from wandering thoughts of that hip and bowed his head. "Are you familiar with the tropics, then, Miss . . .?"

She offered her hand with a frown and pulled her fingers from his grasp before his lips grazed her glove. "I've read extensively on the islands and their culture. Virginia's colder seasons aren't conducive to plants of the tropical variety. So unless you've a greenhouse the size of the Crystal Palace, your boasts are unfounded."

The lady was prickly, decidedly not taking his hint for introductions. Clever, then, too.

Percy found he could spare a moment more before he must leap into a knife fight. The delicious opponent in front of him deserved attention. And Percy never said 'no' to anything delicious.

"Reading is not the same as visiting." His condescending tone was enough to send most women spitting fire. He added a flourish of his hand for extra effect. "Women should not speak of things they do not know."

The lady didn't so much as nibble at the bait. She grinned instead, her teeth flashing against lovely, full lips. "Neither should men."

Percy decided then and there he had to have her.

Lady Blanchett gasped. "Daniella, that is no way to speak to a guest of the esteemed Duke of Lux."

The woman, Daniella, offered a nod of acknowledgment. "Apologies, Aunt. Perhaps I was mistaken." The glare she shot Percy's way said she didn't mean a word.

A thrill went through his chest. What a thinly veiled attempt at civility. If the woman was a niece of Lady Blanchett, that most likely made her *Lady* Daniella, the *ton's* much-anticipated debutante, the eldest daughter of Lord William Deime, Earl of Bromley. Yet there was no charm, no airs. The woman stared him down like they were rifled combatants on a battlefield, and he was in her scope.

He was delighted.

"Very good." Lady Blanchett nodded. "Mr. Seymour, may I present my niece, Lady Daniella Deime. Daniella, this is Mr. Seymour from America, a friend of the Duke of Lux."

This time, the lady had no choice but to offer her hand again, which Percy took with no small amount of satisfaction, and he brought her knuckles to his lips, where the heat of her skin through her glove sank into his soul.

"What of the animal variety?" husband-or-lover said. "With all the wilds in America, hunting must be a fine fare. What breeds do you keep?"

Lady Daniella's hand was so tense, and the insulting limp wrist was such a tantalizing challenge. Percy wished the other man would choke on his lemonade for interrupting. "Breeds?"

"Dogs, of course."

Percy reluctantly released Lady Daniella's hand and refrained from rolling his eyes. A gentleman wouldn't understand most people had to work for a living. Brutally hunting down innocent animals was of no appeal. Hunting down the guilty and treacherous of the human variety, however . . . "Can't stand the beasts. I keep cats on my farm to control the vermin, but then they are barely tolerable in their illusive manners."

"But dogs are so loyal, and so economic," Lady Blanchett

said.

"And far too fond of coconut for my taste." Percy shot his next statement towards the lovely lady in blue. "Can't get the dogs from the adjoining estate to stop digging up the coconuts as they drop and swallowing them whole. A terrible inconvenience."

Lady Daniella stiffened, no doubt ready for another volley of insults at the ludicrous idea of coconuts being the size of seeds.

That hint of fiery temper earlier needed no kindling. If only he could invite her into a quiet room, he'd see how hot he could stoke those flames. Away from all these simple-minded automatons, he'd no doubt she'd set the entire world ablaze.

"Is that the Duke and Duchess of Camine leaving the ballroom?" Lady Blanchett asked.

Lady Daniella nodded, as if she knew firsthand. "Her Grace was overcome with the heat."

"Will they return?" Lady Blanchett craned her neck to look over the heads of the crowd. "I have yet to offer my congratulations on their recent marriage."

Percy, a head taller than most of the guests, watched Her Grace vanish into Lord Leishire's library, a concerned Duke of Camine in tow, and right on time.

Duty called.

"Apologies, Lady Blanchett." Percy bowed to his companions, his mind racing ahead to what came next. "I must take my leave."

"So soon?" Lady Blanchett exclaimed with abject horror. "But you've not met anyone!"

"Alas, I depart tomorrow for America, and vessels are notorious for early starts on long voyages." He took her offered hand and brushed a chaste kiss upon her knuckles. "Now that I'm privileged to know such charming women on this side of the ocean, I'll be sure to visit more."

Lady Blanchett preened and snapped the fan attached to her wrist open with a womanly flourish. "Mr. Seymour, you are incorrigible."

He winked and glanced at Lady Daniella's lovely, scowling face before offering another bow. A tip of his hat to his opponent, and a goodbye that left a hollow feeling in his chest he could not fathom. "A pleasure."

The ballroom's insufferable heat vanished as soon as he extricated himself from the crowd. Bypassing the main hall, he slipped down a darkened hall and into a central courtyard that would lead him the long way around to the back rooms, and a particular room that adjoined the library from the southern side.

Taking a moment to collect himself—and rid his mind of a particularly distracting pair of eyes—he looked up at the full moon above and breathed in the fresh air and slight dampness from the nearby fountain.

His head was spinning, and it had nothing to do with the heat. Lady Daniella was special. It didn't take a trained agent to see the confidence in her stance or hear the authority in her speech, none of it to do with position or title.

She was a woman who knew her own mind and spoke it without shame. What a treasure to find in this jungle.

"Ha! I knew it. You aren't leaving," a woman said.

Percy snapped out of his reverie and groaned. Here he was too busy imagining plundering the chit to hear she'd followed him. Damn silent slippers. Women should be made to wear boots and bells at all times.

He turned to see Lady Daniella bathed in moonlight, her satin dress looking like waves rippling over her body. His groin went sail taut and mast hard.

"I appear to be lost." He used his best chagrined smile. "You wouldn't be able to point me in the direction of a water closet, could you?"

"Are you here to rob Lord and Lady Leishire?"

Percy blinked. No games, no misdirection. Another time, another place, he'd have fallen at her feet and begged for a direct assault. "Lady Daniella, I fear we've gotten off on the wrong coconut grove. I am here as a visitor, a friend of—"

"The Duke of Lux. Yes. I met the Duchess of Camine but a quarter of an hour previous. His sister, if I'm not mistaken? I wonder, are you not a friend of hers as well? She took ill on the dance floor and went to a quiet room. But I'm sure you're aware of that."

Percy's gut instincts roared at him to end this conversation now. The gleam in her eye was trouble, not only for the fact that her reputation—like that of all ladies—was as flimsy as crinoline. If they were found here together, in the dark and secluded courtyard, she'd be ruined. What an impetuous creature. Any decent man with sense would have walked out.

He stepped closer. "And what has that got to do with me?"

Her breath hitched at his nearness, and Percy fought the urge to close the remaining inches between them. "Come, then, Lady Daniella. Pray tell, what nefarious deeds am I to commit?"

The lady bit her lip, her confidence slipping for the first time. "Y-You hope to rendezvous with your friend's sister."

"You object for morality's sake?" He smiled at that. "Too bad the lady is very much in love with her husband."

Pause. "Do you mean to deface Lord Leishire's home as a political statement?"

"Petty vandalism? Not my style. Try again."

She scowled, a charming puckering of lips and brows. "You are up to no good, sir. Prevaricate all you like, but there is no use denying it!"

"I've no intention to. Please, continue. Shall I rob the baron and baroness of their priceless jewels and paintings?"

Her eyes narrowed. "Perhaps."

"And slip out the backdoor, the pilfered items tucked beneath my arm?"

"I wouldn't put it past you to leave all the items in the attic and worry the authorities for nothing. Then flee through the garden and ruin Lady Leishire's prized roses in spite."

He laughed, unable to hold in his delight. She'd pegged him

right. Brazen, insulting—the woman was a revelation. "A capital idea," he said. He was quite determined to do just as the lady envisioned if there was time. "What a wild life I lead." He glanced down at his Hessians. "Though my boots would be utterly ruined climbing down the garden trestle."

"Feign innocence all you like." She crossed her arms over her chest, her pout indignant. "I see through you, sir."

He played with a curl that had escaped her coif, no longer able to resist. "Let's hope that's not true."

Her breath hitched at his touch, but her voice remained steady. "You hide behind grins and sarcasm. Your fallacies of American crops are idiotic. And I've never heard an American pronounce 'America' in a decidedly English manner."

Percy flinched. He never could remember to keep his 'e's short and nasally when impersonating Westerners. She was a marvel for noticing his perfectly rounded vowels. "Name-calling isn't nice."

Her hair was like silk. Would the rest of her feel as smooth?

"You mislead people from even the smallest truth."

He made a grunt of agreement, then caught himself. "Truly, your imagination is getting the best of—"

"You like dogs," she said.

Percy froze and that tantalizing curl fell from his grasp.

She nodded at his silence. "And cats and even, I daresay, fish. And you *hate* potatoes," she said. "I'd wager my life on it."

His normal, stone-cold calm cracked with a chest full of unknown emotion that tasted like coal and sank into his gut with truth. "Don't waste something so precious on such poor odds."

"You're a scoundrel." She poked him in the chest, her finger not nearly as sharp as her tongue. "I shall expose your plot. You won't get away with whatever scheme you've planned."

Percy pushed the strange feeling away and dropped his mask, letting his easy smile turn cold. The lady didn't know whom she threatened, and he'd been on the receiving end of a gun enough times to know when it was loaded. "I wish you'd have left your thoughts unspoken, my lady. For now, I must do something unpleasant."

She stuck out her chin. "You won't hurt me."

"No?" He closed the space in an instant, catching her by the arms and pinning her to one of the stone pillars before her gasp finished. "You don't know me, Lady Daniella. A woman as perceptive as you should know better. Corner an animal . . ." He nipped at her nose, tasting clove on her skin. "You'll find we bite."

UNDERSTANDING COOLED THOSE lovely, blazing eyes. She swallowed audibly, but her gaze didn't stray from his.

She was bricky. He'd give her that. To accuse him of such things, in a private courtyard, no less. The last man who'd found himself in a similar position hadn't left the yard, open or otherwise. Not in one piece, anyway.

Pulling a knife from his vest, he ignored the internal war raging inside at treating her thus. "Now, how shall I keep you quiet?"

The lady's pulse jumped beneath his palm where it lay indecently against the bare skin at her throat—as silky as he'd imagined—but her eyes didn't widen in panic like they should have.

An expert at deciphering body language, he took in her parted lips and dilated pupils and jolted. "You're aroused?"

Her gaze jumped to his.

He saw the answer there, and his own body coiled into a hard spring.

He'd heard of people having particular tastes, usually revolving around dominance and submission. His friend, the Duke of Camine, had a rather unexpected taste for restraints, but Percy had never heard of a woman finding such things palatable.

Percy laid the flat of the blade against her mouth and watched, mesmerized, as her tongue flicked out to lick the metal.

His body sprung apart. He gritted his teeth and imagined cold storms and that insufferable genius, Gregori, and his less-than-desirable ideas of house cleaning, willing his arousal to deflate.

He forced his mind back to task. Any one of the Leishires' guests could happen upon them in pursuit of their own pleasure.

Feeling the mental power back in his control, he leaned down and whispered in Lady Daniella's ear, "That's a dangerous secret you've got there, my lady. What would your precious *ton* think of such a naughty obsession?"

Shame cleared the lust from her expression.

Percy hated himself for being the cause.

No. He needed her scared, ashamed—anything to awaken the monster she'd unmasked. She was just another mark. Not a person. She couldn't be unique or beautifully intriguing. That was how someone like him got stupidly garroted in a gentleman's townhouse.

"Go on." She pushed against the blade still at chin level with her jaw. "You've drawn it. Go ahead and use it."

As far as bluffs went, it was magnificent. Too bad the haunted look in her eyes ruined the play.

His smile was real. "You shouldn't say such things to a hardened killer. I won't hesitate."

"Then why are you shaking?"

Percy took note of his trembling hands with interest. He didn't remember the last time he'd displayed so much as a tick with a knife at someone's throat.

First, he'd dropped his guard, and now this? Masquerading as the Duke of Camine's bodyguard and runner had made him soft.

Percy released her as if burned, dropping the knife atop the flagstones with a flash of sparks, and stepped back. "Run, my lady." His voice was robotic, his body a maelstrom of confusion. "Run back to the lights and sparkle of polite society, where you belong."

She watched him, her fingers pressed to her neck where his hand had been, but she made no attempt to flee. "You're letting me go?"

Was there a note of regret in her tone? He was the one imagining things now. "There's no need to hurt you, Lady Daniella." He said her name slowly, sounding out the syllables in an unspoken threat so the woman would know he'd not forget. "Not when you'll never see me again."

He turned away, needing her out of view to keep from reaching for her and the forbidden fruit she represented. His excuse was paper thin, and he knew it.

The truth was, he didn't want her hurt. For a terrifying moment, staring down at those sharp eyes and smart mouth, the black heart in his chest had risen from the shadows and given a red-blooded thump of approval.

"What if I don't want you to go?"

Percy closed his eyes at her words, whispered and husky, as if she asked in self-consciousness. *Definitely imagining things.*

"What would you ask of me if I stayed?" He kept his back to her. The lady was bluffing, like before. Did she expect him to turn himself in? How he wished she'd ask something else of him, something far less likely and appropriate. It was his imagination that ran rampant, conjuring scenes of wanton embraces and mutual pleasure.

"I won't say a word," she said.

He huffed. "If?"

His ears strained too hard not to hear her next words clearly.

"A kiss."

He froze. His mind repeated her request over and over until the meaning sank in.

"Fuck." He spun around and sealed his mouth over hers, pressing her against the pillar and running his hands down her arms before interlacing their fingers. Silk and fire. Percy never imagined sparks could ignite against something so smooth, but the friction did more than catch. It blazed.

He needed to leave. Needed to set this woman aside. Even if he didn't have a pressing engagement with the end of a knife, this woman was nothing but a danger.

He knew everyone and, more importantly, knew their secrets. It was his business to know. And when it dictated a gentleman's ruin, it was a true pleasure, but he didn't know *her*. Alarming was an understatement. She could have been an opposing agent. Some of the more progressive foreign offices employed women and children. Lady Daniella Deime could be as she seemed, and still be just as dangerous.

It was her spirit that had snared him. The way she challenged him, questioned him, the way her lips and tongue pressed unsurely against his own. The essence of her was in everything she did and said, and Percy was defenseless against such blatant honesty.

She could go straight to the authorities with his description. Not that it mattered. He changed clothes and demeanor as often as socks as it suited him.

Her tongue flicked against his, her confidence growing.

He could teach her everything.

He broke the kiss and a piece of his soul broke hearing the strangled sound that emerged from her. Years of honed cruelty and coldness were the only things that kept his gaze and voice steady as he looked into those heavy-lidded eyes and told the greatest lie of his life.

"Now keep your mouth closed about me, or I'll kill you."

He fled into the dark, leaving her alone and flushed and God above hopefully as aching as himself.

This had never happened. He'd strike the memory from his mind like so many others. He wouldn't form intimate attachments, so he'd have no regrets and no concerns over what the lady might do.

She'd never recognize him again because she would *never* see him again. No one saw *him*. Lady Daniella may have thought she wanted to play with the shadows and live off the thrill of escaping a blade's edge, but no one stared into the darkness after facing a monster and wanted more.

He'd done her a favor.

Percy ducked into an adjoining room off the library and listened to the sounds of male voices through the wall. He tore off his wig and unbuttoned his coat for easier movement and prayed his friend, the Duke of Camine, wouldn't resemble a pin cushion when he jumped into the fray.

Easing out of the room, he pressed an ear to the door and waited for the sounds of raised voices, knowing there was a fifty-fifty chance he wouldn't walk away from the fight to come. Nor would anyone be the less over his corpse. He cared for nothing and no one.

Lady Daniella's face flashed in his mind, along with an asinine vision of a warm home in the country and her waiting arms.

Hands clenching into fists at his sides, Percy shredded the image with the edges of reality. He was not a gentleman, not a wealthy merchant, certainly not a blasted coconut farmer. He'd never be welcomed in polite society, nor would he have anything save for shadows and death to offer a woman of any station.

He preferred the shadows and lies. No amount of leisure or fantasies of a quiet life in the country would change who and what he was.

Even if some traitorous inner voice whispered for a woman of silk and fire.

Sounds of a scuffle on the other side of the door had Percy pulling a knife from his waist, thoughts of being in the same room as Lady Daniella as he was now laughable.

In what world would the starched and pressed fools of the *ton* ever accept Percy Cole, humble thief and murderer?

CHAPTER TWO

Three years later

"C OME AGAIN?" PERCY said.

"You are the new Duke of Grandfellow," the solicitor repeated, his sneer tempered, no doubt by the prospect of Percy's newfound and obviously fabricated power and fortune.

And if the list of properties were any indication, they were *immense* fabrications.

Percy looked around the small office, checking for feet hidden under the ghastly green drapes or in the corners between overfilled bookcases.

When the Duke of Camine had sent him on his "errand" this morning, Percy had been sure it'd had something to do with a fraudulent claim to the estate or something equally mundane. Now he was certain Hamish was having a go at him as revenge for some previous grievance.

"Your Grace?"

Percy turned on the solicitor, knowing exactly where his knife would fit between the man's third and fourth button of his silk vest.

The man swallowed audibly. He cleared his throat and laid a stack of papers on the desk between them. "The list of properties and tenants are here for you to check." The man looked up and hastily added, "At your leisure, of course. You'll find no indentures. It is entailed, of course, but I've served as solicitor for the Grandfellow estate for forty years," he said with evident pride. "The land and farms were left in fine order by the previous Duke of Grandfellow. I trust you'll find no area for complaint. If you'll sign the deed to the estate, I will send the rest of the paperwork after you are settled."

Percy shook his head.

This had gone too far. He'd wasted half the morning coming to this side of London, and even more time finding a presentable vest and coat, complete with a nauseating top hat and cane, as good a disguise for a gentleman's associate he'd ever worn.

The Duke of Camine may have forgotten Percy's former partner, the lunatic hellbent on murdering the lot of them while they slept, but Percy had not. After Nic's appearance at the Leishires' ball and his subsequent capture by the Merry Men gang, then his break from jail and attempted kidnapping of Camille Louis, Duchess of Lux and also Hamish's sister, at the Cock 'n Hen tavern, Nic had escaped by jumping headfirst into the river. That had been three years ago. Their small group of friends—Hamish and Charlotte, and Renard and Camille—may have been gullible enough to believe Nic had drowned in the Thames after being cornered once again by the Merry Men, but it would take more than a poisoned bit of water to rid the world of that rat.

Percy cracked his knuckles. If Hamish had time to come up with such elaborate pranks, perhaps it was time Percy reminded his friend how he'd earned his street nickname, Vengeance, and how aptly the description fit.

He pushed back his chair and stood. He made it as far as the door, when the other man shouted.

"Wait!" The solicitor scrambled after him. "Where are you going, Your Grace?"

Percy didn't bother turning around. "I've more important things to do with my time than be a part of this farce."

"Farce? Sir, the title and land pass to you, whether you wish them to or not. As the only living male relative of the previous duke, there is no one else to inherit Grandfellow. As the law of primogeniture states, the land is yours by right."

Percy scowled. "You mean by control." He had to hand it to the old man, he *sounded* haughty and put out, like any decent gentleman's solicitor. Whichever thespian troupe Hamish had found him in, Percy would make sure to hire the little man the next time he decided to infiltrate the Home Office. Even the man's facial hair, mutton chopped and sharply groomed close to the chin, had an authentic combination of white and grey.

Guess it wouldn't hurt to play along for a few minutes while he devised the best plan to make the Duke of Camine bleed from his ears and nose.

Percy leaned against the office door and crossed his arms over his chest. "And how exactly am I related to the duke again?"

The man frowned. "One moment." He went back to the stack of papers on his desk, making a grand show of selecting a particularly fine piece of parchment.

This should be good.

The man placed a monocle in his left eye and read, "Jackson Cole, Duke of Grandfellow, son of Frasier Cole . . ."

Percy frowned. Why did that name sound familiar?

"Cousin to Jackaby Cole," the man continued. "Whose son was Jack Cole, father to—"

"Me," Percy said. "You say the previous duke was my grandfather's cousin." The names certainly sounded familiar. He did have a vague memory of a man called "Grandpappy Jack."

If this game hadn't been at his expense, Percy would have applauded the other man's dedication to detail.

But the charade *was* at his expense.

His gaze narrowed. "You certainly did your research."

The man squinted back down at his papers. "The line of succession is verified. Seeing as the duke had no heirs and you are the only son of Jack Cole, you, Percival Jackaby Cole, are the new Duke of Grandfellow."

Percy froze at his given name. No one knew his full name. He'd made sure every scrap of paper or person that could be traced back to him had conveniently burned up, in pieces.

Stomach flipping, a new, and unacceptable, thought dawned. "I'm a duke."

The other man sighed. "As I've been trying to tell you, sir—er, Your Grace."

The man removed his monocle and handed Percy the Cole family ancestry.

Percy took in the sweeping lines and fine calligraphy of an official family registry of the *ton*, and stared at his full, legal name in charcoal black.

"That's impossible," Percy said.

"I assure you, Your Grace," the solicitor said, his expression tired. "Nothing is impossible when it comes to your family."

⋙✕⋘

MR. FRENDSTONE, THE Duke of Camine's butler, personally delivered Percy to the drawing room, where he found Renard Louis, Duke of Lux, lounging on the window seat.

Renard and his duchess, Camille, had been married years ago in a simple and secret ceremony in Scotland. They'd come back to England, holding hands and smiling at one another like lovestruck idiots ever since.

Percy was in no mood for sentimental nonsense. "Shouldn't you be at home, making cow eyes at your wife?"

The other man sighed, his gaze fixed in the direction of Lux estate, twenty miles to the west. His coat and pants were smart in hunter green and charcoal grey, but his sand-colored hair lay curled and unkempt on top of his head. "I was told, in no uncertain terms, to make myself scarce or risk violence to my person via footwear."

Percy smirked, feeling for the first time the world wasn't on a personal mission to ruin his day. "Surely, after the second throw, there would be less of a threat?"

"My lady owns twelve pairs of indoor slippers alone."

"That's excessive."

"Not to her."

Percy felt for the man. Aside from the Duchess of Camine, whom he had a small soft spot for, women were tiresome and fickle.

He pushed away the sudden image of a young woman, dark haired and full of fire.

Hamish Hurstfield, Duke of Camine, entered the room, breeches and coat starched into dangerous angles, making his large build and tall height as intimidating as his title. He smirked upon seeing Percy.

"There you are, Lord Grandfellow." He thumped Percy on the back. "Enjoy your errand?" He rubbed his hands together. "I can't wait for the first ball so I can watch the ladies run screaming for the door." He smiled. "Or watch you do the same when said ladies' mothers dig their claws into your eligible hind."

Percy extracted himself from his friend's reach and remembered he had six knives hidden on his person. "I *will* kill you."

"Be careful, Camine," Renard said from the window. "He looks serious."

Hamish eyed him, and then shook his head. "No, he won't. He's too fond of Charlotte to make her a widow."

Renard snorted. "You mean too fond of his person to risk her seeking revenge."

"And who exactly am I to seek revenge on?" Charlotte sailed through the open door in a lovely blue day dress and glanced at each of them in turn. Eyes huge behind wire spectacles, her gaze flicked from the two guests before settling on her husband with a warmth that rivaled the sun.

Hamish crossed the room and wrapped an arm around his duchess. "Anyone involved in my untimely death."

She pulled back and raised her brows. "Is there a concern

from any company present?"

"Not at the moment."

She nodded. "Good, because your son would like a word with you."

Hamish came to attention, putting on his 'master-of-the-house' frown and taking the request seriously, as every good father of an almost three-year-old would.

"Leopold!"

"Yes, Papa?" a small voice said from the hall.

"You may come in now."

The little boy appeared in the doorway, the very image of his mother with light hair and a stubborn chin . . . and concealing a familiar Y-shaped weapon in his back pocket if Percy's childhood memories of slinging rocks at the local drunks were accurate.

Judging by the nicks Percy glimpsed in the bit of wood revealed in the gap between his godson's shirt and knickers, the boy wasn't a half bad shot.

"Am I to assume you have a request?" Hamish asked.

"Yes, sir."

"Let's hear it, then."

The boy squared his shoulders. "It's sunny, Papa."

Hamish's master-frown twitched with suppressed amusement. "It is."

"And Mama says sun is good for adventure." The word 'adventure' came out 'atentor.'

Percy felt his own mouth curl upwards. The boy had inherited his mother's fine words *and* taste for trouble as well if the slingshot sticking out of the boy's back pocket was any indication.

"Mama is never wrong," Leopold said.

Hamish didn't hesitate. "That's right."

Leopold looked his father in the eye. "We should have a picnic."

Hamish made a good show of covering his smile under the guise of scratching his nose in thought. "Would you say the lake would be a good destination for a group setting?"

Leopold nodded enthusiastically.

"I see." Hamish set out his hand for his son to shake. "The preparations are your responsibility. A gentleman must take his guests into consideration."

The boy's grin was all teeth. He glanced at Renard. "You come too, Uncle Renard?"

"An adventure, you say?" The Duke of Lux glanced at Charlotte, and the two siblings shared a conspiratorial look. "I believe I can free my schedule."

"Capital!" he said, the word sounding more like 'captal.' Leopold's gaze flicked around the room. "Where is Aunt Milly?"

Renard sighed again. "The doctor has ordered her to stay abed until her condition is over."

Hamish clapped his brother-in-law on the shoulder. "Better double the servants' pay now, or you'll lose half by week's end."

Leopold's face fell. "She not coming?"

Percy couldn't blame him. Despite a general dragon nature of treating every man within spitting range with contempt and projectile footwear, the Duchess of Lux doted an offensive amount of time and attention on her nephew.

"But cook made lemon tarts special." The little boy shook himself, regaining his good mood. "We send some to Lux later, so she no feel bad for missing our picnic."

Renard, his appetite having returned along with his new bride, came alive at the mention of food. "Lemon tarts, did you say?"

He came off the window seat like a hound on the scent. "Now wouldn't you think it prudent, young Leopold, to sample the cuisine before making the long trek to the lake? We wouldn't want to get there, only to realize the sustenance wouldn't sufficiently restore our energies."

Leopold gazed at his uncle. "Oh." He glanced at the Duchess of Camine and pointed to her stomach. "Mama, will baby be okay?"

At the startled gaze of his brother-in-law, Hamish sighed.

"There goes that surprise." He shot Percy a smirk. "You knew already, right?"

"Of course."

Her Grace's recent sour complexion had turned into a healthy glow over the past few weeks. Along with her natural gait increasing, as well as her appetite, that would put her at about . . . "Twelve weeks."

"Amazing!" Charlotte said.

Hamish regarded him like a specimen under one of Gregori's glass slides. "Inhuman."

"Come along, Leo." Renard had his nephew by the hand, the other rubbing his surprisingly flat stomach. "We've tarts to taste."

Charlotte smiled at the pair when they paused for approval. "Go ahead. We'll be along shortly."

The two's continued conversation could be heard all the way down the hall.

"Now, Leo, there is something vitally important you must know about tarts before we go too far." Renard's voice was utterly serious.

"What?" Leo asked.

"When offering a lady one, always bring extra."

"Why?"

"That is a way to win her heart."

Hamish shook his head as the two voices faded into the depths of the house. "I shudder to think what the Duchess of Lux will teach him when her confinement is lifted. Between aunt and uncle, he is sure to be a rogue."

Charlotte slipped her arm around her husband's waist and smiled. "Just like his papa."

Hamish lifted her chin and placed a soft kiss on her lips. "Just like his mama."

Percy looked away from the tender display and prayed the couple wouldn't ask him to join their merry parade. Though it was a damn shame he'd miss the tarts.

He thought he'd excuse himself quietly while the duke and

duchess were preoccupied when Leopold came rushing back in the room and stopped right in front of him.

"Uncle Percy." The boy gave him a big grin. "Will you come on our picnic, too?"

So close. Percy offered his godson a smile, the words 'Uncle Percy' doing something uncomfortable to the husk of muscle in his chest. "Of course—"

"Not today." Hamish placed a hand on his son's head and threw Percy a look as if to say, *"I apologize for my role in this morning's derailment of any future happiness."*

"His Grace will be anxious to oversee his affairs now that he's inherited. Isn't that right, Lord Grandfellow?"

The man deserved a slow death. A live burial in the peach grove he loved so much.

Leopold swung to face his father. *"Lord Grandfellow?"* He turned back around. "But you are a spy?"

"Leopold!" Charlotte said.

The boy frowned. "Mama, you say—"

"I *said* Uncle Percy is a man of mystery," Charlotte clarified. "And even if he *were* a spy, it isn't polite to ask outright."

Percy chuckled. "You think I'm a spy?"

Charlotte shrugged.

"I'm not a spy," he said. *Not anymore.*

Leopold's face fell. "No?"

"No." Percy leaned down and gave the boy a grin. "I'm a runner."

Leopold's eyes turned into saucers. "What—"

"That's enough, dear." Charlotte scooted her son over to the open door and threw Percy a scowl over her shoulder. "Thank you, *Uncle Percy*. Do enjoy your new title and running such a large estate."

He waved her out the door, his mood lifting. When she'd left, he turned to Hamish. "She adores me."

Renard came back through the door, a tart in each hand. "I thought we were picnicking. What's the delay?"

"Have you left anything to picnic with?" Hamish shook his head. "Positively criminal how much you eat."

"No need to ship me off to Australia just yet," Renard said. "You've set your sights too low, Camine. Surely, you can do better?"

Hamish barked a laugh, but his expression was hard. "Any day, the Australians will regain their dominion and England must set her sights back on her own borders and the people suffering for the cause. I suggest you do the same."

"Social reform?" Renard popped a mini tart into his mouth and said around the pastry, "What's next? Workhouses? Charities?"

"For starters."

Renard swallowed and eyed his friend contemplatively. "Become a revolutionary while I was busy winning over my duchess, have you?" Hamish nodded. "Where do I send the donations to?"

Hamish gaped. "You'll aid me in relief efforts?"

"With my duchess's pet projects at that forward-thinking home of hers, I must find my own call to arms or risk becoming the exact useless gentleman she once accused me of being."

"How revolutionary of *you*."

"I'm glad you approve, but really, I can't stand it when she's right." Renard grinned. "Just, no more speeches on the public, please. If my lady makes me sit through one more of Ruskin's lectures of bringing England into a welfare state, I may take up gathering in the streets in protest for the cause, and no speech of mine would win any sympathy."

Hamish clapped him on the back. "You've grown, old friend."

Watching the two lifelong friends discuss the ways in which their insurmountable influence and wealth could better the community, Percy knew they'd both grown, and he knew the exact two ladies to blame. He muttered as much. Was this what matrimony did to intelligent men?

Noticing their companion's frown, both dukes offered him sympathetic expressions.

"You're next, *Lord Grandfellow*," Hamish said.

"Thank you, no," Percy said. "Gentlemen acting noble. Ladies running businesses." Lowly street urchins gaining a title . . . "I've witnessed and experienced enough of this upside-down view to last me years of complacency." The last thing he needed was some wife nagging him into a role he had never been meant to play. He'd suffered poverty, starvation, and war, and yet the life of a gentleman might very well be the thing that did him in.

"Love will change you without you trying," Renard said.

"What nonsense."

"He'll fall hard when it happens," Hamish said.

Renard nodded. "Indeed."

Percy scowled. "Don't you two lovestruck fools have wives to placate or shelters to build for displaced families? Little kittens to rescue from nearby trees?"

"Shelters?" Hamish looked at Renard. "There's an idea."

Percy stalked towards the door. "I'm leaving." Before the men decided to rope him into building a church in the foyer for refugees in the name of Utilitarianism. Good men of sense gone to waste over *feelings*.

"Keep an eye out for her," Hamish called to his back.

Percy opened the door and peered into the hallway, expecting to see Charlotte ready to cut him down with a trademark insult. The hall was empty. He glanced back. "Who?"

Hamish's smile was smug. "The future Duchess of Grandfellow sent to ruin you into decency like the rest of us."

The image resurfaced again. A woman, dark haired and dressed in a provocative navy dress, along with the memory of a stolen kiss and a forgotten knife.

Percy *hmphed* and slammed the door behind him, cursing dukes. As nosy as any women he'd ever met.

CHAPTER THREE

LADY DANIELLA NEVER understood why a woman of twenty was considered 'on the shelf.' She was neither a book nor a dish, and, with every passing year as the weight of societal expectations fell away, she felt more invigorated than ever.

She'd had her fair share of proposals. Eight, in fact. An unheard-of number of offers with no acceptances. After the first refusal, society had congratulated her on her sensible and discerning taste. After the fifth, society had dubbed her the less complimentary title: 'London's greatest tease.'

Her mother was beside herself with exasperation. Her papa merely shook his head each time a suitor left his office, knowing whatever dandy came to call, fortune hunter or saint, his daughter would never have him.

It had been rotten luck to find the perfect man at the end of her first season. After a disappointing round of balls and rides in Hyde Park with people far too charmed by their pretentious outlooks, the dark and mysterious man—though not to her—had disrupted her life with adventure and passion, subsequently ruining every other man in recent and future acquaintance.

And then he'd vanished into the night, never to be seen again, and leaving her with a kiss that was seared in her memory for all time.

Danny sat in the Deime Townhouse drawing room, her book open in her lap and her concentration broken—a travesty Lord

Mullbury had ruined her reading since her most recent study on the growing industry of America was fascinating—when her papa entered.

For a man of five and fifty, he was quite square jawed and shouldered, adding another layer of intimidation to his six-foot height and esteemed title.

Lord Bromley nodded silently to her chaperone—a matronly woman by the name of Mrs. Pebblestone, the woman and her name a credit to her inflexible outlook on propriety—and the woman quit the room, leaving Daniella alone with her papa.

"You refused him," Lord Bromley said. It wasn't a question.

The Earl of Mullbury had left, coattails flung behind him, with a loud shout of, "What an insult!"

She was sure the neighbors had heard the disgusting outburst through the brick and mortar.

Her papa, the Earl of Bromley, picked up his pipe from the fireplace mantel and glanced her way as if to check her current state. "He was rather vocal." He shook his head. "No, it wouldn't do to have a son-in-law so in love with his own voice. Better to wait for someone more reserved."

Danny closed her book and rose. She crossed the room and took his outstretched hand, eternally grateful for her papa's revolutionary ideas on his daughter's happiness—as in, believing it mattered.

Her mother may have thought Danny was the manifestation of past sins—the reason Lady Bromley was currently church-bound on a Tuesday morning to pray for a more pliable and obedient daughter—but her papa never gave reproach. If the earl thought anything unbecoming of her refusal of eight proposals— nine, including Lord Mullbury—he hid it behind genuine humor and an unfashionably oiled mustache.

"Thank you, Papa."

He released her hand and turned to the fireplace. "I believe you are a woman of sound mind and impeccable character. If you were a son, I daresay you'd be a force unparalleled by your peers." He shook his head. "But you are not a son, and a father does wonder." He patted her shoulder. "You are of fine design and good humor. It is of no wonder why men seek your hand. Old, young, rich, connected. Lord Mullbury, while a honking goose, has an income any man would covet."

Danny waited. She'd learned men—especially the more internal and cautious of speech, like her papa—had a tendency to speak plainly when given a reflective partner.

He sighed. "Your mother wishes you to marry."

Danny cringed. "And you, Papa?"

He huffed and put the pipe in his mouth, though he would not light it until she'd left the room. "I wish for your brother to take over my seat in the House of Lords. I wish for your sister to remember her place in public. You . . ." He smiled. "My wishes for you are selfish ones, my Danny. If you were to marry and leave, I would need to immerse myself in modern employment to avoid your siblings' natural inclinations towards dramatic nonsense. And I am far too old to start any new endeavors."

It was not an uncommon statement for her papa. Her siblings were indeed full of sport and vigor, but his cadence held a note of reservation that normally gave way to humor. Today, it gave way to silence.

"Something is troubling you?" she said.

He waved her concern away. "It's of no importance."

"Papa." She waited.

He smiled and relented. "There's been commotion over the succession of the Grandfellow title and estate."

"No heir was found?"

"One was found. By Bernard's estimations, a most suspicious man. Didn't believe the truth of it until the old man had given the full family tree."

Their families as close as blood, her papa and the late Duke of Grandfellow had been friends since boyhood—both sharing a neighboring plot as well as the use of the same puffed-up solicitor. Danny took her papa's hand again. "I'm sure the man was surprised is all."

Her papa smiled over their clasped hands. "Just so. I plan to ride over this afternoon and offer my support and aid as the new duke settles in."

Danny's heart gave a squeeze thinking of a stranger living in the house of the man they'd all loved so dearly. The former duke wouldn't hear of his neighbors and friends using his title. As a child, Danny had known Lord Grandfellow only as 'Uncle Jack,' the man who'd boosted her into trees when her little arms couldn't reach the branches, or the man who'd offered her lemon candies before dinner when nothing but gamey pheasant and boar had been on the menu.

When her governess had scolded her for her informal greeting to His Grace, Danny made sure to use the proper honorifics at their next weekly dinner. To which she'd received the greatest lecture of her life, from a man—the refined and honorable Duke of Grandfellow—as he'd rolled up his sleeves and pointed to every scar he'd 'earned' chasing around his beloved goddaughter.

The man had been a staple in her life for its entirety. And now he was gone.

Danny pushed away her grief and offered her papa a smile. "Uncle Jack would approve of your charity and neighborly concern. Shall I accompany you?"

It wouldn't be proper, she knew. Gentlemen greeted other gentlemen as strangers before formally introducing acquaintances, but the Grandfellow and Bromley estates had a long history of friendly connections, and the rules of propriety were laxer in the country than in the city. And, frankly, she didn't want her papa to be alone when he rode by the family cemetery and saw his friend's name carved in grey stone.

"Thank you, my dear," he said, his smile warming. "You know I'd never turn down your company." His smile turned sly. "We'll take the curricle, if you don't mind? I'd like to drive today."

Knowing the two-person carriage would make it impossible

for one rock-named chaperone to accompany them, Danny returned his smile. "I don't mind at all, Papa." She dropped a kiss on his cheek. "I'll go change."

She headed for the door, prepared to clip any emotional threads if it meant staying strong for her papa's sake. She'd be civil and charming no matter what the new duke was like.

But as she glanced back at her papa, his pipe forgotten in his hand and staring into the cold hearth with that same blank expression he'd had when he'd received news his oldest friend had passed, her heart gave a painful ache. She vowed, duke or not, whoever the new Duke of Grandfellow was, if the man so much as insinuated insult to her papa, she'd take the dandy by the ear and give him a tongue lashing to rival those of her dearly departed Uncle Jack.

DEATH HAS TO be better than this, Percy thought.

Standing in the drive, Percy sneered up at what had to be the grandest house in the English countryside.

Columns—taller than the mighty oaks along the drive—lined the front of the house in startling white marble and supported a triangular overhang that had to run a mile long from edge to edge. The yard in front lay green and lush, broken only by a staircase that had been impressive even from the bend on the carriage ride over.

With the inconvenient death of the previous Duke of Grand-fellow—a pretentious name if ever he'd heard one—and a rather annoying family relation, Percy was expected to move into this ghost mansion, or whatever pompous name the structure was given: Grand Manor. Grand Hall. Kill Me Now Estate. Damned nuisance!

As if he needed the trouble of a big house and a nosy staff gossiping to every wagging tongue and grocer about his comings and goings.

And then there'd be the introductions. As misfortune had it, with the season being two weeks from over, every lord and lady would migrate to their country estates—too close to not stop by—and offer their names to the new lord in residence. There'd be country balls and weekly fairs, and idle chitchat.

Forget the blasted servants. He'd cross the border into Scotland and leave the title to rot.

"Your Grace?"

Percy eyed the man approaching in pressed pants and a sharp tailcoat, the grey at his temples and in his vest stating for the whole world the man was the butler of this monstrous house. The man didn't even have the decency to be overweight and balding. Lean and clear eyed, he no doubt would be a credit to his position and impossible to tolerate.

Percy rubbed the ache in his temples seeing the other servant in the butler's wake, a woman in middle-age wearing a frown sharp enough to cut a would-be duke in two.

Remembering the names from the solicitor, he asked, "Which of you is Smith and which is Lancaster?"

The woman stepped forward. "I am Mrs. Smith." She nodded in the direction of her counterpart. "This is Mr. Lancaster. Would you care to meet the rest of the staff, or would you prefer a tour of the house and grounds, Your Grace?"

The noose or the firing squad? There were forty-two servants lining the front stairs—he couldn't help counting—starting from the top step all the way down to the rough gravel drive.

It would take a man half a day to make that climb. "Grounds," he said.

Mrs. Smith nodded and called a man in a smart frock coat and brown gaiters over. "This is the groundskeeper, Your Grace. Any questions you have about the property, Mr. Brinkley can answer. I shall be in the study working on the household accounts when you wish to address the running of the staff."

With a single clap of her hands, the servants dispersed, revealing the full scale of the grand, stone steps. A mountain of limestone to ascend after miles of walking across meadow, moor, and whatever auspicious topiary garden an estate like this had to have somewhere to impress people who wouldn't know the difference between a maple and a bonsai tree.

Percy groaned, his feet aching already. "Let's go in the back entrance when we're done."

Mr. Brinkley nodded. "As you like, Your Grace. Where would you care to start? Gardens? Stables? Lakes?"

Percy didn't miss that all options came in the plural. He should've changed into his moleskin instead of the coat and boots he'd worn into the solicitor's office. Any jaunt in nature and his ensemble would be hopelessly ruined, along with his feet. "What's closest?"

"The hedge maze," Mr. Brinkley said, nodding towards the south side of the estate, where Percy had mistaken a massive wall of trimmed shrubbery for a single-level addition.

The full scale of the maze indiscernible from this angle, Percy sighed and waved the man on. Maybe he'd get lucky and find himself lost in the maze for the next decade, where he could grow monstrous and wild. A damning Minotaur let loose to pass judgement on unsuspecting heroes. Not that baring his torso and legs would work. He was far too fond of his toes to skulk around naked when the snow hit.

No, he would be a wraith, darkness lingering in the shadows of his victims. He nodded to himself, sure if any of these refined servants were privy to his thoughts, they'd run screaming for the hill of stairs before disappearing into the house. An option for later if the staff became unmanageable.

He smiled. Yes, he would do nicely as the ghost of . . .

"What is the name of the house?" he asked.

Mr. Brinkley pushed aside a low-hanging vine to reveal a small opening between the hedge, where a neat, wooden gate stood open in invitation. "Fellow Hall, Your Grace. Though the parks on the grounds all have different names."

To make it easier to identify to which their lord and master referred when demanding trimming or sprucing, no doubt.

Percy rolled his eyes. "Fellow Hall." That wouldn't do at all. No one would flee in terror from *the Ghost of Fellow Hall*. Not when it sounded like an advertisement for recruiting militia.

"Any way to change the name?" Percy asked, three darker, albeit inappropriate for society to mention, descriptors coming to mind.

The older man scratched his head, displacing his cap and revealing disheveled, greying hair.

"Not sure about any of that. My knowhow is for greens and horses. You got questions about those and I'm your man. The rest . . ." Mr. Brinkley shrugged. "Seeing as the place is yours, don't see why you couldn't call it anything you like."

Percy spied another door at the far side of the entrance to the maze, impenetrable walls standing seven feet on all sides in spiny-looking shrubbery sharp enough to draw blood. Renaming the maze 'Fellow Prison' wouldn't be out of the question.

"If you're up for suggestions?" Mr. Brinkley said.

Percy cocked a brow, hoping he hadn't imagined the spirited tone in the other man's voice. "Eh?"

Mr. Brinkley nodded in the direction of a stone statue of a woman tipping an urn, the contents a mystery.

"That there is called *The Grieving Woman*."

Not so mysterious, then. How gothic and morbid. Perhaps the place wouldn't be so insufferable. Percy asked, "The previous duke commissioned it?"

"Nah." The other man rubbed his chin. "Been here since the original construction." He shuddered. "Always gave me the creeps as a kid." Mr. Brinkley ducked his head. "Pardon, Your Grace. I was raised on the grounds. Took over from my father when he passed."

Percy waved his apology away, along with an unpleasant sense of kinship to the man's circumstances. "No need to placate my sensibilities, Mr. Brinkley. The whole place looks like a marble mausoleum."

The older man grinned. "Not a bad name there."

Percy's smile was a surprise, as was the man's informality. "Shall we compromise? How about 'The Woman's Crypt'?"

Mr. Brinkley returned the smile. "I'm partial to the Grieving Mausoleum myself."

"Then 'The Grieving Mausoleum' it is! Well done, Mr. Brinkley. I say, you've a new skill to add to your repertoire. I shall have you rename all the parks on the estate by the end of the day." He twirled his hand to encompass the whole around them. "I assume they're all just as bad?"

In his element or finding solace in the new duke's relaxed demeanor, Mr. Brinkley leaned in conspiratorially and said with no shame, "Wait until you visit Fellow Pleasure Park. It has so many nude sculptures, the name is justified."

Wondering if any of the sculptures depicted a goddess in a tight-fitting dress with hair that looked like coiled silk, Percy inclined his head. "Lead the way, good man. Daylight is wasting."

CHAPTER FOUR

DANNY WATCHED THE landscape change from the wild heath and forgotten moor of southern Kent to the fastidiously cared for and maintained trimmings and plantings of birch and oak along Fellow Hall's drive.

She'd forgotten how long the journey was from estate to estate. Bromley Manor may have abutted the grand neighboring acres for hundreds of miles along the western side, but that short walk from back yard to back yard meant nothing when an introduction required the conveyance of a proper carriage and a roundabout trip through the front gate.

Etiquette never failed to inconvenience everyone. At least her papa had elected to put the top down on the curricle to let in the warm, July air.

Lord Bromley shifted across from her—one hand fiddling with the reins while his other drummed rhythmically on black trousers—clearly as eager to exit the carriage as she.

"We're nearly there, Papa," she said. She spied the Grandfellow family cemetery up ahead, the trademark stone angel visible through a picket of dark iron. Heart suddenly heavy, she drew attention away from that side with a cheerful laugh she did not feel. "What a lovely day! Perhaps we shall be asked to have tea on the veranda. I've missed Cook's apple honey scones."

Lord Bromley rubbed a hand on his belly as if remembering how he and Uncle Jack used to eat the pastries until they'd been ill and had encouraged her to do the same. The grin he shot her way was full of youth-filled mischief. "That woman could make a strip of leather taste like braised beef."

Danny would give her right arm to keep that spark in his eye. "I bet we could steal her away with the promise of a new kitchen."

"Daniella." He frowned, though the spark hadn't faded. "It is bad form to steal servants away from a lord as he gets his bearings."

Danny bit back a smile at the half-hearted reprimand. "Shall we wait a month or so and *then* steal her away? It would give us time to order the necessary equipment for the range."

Her papa threw back his head and barked a laugh. "Devious daughter."

She inclined her head at the compliment and let her smile surface.

She'd missed the easy smiles and easier laughter. Her papa never failed to teach her the complexity and beauty of open communication and unconditional love, two things she demanded for herself and her future, and two things horribly lacking in the nine offers of marriage she'd received thus far.

There'd been some fine proposals. Mr. Pendor had offered no less than six horses—with an accompanying phantom—for her pleasure, and Mr. Richmund had written such a lengthy poem about her beauty, she'd truly felt her worth in such an arrangement. But what men misunderstood, gentlemen especially, was the interactions never failed to sound like the haggled buying and selling of merchandise instead of the foundation of a marriage.

Her thoughts strayed to a different man, one of mystery and danger in a moonlit courtyard, and somehow the most honest person she'd ever met. The man had made every effort to deceive with words and flattery, but his actions had been true to character, whatever that character was.

She blew a strand of hair from her face, one of several that had escaped her coif with the unpredictable wind and berated her lack of restraint. How irritating! She should not be thinking about some criminal she'd threatened in the dark. Her intuition had never failed her. She believed in it wholeheartedly, which made her feelings about Mr. Seymour—undoubtedly a false name—even more vexing. He'd as much as admitted he'd been at the Leishires' home for mischief, but she'd have sworn the man's intentions had been noble.

And that kiss. What humiliation that she thought of it years later and her skin still went warm beneath her dress.

"You're frowning, my dear."

Danny forced the downturned corners of her mouth to lift. "'Tis nothing, Papa. I but fear what Mama will say when she learns I accompanied you today on your visit."

He flinched. "Let's hope the new Duke of Grandfellow is young and handsome."

Because youth and title forgave all. As if her mama would not hope for a match for her eldest daughter if the man were old and as homely as a bilberry bush. Danny was torn between hoping for the latter and dreading the former. Younger men were harder to dissuade.

As the carriage rumbled around the bend and out of sight of the cemetery, Danny breathed a sigh of relief. If nothing else of this visit went to plan, she'd be a successful distraction. Now if only the young and handsome, or old and weed-like, duke would be so accommodating. Danny patted her reticule in her lap, the healthy weight of her newest read—a collection of journals by adventurers explaining the proper footing and mechanics of glissading—and her trusty hand pistol a comfort like nothing else.

Over the vine-covered bridge, through the copse of thick oaks, and out the other side, and Fellow Hall rose up in all its majesty of towering pillars and formidable stairs, the afternoon sun casting giant shadows across the front drive, the same front drive she'd played in as a girl, stacking rocks and earning disapproving glares from Mrs. Smith.

The carriage stopped at the base of the stairs and her papa

handed his card to Lancaster as the butler appeared as if from the limestone itself.

Lancaster bowed. "Greetings, Your Grace, Lady Daniella."

Papa would have none of that. Descending from the vehicle, he clapped the other man on the shoulder and said, "Good to see you, Lancaster. Is the new duke at home?"

"I shall check, Your Grace."

The man made his ascent up the stairs, presumably to do just that, and Danny swore she heard Lancaster sigh. A non-tiresome new duke appeared out of the question. Which left one of two options: The man was old and demanding, or young and arrogant. Both were creatures she'd taken to avoiding for their wayward glances and wandering hands.

Danny glanced longingly at the hedge maze, wishing she'd chosen one of her subdued and modest frocks instead of the vibrant yellow silk that left her neck and arms bare.

Her papa missed nothing as he helped her down. "It may be some time before Lancaster sends word back. Perhaps a stroll in the gardens is in order?"

She hated refusing. "It isn't proper to enter someone else's property without permission."

"Nonsense. Mrs. Smith accepts visitors all the time. You would do her a service by taking yourself. Besides, no one will be in the maze this time of day." He tweaked her nose when she sent him a grateful grin. "Run along now."

She kissed his cheek and made her escape.

There was a trick to the maze, like all great puzzles. Having learned the six lefts, two rights, and four lefts pattern by the time she'd reached eleven, Danny wove through the hedges with confidence, her destination the center of the maze, where one of her favorite statues stood guard over a three-tiered fountain, and a lovely oak bench perfect for avoiding all manner of unpleasantness.

So many of the figures were women, struggling to free themselves from the embraces of devils and men. With Uncle Jack's weak knees and past year of failing health, no one seemed to mind how the hedge had started to encroach on the path, or how the statues along the way sported patches of mossy neglect. A pity that, since the brilliant greens of the leaves had given way to early oranges and yellows of autumn, leaving the entire surrounding feel of a world apart, where at any turn one could stumble upon a mythical creature wandering through the fire of color.

Danny made her second right and came up short at the tall creature standing under her beloved fountain, barely managing to keep her cry of surprise inside. She composed herself and laughed at allowing her imagination to make her a ninny, and instead turned her attention to the most certainly *human* person who seemed to find the fountain as engrossing as she.

Upon further study, the human was far too well dressed in a top hat and navy overcoat to be anything but a gentleman. Perhaps another neighboring peer visiting to admire the grounds?

The man turned to seemingly get a better view of the sculpture in front of him, revealing a strong-chinned profile and black hair that curled below the ear.

Danny gasped. The hair color was different and the ensemble more refined, but she was certain she recognized that mouth and chin from a dark memory that had plagued her every waking fantasy for the past three years.

The man was no gentleman at all, but a devil in a nice coat.

⋙⋘

PERCY DID, IN fact, get lost. While admiring a rather unseemly statue of a man groping an angel's leg, he hadn't heard Mr. Brinkley move on. When he'd come to see the other man had disappeared, he'd shot off through the maze, taking several senseless turns before he'd realized he should have stayed put.

The nearby sound of water prevailed on him to take the next right turn and he found himself at what must have been the heart of the maze, three-tiered fountain front and center.

Overheated from his rush, he stepped up to the water's edge and let the fountain's spray cool him, admiring yet another ridiculous statue of three women twisted into such a knot, it looked as if their feet had fused into a long serpent tail. And the faces: Brows drawn, mouths open in silent screams. Were the women in the throes of passion or pain?

Click-click.

Percy froze. He could've gone the rest of his life without hearing the telltale sound of a gun cocking.

"Turn around," a voice said. "Slowly."

Percy did as commanded. Shielding his gaze from heaven's glare, his eyes adjusted slowly, and the vision of an angel cleared. The lady from the Leishires' ball.

He glanced around, certain a piece of the sculpture had fallen on his head, and he was hallucinating. Checking and finding his head free of bumps, he pinched the top of his hand to find only located pain. This was real. *She* was real.

The same dark curls framed her tanned cheeks. The same burning gaze stared through him, leaving a man to envision the wildest and naughtiest of fantasies. And the same frown, marring an otherwise perfect full set of lips. Lips he remembered tasted like forbidden fruit.

And she was training a Remington Model 1890 at his chest, hands rock steady, like a veteran revolveress's.

Her hands weren't the only things resembling a rock at the moment. Whatever reaction to the fresh air had addled his brain to conjure the image of Lady Daniella, stunning in yellow silk, holding a pistol like she knew how to use it, Percy would never leave the country again.

"Lady Daniella." Even her name was a lesson in temptation. "What are you doing here?"

"That's my line, sir." She leveled the barrel higher, no doubt a sight between the eyes. "I let you get away last time, but I won't forgive you if you mean any harm to this estate."

Let him get away? Looking at her face, remembering how her body was soft and responsive when against a hard chest—*his* hard chest—his body was strung as tight as it'd been the night at the ball. Despite all his best efforts, the truth was he'd never gotten away, not from thoughts of her. But unlike that night, there was no flirtation in her voice, no excitement. She sounded as if any actions he'd take in this place would be a personal assault on her person. Fellow Hall meant a great deal to her.

Percy's stomach dropped out. He hadn't heard anything about the previous duke marrying. Was she the Duchess of Grandfellow?

"You didn't marry the duke, did you?"

She startled, dropping her arm. "Do you mean Jack?"

Jack? Percy's insides revolted against the affection and familiarity in her voice. Good thing the man was dead, or he'd be tempted to stretch his killing muscles and make the old duke bleed.

Her laughter cleared the red haze. "No," she said. "Jack was a good family friend. I grew up coming here." The humor in her gaze evaporated. "If you even think of using the man's death to your advantage, I will drown you under *Athena's Justice.*"

Percy didn't like the idea that she called down the power of the gods against him. One goddess before him was bad enough. He raised his hands in surrender. "I have no intention of ruining anything." At her narrowed gaze, he said, "I speak the truth."

"Really?" She stuck out her chin, as her words struck their mark. "So much for your American accent."

Percy winced. *Damn it!* "Yes, about that . . . There were extenuating circumstances that dictated a more *covert* character."

"Such as?"

Percy blinked. She was asking for details? "They're personal."

She tried again. "Who are you, then?"

He grimaced, but his answer was honest. "Hard to say anymore."

She snorted and shook her head, and Percy didn't like the

new spark entering her eye.

"Well, then." Her sweet smile was terrifying, as was watching her place her gun away in her reticule as if she no longer needed it. "I'll leave you to your personal endeavors, then. Spending the next few hours finding your way to the exit will provide ample time for you to contemplate your *circumstances*, and for *me* to contact the proper authorities."

She turned to leave the way she'd come.

Percy watched, mesmerized at her fierceness, and then remembered he hadn't had breakfast or lunch. "You would leave me here?" he asked incredulously. "With these monstrous statues? To fade away from starvation and thirst?" He'd be impressed by her callowness if he weren't so hungry.

She scoffed, clearly affronted, and pointed at the fountain. "*That* is Athena, the Goddess of War and Wisdom, as she battles her sisters for the good of mankind."

Athena's Justice. Ah.

She wasn't conspiring with the gods, then. Small mercies.

"I am to perish in agony *and* be at the mercy of the gods? You are cruel."

Her brow cocked on one side. "Dramatic, aren't we?"

How he loved that saucy tone, loved how it parted those ripe lips and drew them to one side.

His hunger shifted. It was suddenly imperative she did not leave, not until he got a taste of her. A small one, he promised himself. Not so much he'd ruin her, but enough to last him another three years. He'd go mad if he didn't partake.

She turned away again.

"Wait!" He angled himself between her and her chosen exit. "If I am to be lost here," he said as he stalked closer, feeling his body coil in tight anticipation of her skin against his, "I have a boon to ask."

She eyed him suspiciously, but she stood her ground like a general on the battlefield. "You don't deserve a boon."

She had him there. "True." He smiled, not missing her quick

inhale when he was close enough to run a finger down her arm. Would she make that same sound in bed, when he nudged himself between those lovely thighs . . . He shook himself. A chaste kiss was all he'd take. All he'd allow himself. She did have a loaded gun, after all.

He dipped his head and brushed his lips against her ear. "But I did accommodate you once, did I not? 'Tis only fair to return the favor."

She shuddered.

Percy's blood pumped hot. If he didn't take her in his arms this instant, he'd really turn into the maze's monster, a frustrated beast denied by an angel. But still, he did not act. If she said 'no,' he would not force her or further tempt the temptress. Seduction was for underhanded gentlemen. When he won a woman, it was with a clear head.

He stepped back to give her space. "What do you say, Daniella?" Her name was sin on his lips. "May I kiss you and save us both the unbearable waiting?"

He didn't have to wait long.

She flung herself into his arms. "God, yes." Her fingers curled into his hair and dragged him down so she could demand against his lips, "There's no escaping me this time, sir. I will kiss you until I am satisfied."

God help him. He cupped her bottom and lifted her against him, throwing his pesky morals into the illy-decorated fountain. He was a gentleman now, and it was his responsibility to see to the lady's demands.

He found the duty was no task at all.

CHAPTER FIVE

T HIS WAS MADNESS.

Danny unthreaded her fingers from his sable locks and still could not pull away. His hard stomach and wide torso stretched her hips and bruised her thighs. His hands dug into her bottom, pressing urgently and painfully even through her thick skirts. His tongue and lips were incessant and demanding and even then, Danny wanted more.

She clutched his shoulders and ran her tongue along the top of his mouth, tasting something smoky and complex. The essence of the man himself.

What he was doing here and why didn't matter. Not after she'd spent three years comparing him to every other man in her life and finding no one measured up. She'd convinced herself she'd fabricated the feel of his masculine hand on her neck and the heat of his tongue in her mouth, but she'd not exaggerated his skill or the passion he aroused.

In the fading light, in the middle of Uncle Jack's garden, she was one more fallen woman, another statue frozen in the moment and helpless to break from the demon responsible.

Nothing but a tease.

The thought didn't stop her, it egged her on. There was nothing teasing about his kisses or the grip he had on her hips. This was a man of decision and uncontestable action. And it spurned her wilder inhibitions like nothing else in life ever had.

His hold lessened and her body slid down his stomach and over the ridged protrusion in the front of his trousers. The sensation was exquisite.

She groaned and rubbed the aching muscles between her legs against the length of him until he hissed her name.

He tore his mouth from hers and rested his forehead against hers, the breath in his chest ragged. "You must not do that, love."

His passion thrilled her. "Or what?" she asked, just as breathless.

His teeth flashed in a grin or grimace—it was hard to tell.

"Or I will be forced to lay you down before your precious Athena and fuck you until you have no more use for gods and their justice."

She gasped, not from his blasphemous language, but from the flood of heat between her legs they elicited. Clenching her thighs to keep the wetness contained, his arousal pressed tight to her, bringing another wave of heat and want.

"Damn it, Daniella!" His words sounded painful. "Stop at once, or I will make good on my threat. A man can only bear so much perfection."

Her heart fluttered in her chest. "You think I'm perfect?"

He huffed a laugh, his arms still tight around her. "If no man before me has told you as much, the entire sex is dumb, lame, *and* blind."

That flutter turned into a rabble of wings. She'd been called many things. Over nine proposals, she'd been likened to fairies, goddesses, and Mother Nature herself. But no man, ever, had made her believe the words were true.

"Thank you."

The gratitude seemed to startle him. He chuckled again, a deep rumble she felt in her own chest.

"You're welcome, my lady."

His gaze held hers, the dark grey giving way to a softening of expression and changing the air between them. With his face uncovered, she could see how lovely and warm his eyes were.

He leaned in this time, his kiss unexpectedly soft, and the responding warmth in her chest sank into the very center of her heart.

She was in a great deal of trouble.

Footsteps scraping along the path to their right had his arms instantly setting her aside.

Desire giving way to panic, Danny gasped and fussed at her skirts. They'd had but a moment to catch their breaths and set themselves to rights before a man in brown gaiters drew short at the sight of them.

His gaze bounced from one to the other. Seeming unconcerned by the presence of the man next to her, he turned to her, recognition widening his eyes. "Lady Daniella. What a surprise."

She smiled, hoping her cheeks weren't as flushed as they felt. She willed her voice to remain steady. "Hello, Mr. Brinkley."

The man removed his cap and sketched a bow, revealing an ever-increasing number of grey hairs. "Pardon my manners, my lady. I saw your papa up at the house, but I had no idea you had come to call as well." Sincerity warmed his voice. "It was good of you to come and check on us."

Tears burned the back of her eyes, and guilt churned her fading desire to regret. "I stayed away too long."

She felt the object of her guilt shift beside her, but she focused her attention on Mr. Brinkley, a man she'd known since infancy. "How's your arm? Did it heal after that fall in Fellow Pleasure Park?"

Mr. Brinkley's unbridled smile did wonders for her conscience. "All healed." He rotated his shoulder to demonstrate. "That salve you used on it did wonders."

This time, Danny could not ignore the shifting wall of maleness beside her, not when the air around them seemed to drop twenty degrees at the movement.

She whirled on him, irritation and frustration making her blunt. "What?"

He didn't balk at her tone. His own was too quiet when he

asked, "You put salve on his shoulder? Wouldn't that be difficult with the man's clothes on?"

Her brows scrunched. Was the man daft? "That's asinine. Of course he removed his shirt before I applied the medicine."

His voice pitched lower. "Is that right?"

Danny took in his clenched jaw and hard gaze, disbelief coloring her voice. "You're angry with me?" He couldn't have been serious. "That's ridiculous!"

"Let's leave my ridiculousness out of this, shall we? You admit that you rendered aid to this man without proper dress." He tilted his head, looking like an owl prepared to swoop down and gore his unsuspecting victim.

Good thing Danny smelled the rat.

"Where was this exactly?" he asked. "A crowded garden party? At an evening meal with the entire household staff present?"

She clamped her lips together, willing to give him the details when hell froze over.

"We were in the back shed," Mr. Brinkley said, confusion plain in his voice. The grateful smile he threw her way didn't help. "I'd fallen, as Lady Daniella said. A bad one. My shoulder was so sore, I barely managed to get into a sitting position. But she heard my shout and came running from the maze, used her own handkerchief to wipe the sweat from my face and helped me find a seat in the shed." He shook his head as he regarded her with that same warm smile. "I never saw a lady run like that." He turned now to the predator next to her, where his kindness was not so well received. "Ran all the way back to the house, strong-armed Cook into giving up a canister of her miracle herbs and rushed back. A right heroine."

"Yes." There was no mistaking the sarcasm in his voice. "A regular lady turned saint."

Danny's temper snapped. "That's rich coming from a man who claimed he was an American merchant. What are you supposed to be today? A baron? An earl?"

They stared at one another, ready for a lengthy stalemate.

"He's a duke, actually," Mr. Brinkley said.

Danny startled. A quick glance to confirm he was serious, and she spun around to look at *the duke* in his lying face. Was that how he'd gotten onto the estate? "Since when are you a duke?"

He sighed, the sound tired and full of emotion Danny swore was resignation.

"I don't know. Does the title pass as soon as the paperwork is filed or upon stepping foot on the premises?" He ran a hand over his face. "If the latter, then this morning. A decidedly long morning."

Mr. Brinkley—clearly unaware of the tension—rubbed the back of his neck, looking sheepish. "Sorry about running off, Your Grace. I'll be sure to keep you in my sights when I show you the rest."

Show him the rest? "Mr. Brinkley, you can't seriously be catering to this man's whims?"

Mr. Brinkley nodded, seemingly without taking offense. "Who else would show His Grace the grounds?"

Danny felt the blood drain from her face. He'd become a duke this morning? A bad feeling wormed its way through her stomach. Whatever outrageous thought her imagination was conjuring, it couldn't be true. When Papa's solicitor had said the new duke had been disbelieving, surely, he couldn't have meant . . .

At a shout originating from somewhere outside the maze, Mr. Brinkley winced and asked the man beside her. "Apologies, Your Grace, again. But if I may be excused? There's a fallen tree in the yard that has the stablemaster hot around the gills." He nodded to her. "Lady Daniella knows the maze better than any of us, and seeing as you two are already well acquainted—"

"We're not acquainted." Danny couldn't believe it. There was no way Uncle Jack's precious home and grounds had anything to do with the man beside her. She *wouldn't* believe it.

Mr. Brinkley blinked. He glanced between the two of them, seeming to write his own scenario of them stumbling upon one another in the maze, both alarmed at the intrusion and unable to continue without proper names. He straightened his shoulders and seemed to remember his exalted position as a duke's servant as he said with great formality, "Then if I may? Your Grace, may I present Lady Daniella Deime, daughter of the Earl of Bromley." He turned to Danny.

She held her breath and prayed.

"Lady Daniella, may I present to you Percival Cole, Duke of Grandfellow."

"NO," SHE SAID.

Mr. Brinkley followed Percy's suit and turned to watch Lady Daniella clench and unclench her fists at her sides.

"No," she repeated.

How beautiful she looked when enraged.

"I'm afraid so," Percy said. When the lady said nothing more, he addressed Mr. Brinkley. "Do what you will. Mustn't keep the gills waiting. We'll continue the tour another time."

"Aye, Your Grace." Mr. Brinkley tipped his hat to Lady Daniella, who was decidedly nowhere in the present mind to respond.

Percy sighed. "Might as well go," he said to the other man. "The lady seems to have taken the news hard. I'll wait until she has recouped and then we shall return to the house."

Mr. Brinkley hesitated and fiddled with his cap, his gaze darting back to Lady Daniella. "Can I trust your intentions, sir—er, Your Grace? I've known Lady Daniella since she was weaned. Loved her like a daughter." The last was said with a pointed look. "We all do around here."

Percy appreciated the man's guts—and his fatherly tone— glad he didn't need to disembowel the man for being in love with Lady Daniella. He really liked these boots. "You have my word. The lady will be safe with me."

His last statement seemed to at last shake said lady from her stupor.

"Safe? Safe!" She advanced on him, not seeming to notice how Mr. Brinkley resisted a smile before making his escape into the maze.

Traitor.

Percy faced her head on and raised his hand, understanding the situation perfectly now. "On my honor."

The face she made, he'd once seen that same expression on a sailor who'd lost his boot in the beak of a giant squid.

"If you had any honor," she spat, "you'd relinquish your false claim on Jack's title and give the rightful duke his place."

Wouldn't they all prefer such a scenario?

"Awful as it is," he said, "the claim is real, and I cannot pass it off, no matter how many times I threaten that peacock-vested solicitor."

She'd really loved 'Uncle Jack.' He could hear it in her tone. *Guess the old man couldn't have been all bad.*

"I'm sorry," he said and he meant it. "Clearly, he was dear to you."

Her lip quivered, and he didn't imagine the glassy quality in her eyes. But Lady Daniella wouldn't stoop so low as to cry and let a cad like him off the hook by bungling a comforting gesture.

Instead, she made a graceful turn and walked from the place without a word, leaving him to awkwardly follow her to the rear exit of the maze and onto a fully furnished and gently vined veranda complete with a man in a dark suit who sat drinking tea as if he were a cushion that had always been there.

The man glanced up at their approach and smiled. "There you are, child. Come and sit down before I eat your share of biscuits."

Lady Daniella kissed the man on the cheek, her smile sadly tempered. "I can't believe there are any left."

The same brown eyes and dark brows, the same smile lines around a wide mouth . . . This must have been her father. One glance her way and Percy knew a single word out of line, and he'd feel that goddess's justice she was so fond of.

Finally noticing him, Lord Bromley's gaze widened. He shot to his feet and stumbled towards Percy, arm outstretched. "Jack . . ." The man stopped and collected himself with a clearing of his throat. "Apologies." He ran a hand through his hair, the gesture tired. "You look so much like—"

"Like Uncle Jack," Percy finished. So, the old man had been a looker.

For the man to have gained the respect of these people, it was clear Percy hadn't gotten the entire picture from his late father about their family's estrangement, or lineage.

Lord Bromley's gaze shifted uncomfortably at his silence. "I must beg your pardon for taking tea. We did not mean to intrude."

Percy waved away his concern. Truth was, he could use help navigating how best to conduct himself now he was here, and how best to avoid more calls. He stuck out his hand, getting a feeling the Earl of Bromley wasn't one for ceremony. "I hear you were close as brothers. It would mean a great deal if we could sit down some time, and you'd tell me about him?"

In his peripherals, Percy saw Lady Daniella relax, and he was surprised his words were for more than her relief.

"I'd be honored." Lord Bromley nodded to Lady Daniella. "I see you've met my daughter already."

Percy waited for her to elaborate on what details she wished to confess about their 'meeting,' but she remained silent, ever the cruel creature he was coming to adore.

Good God! Adore? The warm afternoon was curdling his brain.

"Yes," he managed. "She saved me from a fate of wandering my life away in the maze."

The man looked at his daughter and smiled. "That's my girl. Always saving people."

Her returning smile gentled her words so the oblivious

wouldn't feel their bite. "Only the foolish ones."

There was that tone he loved, proper but barbed. 'Foolish' may not have been far off. Good thing estates like these were far between. Only the closest of neighbors would be trouble to avoid, and what was the chance of Bromley's country seat being next door?

He glanced at Lady Daniella, her every skirt rustle and fleeting smile like an assault to his system he couldn't help but feel like a blow to the chest. Having her proximally close would be far too great a temptation. What cruel fate she stood so close—their positions in society at last acceptable for acquaintance, and yet she remained so far above him, he'd never be fit to be seen at her feet, no matter his new title.

And he was the biggest fool for dwelling on it. As the introductions had now been properly made, he need only hold out the next quarter hour or so until she left and he'd never cross paths with her again.

Might as well make the best of the situation at hand. He indicated they should all sit and asked, "Perhaps if it is not so much trouble, you could return in the next few weeks, and we could discuss the estate? I'm sure you have a great deal of insight?"

Lord Bromley looked to his daughter, pride swelling his chest. "No trouble at all, Your Grace. I could come as early as tomorrow. 'Tis less than a ten-minute walk through the woods."

Percy's hand froze, reaching for the tastiest biscuits he'd ever seen, the golden honey spread on top taking on a sickly yellow tint. "Ten minutes?" His gaze shot to Lady Daniella, whose expression matched her deadpan tone.

"We're neighbors, Your Grace."

Dear God, no.

CHAPTER SIX

"WHATEVER IS THE matter, Danny?" someone asked.

Looking up from the book in her lap, Danny became aware she'd not only *not* read a single word of her book since coming out to the lake but had been here for an alarming amount of time if the darkening sky was any indication. Her lengthy visit to the lake the only reason her brother, Lord Donald Herbert Deime, would dare leave his rooms before sundown.

She smiled at her brother's overly long hair—the same shade and texture all the Deime siblings shared—and unshaven cheeks. At least he'd remembered to put on a vest underneath his buckskin coat, though the lime green color meant he'd dressed in the dark once again. "Are the bats out already, Don?"

He paused on the hill and pointed to the treeline beyond the lake, where Danny could make out small shadows gliding back and forth between the spruces.

He hadn't come out here for her. "Oh."

He finished his descent from the hill and sat beside her on the grass. "I saw you from the window. I grew concerned when it had been over an hour, and you hadn't turned a single page. What are you reading?"

Don was always one for details.

"*Savage Animals of the Jungle,*" she said, finding the title more telling about the author's ignorance than the actual temperament of most animals.

"Boring book?" Don asked, sounding scandalized. "Or did you receive and decline *another* proposal that will have us all fending off Mama's attempts to drag us to church?"

Danny ducked her head at her brother's assumption. Though her mama's merciless natter picking had nothing to do with her wandering thoughts. She'd forgotten about the earl's visit earlier in the day. "I'm merely lost in thought." The day had been a whirlwind. "Papa and I visited Fellow Hall this afternoon."

Don looked out at the lake, the first stars visible in the sky reflecting in its placid surface. "How is Father?"

She smiled at his tone, the same reserved concern their father had when asking about his son. "You'd know if you spoke with him."

Don leaned back on his elbows and considered the sky. "He only wants to discuss how I am duty bound to take up his seat and draft bills of institution and charity."

"Or pass laws on animal habitats and integration of understanding into the schools."

He glanced her way and quirked a brow. "Always the peacekeeper."

She nudged him with her shoulder. "I'll have you and Papa reconciling over one of your revolutionary vegetable dinners before Michaelmas."

He laughed.

"Who's reconciling now?" Lady Denise Eloise Deime, their younger sister, appeared beside the reigning willow tree, her slippered feet hidden in the ankle length grass. She glanced around, her mass of curls on her head dangling dangerously to one side. "Has Mama prepared one of her sermons? If so, I can arrange for bedrolls and a lantern, and we can stay out here indefinitely."

"You, stay outside?" Don glanced Danny's way. "Did we get a new sister while I was working in my study?"

"Working?" Denise glowered. "You mean sleeping all day and lurking through the dark woods at night like some creature from a gothic novel?"

"Creature?" Don quirked his head to one side, clearly intrigued. "What kind of creature? *Canis*? *Catus*? *Aves*?" He paused and considered. "That's Latin for—"

"I know the Latin terms for dogs and cats." Denise frowned at Danny. "What was the last one?"

"Birds."

Denise nodded, as if she'd known the answer all along. "And birds, of course."

Don clapped his hands together. "That's marvelous! If you've taken an interest in species, you can help me with my research."

Denise snorted. "I'll take Mama's sermons, thank you."

Danny hid her smile behind her hand. While the three siblings had always found a way to co-exist with minimal bloodshed, recent changes—Don's grant to study nocturnal habits from Cambridge, Denise's forthcoming debut into society with all the fittings and instruction, and Danny's ever-persistent suitors—kept them far busier than any of them liked.

Denise sat on Danny's other side, leaving the three in ascending order from youngest to oldest. "If we aren't hiding from Mama, then is it another suitor? I tell you, Danny, I can instigate an innocent 'accident' the minute the next one walks through the front door: Releasing the hounds inside, a chamber pot's contents thrown over the banister, a pie to the face."

Danny laughed but quickly added, "No, thank you. There's no need to go that far." With Denise, one should never assume threats were idle.

Denise glanced over her head to share a look with their brother, both seeming to come to the same conclusion when they wrapped their arms around Daniella in an unbreakable grip.

Danny gasped. "What are you doing?"

"You may as well give it up," Denise said. "There're two of us and we're all equally stubborn. Now, tell us all your secrets or we'll be forced to throw you into the lake."

"You wouldn't—" She stopped, reconsidered addressing her

sister, and turned to her brother. "*You* wouldn't!"

He shrugged. "We're concerned."

"And letting me catch pneumonia is your solution?"

Denise shook her head. "She's stalling."

Don agreed. "You take her arms. I've got the legs."

"Stop!" Danny scowled as they released her, both enjoying smug smiles of victory. She cursed under her breath. *Meddling siblings, worse than magpies.*

"Out with it, then!" Denise commanded.

Danny glanced back to the house, knowing she wouldn't make it halfway before they caught her. She sighed. "I met the new Duke of Grandfellow today."

"Oh." Danny made a face. "Is he boring? Old? Snaggle-toothed and smells like herring?"

If only. "He's handsome, mannered, interesting."

There was a pause, and then, "You fancy him!"

Give her sister a list and she'd write a novel. "That's ridiculous."

"I've never heard you mention a man as handsome or interesting," Denise said. "The best compliment you've ever used was 'tolerable,' which I daresay meant he was nothing of the sort."

Danny's cheeks grew warm. "I would never be so critical."

"She said 'moderately tolerable,'" Don confirmed. "It was when the Duke of Wembley proposed."

"Which one was he again?" Denise asked. "The one who proclaimed his undying love from the seat of his carriage?"

"That was the Viscount of Wessex. The duke was the one who'd instructed his gardeners to fetch all the lilies from the surrounding ponds to be placed on our drive, leading up to his white charger."

"Yes." Denise nodded, remembering. "Too bad the man had no notion of water plants and their intolerance for sunbaked gravel."

The ache in her temple wouldn't abate, no matter how hard Danny pushed. "If you've had enough recounting my humiliation?"

"Don't be selfish, sister," Denise said. "The humiliation was entirely theirs."

Don patted Danny's hand affectionately. "It is rare to hear you so complimentary."

"I told you, she's smitten!"

Danny frowned at her sister's squeal. "I don't know anything about him."

Denise waved that rational thought away. "Easily remedied. We'll ask around, see whom he knows, check his credit with the butcher."

"That's all it takes for a gentleman to be a catch? A few friends and a settled account?"

"His account need not be settled," Denise said. "As long as he has the funds to make it current upon notice."

"You sound like Mama."

Denise clutched her chest, horrified. "Take that back."

"Shall I inquire about his character at the club?" Don asked.

"He won't be a member of any club."

The words came out too fast, and her sister leapt at the implied admission.

"You talked a good deal this afternoon it seems. Tell us, what else did you learn about the new duke?"

Danny took the hit and struck one of her own. "He's blessed as an only child."

"Poor fellow," Denise said. "I know! Let's invite him to tea."

"He'll be far too busy managing his estate," Danny said, praying it was true. When Denise caught the scent, it took a blizzard to take her off. "And Papa has already offered to make a social call next week. Too much interference from us and the Duke of Grandfellow will avoid us like gnats."

Don stirred. "Gnats are actually quite fascinating—"

"No, they're not." Denise tapped her chin and contemplated her sister long enough to make Danny squirm. "All right. I'll leave the man be, *for now*. But I'm still going to inquire in town to hear what is to be said for the man." She made a face. "I mean, what if he *likes* herring? Better to know if he will smell like oily sea waste *before* you fall in love."

Love? Ha. No worry over that. Danny smiled and wrapped her arms around her ridiculous sister. "Thank you."

Don's babbling about gnats and how their living cycle made them choice prey for the nocturnal predators petered out as he glanced at their embracing forms. "I missed something."

"We've promised not to encroach on our sister's new suitor," Denise said. "Except to make sure he isn't a lover of fish."

"Herring?"

"Precisely."

Don nodded. "I loathe the smell of brine."

"He's not my suitor."

Both siblings turned to her, brows raised.

"He's not," Danny said.

Denise's gaze narrowed. "But you want him to be?"

"I . . ." Danny's lips and tongue wouldn't make the proper denial. There was still the business of the Leishires' ball and the man's suspicious character. But that hadn't mattered when he'd kissed her. Expert kissing. Not to mention the respectful way he'd addressed her papa. Saying she felt nothing for the Duke of Grandfellow would be a blatant lie. The truth was, she had yet to decipher if her feelings were ones of romance or gratitude or curiosity. The connection between them was visceral, over-whelming. Danny recognized the fire his presence set off in her, but whether those flames would smoke out or burn her irrevoca-bly was yet unknown.

"I don't know," she said finally.

"Then it's settled," Denise said, giving a firm nod. "We will help you figure it out."

CHAPTER SEVEN

DANNY STIFFENED AT the soft knock on her window. Lighting the candle at her bedside, she set down her book and tiptoed to where the moonlight shafted onto the dark floor and parted the curtains to reveal a most unwelcome creature.

Wishing she'd donned her dressing gown over her thin nightgown, Danny pushed the glass open and crossed her arms over her chest, letting her visitor know explicitly how she felt about his presence. "I hope you fall out of that tree and break your lying neck."

"Come now," Percy said, looking insufferably well-groomed for a man who'd just climbed a two-hundred-year-old oak. "Is that any way to greet a man who's come all this way to speak with you? The decent thing would be to invite me in."

"Decent? That's a laugh coming from you." She leaned against the sill, no longer able to keep up that back-bruising posture without her corset. "Believe it or not, you're not the first gentleman to climb that tree and ask for entry into my bedchambers."

Smiling eyes turning hard, his tone held a note of danger when he asked too casually, "And have any been accepted in?"

Why did that jealous glint in his eye, the one that promised the slicing of other men, thrill her so? "That's quite the question. One I believe is none of your concern."

She heard his teeth grinding and felt a sense of satisfaction.

Served him right. First, he'd had the gall to be the heir of Grandfellow, and now he was at her chamber window, at a most unreasonable hour and demanding to know intimate details about the suitors in her life. Ha!

"Smugness isn't an attractive look, Lady Daniella," he said.

She smiled, fully aware of how his gaze kept wandering to the untied ribbon at her throat. "Liar."

His eyes widened, but his lips smiled. "Done with the pleasantries already? Very well, then." He crouched low and reached for the branches just above his head. "I suggest you step back."

Danny's arms dropped in her disbelief. "You can't possibly think you'd land safely?" It was a good eight-foot jump.

"Worried about my welfare now, Lady Daniella?" He placed a hand over his chest. "I'm touched."

"You're touched in the head if you think I will call for aid when you break bones doing something so reckless."

"Leave me to the wild dogs, will you? The same heroine who secured and bound the arm of a most grateful groundskeeper? I think not." He readied himself again. "Another step or so back, would you?"

Heart pounding, she grasped the window's ledge. "Stop this! You'll kill yourself—"

Tumbling back, the only thing that kept her head from cracking on the floor was a set of hands that came around to cradle her neck. Warm hands, big enough to be a giant's, and comforting if not for the boulder weight pressing down on her chest.

She gasped and stared up into eyes the color of hard coal and midnight dreams. "You didn't break yourself," she said stupidly.

Those eyes smiled. "Disappointed?"

She shook her head, still dazed. He smelled smoky, like the maple wood bonfires they lit at the country fair every week. Truly, was there anything about this man that wasn't perfect? From those tender hands to those sinful eyes to the hard contours of his figure that was currently pressed all along her barely clothed body.

Her mind cleared and with it came the knowledge of two *imperfect* traits: He was a liar, and he kissed like a devil without so much as a farewell afterwards.

"Remove yourself," she said, willing her mind not to focus on how his thigh was wedged between her legs and the ache it produced.

Those warm fingers tangled in her hair, seeming to be a different distraction for a different person. "I kind of like it here," he said. "Is it not cozy for you?"

'Cozy' was not a wanton enough word for what it felt like to have his fingers brush against her skin. "You're heavy."

Fingers stopping their divine attentions, he glanced down at their pressed bodies, seeming to realize for the first time he'd trapped her beneath him when he'd broken his fall on her person. But he did not move immediately. Instead, he smiled—the scoundrel—and slipped down her body in a most indecent way before coming to his feet and offering her a hand up.

"You're taking this all rather well," he said.

Danny came to her feet, releasing his hand as quickly as possible, and smoothed down her nightgown. "I've found hysterics unhelpful."

"Don't tell me you've had a man pin you down as well?"

"Would that make you jealous?"

"Yes."

Danny laughed. For a man who'd boasted of killing and subterfuge, he was remarkably straightforward. His presence here should have sparked some panic, but Danny found herself uncommonly at ease. She knew something about following her instincts, and he'd had two opportunities to harm her and had taken neither. Words were important, but actions remained the deciding factor of a man's character.

She made for the chair by the fire and sat, shifting to get the best look at him in the moonlight.

Such a lean man. The black moleskin clung to his thighs and arms, both defined but slight, and yet he'd felt like a mountain atop her, as if there were nothing but muscle and sarcasm under the fabric.

Crossing her ankles, she made a point to look at the blue curtains behind him and not at those eyes that seemed to glow in the shadows and see right through *her*. "Now that you've found out we're stuck with each other, I assume you came here to threaten me to keep my mouth shut again." She refused to glance at her bedside table, where evidence of their last nightly encounter lay hidden beneath her daily correspondence. "On with it, then."

"Don't tell anyone about what we discussed at the Leishires' ball."

She frowned. That was it? "Or else . . .? Really, is this only the second time you've threatened someone? The first time was much better."

He chuckled and took her place leaning against the windowsill. "Most people find me terrifying, you know? I'm quite famous in the rookeries."

"Most people believe coconuts are small enough for a dog to eat whole. Besides, I can always shoot you if you do something I don't like."

His gaze flickered to the reticule on the table beside her, her choice of seat in proximity to her weapon now evidently clear.

His teeth flashed into a smile, and Danny was glad for the chair's support.

"I won't tell anyone," she said, rising. "Happy? Now you may go out the way you came or risk a very real possibility of running into our housekeeper, Mrs. Norman. For your safety, I'd choose the window."

He blinked. "That's it?"

She cocked her head. "What were you hoping for? Refreshments? Shall I wake the whole house and invite you to tea?" Really, were men nothing but fools? "If Papa didn't shoot you on sight, my brother certainly would. And blood is such an affair to wash out of the rugs."

When he spoke, it was not with wounded pride, but with something darker, deeper. "What a sharp tongue you have, Daniella."

Why did he have to say things in that whispered tone? And why did her toes curl hearing it? She pressed her feet against the cold floor and nodded to the window. "You should leave."

He didn't move. "And if I don't wish to?"

"I could always scream and wake the household that way."

He came off the sill, shaking his head, and approached with unhurried steps that reminded Danny of the prowling tiger she'd read about just this afternoon.

She held her ground until she had to tilt her head back to keep him in her sights.

He looked down at her, his eyes black and predatory. "You didn't scream."

It was suddenly a struggle to catch her breath. "I did not."

"Why not?"

Her body was floating. His body, his smell, her head spun with it. The man had no right to be so large *and* smell like hidden fantasies.

A slight tug on her hair had her blinking fast and upwards into his smiling eyes.

"Why didn't you scream, Daniella?"

Why would she scream when all she wanted to do was sigh? She leaned into his scent, unable to help herself. "It would not be kind to wake the whole of the house for one inconsequential vermin."

His responding grin was devastating as his fingers lifted her chin. "I'd say you aren't as honest as you claim to be."

The insult in his words, the idea that she was on his same level of deceit, had her feet firmly coming back to the ground.

She batted his hand away, his spell broken. "You make assumptions, sir, and I don't care for it."

He snorted. "My lady likes nothing aside from badgering a man for his right opinions."

"His *wrong* opinions," she shot back, gaze narrowing. This man was an ever-changing path. One minute sensual and agreeable, and the next, completely infuriating. "Arrogance isn't so attractive either, *Your Grace*." She paused. "And I'm not your lady."

"Really?"

His superior grin made her wish to break every mirror in the house, quite a feat since there were at least three dozen on this floor alone.

"Tell me," he said, "do most ladies kiss men without an understanding between them? Or just the ladies you know?"

Danny's mouth gaped. He didn't dare assume such things! "Cad!"

He shrugged. "Better a cad than a tease."

The blow struck true. Danny had heard nothing else from their social circle for years. Lady Daniella, charming and lovely and the worst tease to plague society. *Men beware the succubus's charms.*

She'd never accepted such idiotic labeling for truth. Having standards and being unafraid to lower them didn't make her anything but expectant. And she'd never encouraged a single suitor. Not. A. Blasted. One.

She'd had but three kisses in her life. One a chaste thing by Mr. Pendor that she'd made sure to end quickly and with the understanding made clear a man should wait for an advance to be welcomed. The second and third . . . they had been anything but chaste and with the same man. *This* man. A man she'd let into her bedchambers, barely clothed.

Anger gave way to shame.

She turned her back, unwilling to show him anything less than a warrior's face.

He cursed, and she felt the heat of him through her thin nightgown as he neared.

"Forgive me," he said.

His whisper sent her sizzling.

Never one for girlish outbursts or ridiculous fantasies, she wasn't the naive seventeen-year-old any longer. She was a woman of twenty and she had no illusions of what her reactions to his nearness meant. She'd been courted by nine men, feeling everything from mild amusement to rigid disgust, sometimes all during the same day with the same person. But Percival Cole made her feel nothing but alive. No one else made her want. Made her ache. In the strangest way, feel safe. The rest of the male population may have thought of her as they would: A lady. A tease. Cold and unfeeling. But it would not be the same with *him*.

She knew how this would end. The way *she* chose.

His hands came to her shoulders, hot and big. "Please, Daniella, forgive me. I should not have said such a thing."

She closed her eyes, reveling in the heat and size of him. "No, you shouldn't have."

"I didn't come here to fight."

She shuddered as his lips skimmed her ear. "No, you came to frighten me."

"Is it working?"

It was that final note of vulnerability in his question—so slight, she'd known he hadn't meant to give his insecurity away—that had her twisting around and pressing herself into his hard body. Or was it he who'd twirled her to bring them chest to chest?

When his mouth sought out hers, the who of it ceased to matter. What she'd mistaken as a kindling flame was a raging blaze that had the potential to ruin everyone in its path if not controlled. But there was no stopping the force between them, powered by desire and a blending of iron forged wills that somehow fit perfectly together.

There was no trepidation, only a sense of excitement that should've given her pause.

It didn't.

CHAPTER EIGHT

PERCY BUNCHED HER nightgown in his fists and lifted the fabric until smooth skin met his palms. He shouldn't touch her, shouldn't breathe the same air for the risk of harming her.

But that look on her face had unmanned him. Trading insults like a luscious pirate, he'd mistaken her strength and composure for coldness because he couldn't entertain the idea she was not as frenzied in his presence as he was in hers.

Lady Daniella was not unfeeling or a seductress. She was beautiful and fierce, and Percy knew without asking she'd never encouraged a single man in her life, except one.

"I won't say a word if you kiss me."

He was a bloody arse. Gritty and with the same manners as that of livestock. If he had any decency left in his wretched soul, he'd walk away, leave her in her tidy room with nothing out of place save a few letters on her bedside table.

But his soul had been blackened years ago, before he'd even had a mind to wish it kept pure. He was rough and tasteless, but above all, he was selfish.

"Open for me," he demanded against her lips.

Her lovely legs spread wide and encircled his waist, not what he'd wanted, but perfection all the same. Tongue teasing the seam of her lips, her mouth opened next, and Percy felt he'd found heaven.

He pressed himself against her, feeling every inch of heat

through the thin fabric.

She stiffened in his arms and asked, "What is that?"

Percy looked down at where their bodies met, realizing one of his knives had shifted inside the inner pocket. Holding her against him with one arm, he extracted the blade, watching her eyes track the flash of metal.

Her tongue licked her bottom lip, and her breathing went ragged.

Something close to reverence bubbled up in the dark hole where Percy's heart should've been. What perfection this woman was, to be aroused by something so hard and dangerous. Only a divine creature could love such things.

"Would you like to touch it?" he asked, careful to offer his weapon handle first.

She shook her head, but her focus didn't shift.

His blood roared in his ears. "Shall I do it instead?"

Her gaze shot to his, her pupils large and black. Her little teeth nibbled at her lip, unsure. "It wouldn't be—"

"Please don't say it wouldn't be right," Percy said, the blood in his veins pumping hot. "I'd give up all ten fingers to watch you take pleasure."

Her lips parted, her fingers bunched in his coat. "Yes," she said.

He didn't ask a second time.

Laying her on the rug by the dying fire, he caught the light on his blade and watched her body shudder in anticipation.

Sinking to his knees, he nudged open her thighs and used an arm to steady himself over her.

"Where shall I start, my lady?"

He rested the knife against her cheek, loving the moan that escaped her lips. Lifting the blade away, he moved it to the edge of her nightgown, where it had come untied at the base of her throat. "Here, perhaps?" He moved the blade away again. "No, not there."

"Please," she begged.

The sound was silk against his groin. A small and most unwelcome inner voice told him he was taking this game too far.

He didn't listen.

"I know." He caught the edge of her gown with the knife's tip and neatly cut the fabric away, leaving her exposed to the hips and giving him the most sensual view of her wet folds.

He swallowed and pressed the flat of the blade to her inner thigh.

Years of patience and training kept his attention fixated on every rush of breath between her teeth, every twitch of muscle in her face and hands, anything to indicate she was not pleased with his movements. But with every pass of the flat of the blade against her thigh, she clutched at the rug beneath her, lost in the sensation.

The mewling sounds she made—God, they were erotic.

His erection strained and pulsed in his trousers, nearly spending at the sight of her unguarded passion. Massaging the beast into a more comfortable position, the hand with the knife moved upwards but an inch and her gasp was of unadulterated pleasure.

He watched her head roll side to side and her hips make the most wanton little bucks, moving the blade back and forth, closer and closer to the glistening center of her.

And he couldn't wait a second more to taste her. Securing the blade under his arm, he hooked her legs over his shoulders and ran his tongue along the seam of her sensitive lips.

"My God!" she gasped.

He smirked and blew a stream of air across her bud. "Quiet, my dear. Wouldn't want to inconvenience the staff, remember?"

Her fingers tangled into his curls, nails digging into his scalp. "Again."

He smiled and pushed his tongue inside, the heat of her blazing, the sweet taste of her exquisite.

"Yes! Percival, please!"

His name on her lips was a command of the highest order, and Percy set about his mission with single-minded determination. Fingers parting her folds, he angled his mouth, finishing each thrust of his tongue to lick the bottom of her cleft.

Her pants grew short and breathy. Her hips rose to meet each intrusion as if designed. She was on the edge, waiting for him to bring about her fall.

Without looking, he pulled the knife from under his arm and flipped it, handle first. Timing his thrusts, he buried his tongue into her folds and pressed the heel of the knife against the center of her arousal.

She arched, hands coming to her mouth to muffle screams of pleasure.

Her climax rocked him to his foundation. Every squeeze of delicate muscle around his tongue choked the thoughts and ideas of what pleasure really meant. This woman had lain completely at his mercy—knife in hand—and she hadn't hesitated.

He lapped at her wetness, the taste of her addicting, the sounds of her aftershocks music.

It was blasphemy that such a creature existed without his knowledge. He'd had other women before her—no, there'd been no others and would never be again, not like this. Percy knew it in his bones.

He rocked back on his heels, surprised to find himself unsteady and lightheaded. The woman was a force, taking the very blood in his veins and turning it to euphoric mist.

Quieting, the awe in her voice was not unfounded. "There's no way a mere duke could be so divinely wicked."

He lay back, grinning, and willed his pulse and body to come back to Earth. "A man does like to make an effort."

"Was that normal?"

To think what had just happened between them hadn't been the work of the Devil himself was laughable. "No," he said, not needing to see her to know she was smiling with him. "That was extraordinary."

"Good to know."

He smirked at her prim tone and sat up.

She lay sprawled on the rug, the cream fabric surrounding her tousled hair and angelic face like the backdrop of sun filled clouds.

"You are a marvel, Daniella."

She smiled and the sun shone through. "A lady does like to make an effort."

He laughed and found himself lightly tracing the slope of her calf, completely at ease despite the marital consequences if they were discovered.

And yet . . . "I don't wish to be insensitive, but you must realize, despite what we just did, I have no intention—"

"Of offering marriage?" She snorted, though the flippant sound didn't match the sudden distance in her gaze. "Save the speech, Your Grace. I have no intention of making demands." She rose up on her elbows, her lovely hair draping over her shoulders to provocatively curl around her breasts. "I told you, I'm not one for hysterics." She paused. "*Or* one for gossip."

He believed her. She wouldn't mention their past encounter, or last. She was a woman of her word, a new and strangely appealing trait. But the close proximity of their estates, and the connection with Lord Bromley—the reason he'd left the disgusting equestrian wallpaper and polished checkered floors of Grandfellow in the middle of the night to tromp through the woods and peer into every bedchamber window on the third floor of the neighboring house until he'd found Lady Daniella reading snugly in her bed—complicated what could have been irregular rendezvous as Lord Bromley would no doubt realize his daughter's absences and the new Duke of Grandfellow's happened to coincide. Nor would a routine visit excuse work, seeing as Percy had no siblings, or aunts, or mothers, or women relatives of any kind to use as a front.

He sighed. This had all been so much easier when no one had known who he was or where he rested his head at night.

"What am I to do with you?" he said.

Her voice sounded sleepy when she replied, "I'm up for another apology if you are."

He laughed again, his side hurting from the frequency of use. She understood there'd be no honorable actions on his part and yet she wanted round two. "Insatiable." He was pleased and still painfully aroused. "We risked much doing it once," he said, reminding himself. Any number of household maids could've come at the sound of their raised voices. "It would be unwise to tempt fate a second time."

She huffed. "Tomorrow, then?"

And again, he laughed. Too much more and he'd hurt himself. "We shouldn't."

"We cannot stop!"

No, they couldn't. He'd risk pistols at dawn, hanging, and the altar to taste those silky folds again. Just the thought of what sound she'd make if he pressed the end of his knife's handle into her . . . he needed to leave before logic became the enemy.

She sat up and worried her lip with her teeth, her earlier light and passion gone. "I-If you're disgusted with how I responded to your knife—"

"Don't finish that sentence, or I'll put you over my knee." He softened his growling tone with a quick peck to her lips. "I liked it, all of it. The *you* part especially."

Her sigh of relief irked. Someone somewhere had said something they shouldn't have to make her so ashamed.

He leaned forward to kiss her jaw and promised, "Next time, I'll use three blades, one for each pleasure point."

Her eyes went wide, but her lips parted on a catch of breath. "There's more than one?"

"Many more."

She wetted those lips, and Percy had the urge to begin her instruction on pleasure immediately, starting with how that pretty little mouth could surround his cock and make a grown man worship and curse at the same time.

"Definitely more than a duke," she whispered.

Running his thumb across her lip, he let his defenses slip brick by brick, not seeing the harm now when she had just as much to lose. "I was an officer in the army. Lieutenant Cole of Her Majesty's Third Hussars." He grinned. "Among other stations and titles when it suited me."

Her eyes widened. "An officer?" That beautiful mind whirled behind those eyes before they narrowed. "But you're an officer no longer, not in the official capacity."

Percy blew out a stream of air through his teeth, his reaction alarmingly lacking panic. Who was he kidding? His defenses had crumbled away to nothing years ago in a dark courtyard with nothing but a brush of innocent lips and a will of iron that could pierce his coal-coated heart.

"I'm not an officer in any capacity anymore." He acknowledged her cleverness and loyalty to the promise she'd made him in that same courtyard with a foolish bit of honesty. "But I followed my orders religiously and credibly. I do still, but for a more honorable master."

"So that night at the Leishires' ball—"

"Was its own mission to protect a peer of the realm and his wife."

He waited for an incessant stream of questions. The woman had a knack for interrogation that would make the Home Office question their policy on recruiting ladies of the *ton*. But if he—Percy, the agent who knew everyone's response before they were granted opportunity to speak—thought he could predict the mind of Lady Daniella, he was a fool.

"Thank you." She stood and smoothed down her nightgown before padding to the washbasin and wiping away the evidence of her climax with a strip of flannel.

He watched her, caught between remaining silent to enjoy the erotic view of her lifting her leg while her hand disappeared beneath her torn dress, or asking stupidly, "You're thanking me?"

"Yes, for telling me the truth."

So polite, so straightforward. Then why was he so irritated? "I could still be lying. I could have woven a web of tales you've no hope of untangling to prove I'm right or wrong."

She didn't so much as look up from her task of washing her thighs. "You were honest, I know. You have a tell."

The hell he did!

"What is it?" he demanded.

"If I told you, you wouldn't do it anymore."

His gaze narrowed. "You're teasing me again." She must have been. "There's no way I'd give myself away, not even unconsciously."

She rolled her eyes and dropped her nightgown, sadly, to cross the room and give his left ear a good tug. "Your ear wiggles. Here, at the bottom."

Percy clapped a hand over the offending limb, horrified. "My ear does not *wiggle*." Not a single body part on him *wiggled*, and if it did, it would be a full-fledged shudder of manly presence.

"Flinch? Twitch, maybe?" she offered. "I assure you, it moves."

Ludicrous. Percy prodded at the lobe of his ear, determined magical fairies or haunting ghosts were to blame before his own body would betray him.

Seeing her amused smile, he dropped his hand and his voice. "And your curiosities are satisfied, just like that?"

"Heavens, no," she said. At his silence, she explained, "When I thought you were a criminal intent on harm, I would stop at nothing to uncover your plot. But since you were skulking in the name of Queen and country, I retract my need for sleuthing, seeing as how it is none of my business."

His mouth worked, but nothing intelligible made its way out except, "I do not skulk."

She glanced at him, her face sincerely curious. "Do you creep? Prowl? Who knew a man could be so combative over descriptors that all mean relatively the same thing?"

"I'm not combative—" Percy clenched his teeth together, determined to wipe the smirk from her face. Damn, but the woman could needle him in far too fetching a way. Weren't nagging women supposed to be bothersome and gap-toothed?

Not amusing and entirely too easy to spill one's secrets to. Lady Daniella. He'd rename her Lady Danger . . . specifically in regard to his apparently imperfect poker face. To be taken down by a woman who didn't know how many points of pleasure were on a woman's body . . . "I liked you better naked and moaning."

That smirk curled into a sensual smile. "Me too."

And now he was painfully aroused again. He reclined back on the rug. "You'll be the death of me."

"I was hoping we'd be friends instead."

"Friends!" His gaze jumped to hers.

"Another impossibility?"

"Men and women cannot be friends." He sneered. "There are *emotions* that get in the way of rational thought. Especially when they've . . ."

"Fucked?"

Percy bit his tongue and grunted. It was either that or push her on the bed and taste that dirty mouth again. He wouldn't ask where the lady had learned the profanity. She was known as a friend to the Duchess of Camine, after all.

"What a cynic," she said. "As if a woman couldn't enjoy physical pleasure without turning into a puddle." She straightened and rapped her knuckles on the mantel. "I'll prove it to you."

He didn't like that gleam in her eye, or how his entire body came alert to make sure it never faded. "How?"

"By spending time with me, in public."

"Everything but the public part was amiable," he said. In truth, he seemed to be the fool who couldn't keep his feelings from spilling over into something unacceptable in her presence. It would be better to part ways now and entrust the estate to a more qualified man. "If I so much as think of 'public' in any proper sense, I'll cause a scandal to rival that of D.G. Rossetti."

She laughed. "Then there's no trouble. I have a talent for weathering scandals. And you have a duty to be present in society as the new Duke of Grandfellow."

Mad! She was mad! And damn it, it was catching. "And you'll

be my faithful guide, Lady Daniella?"

"Call me 'Danny.' In private, of course." She nodded. "We'll start tomorrow night."

Private. That sounded promising. "What's tomorrow night?"

"A ball."

"Oh, yes. A ball." If he took a running start, he could leap from the window and break all the bones in his body.

"It will be fun," she said.

He ran a hand through his hair at her bright expression. "I doubt that." Dancing, introductions, *dancing.* Forget the bones. He'd dive headfirst out the window and end all future torture with a quick smearing of the brain on Lady Bromley's bushes.

"Your definition of fun does not sound appealing," he said, hoping to dissuade her.

But the clever minx knew her way around a disgruntled man and how to appeal to his darker side. "Come now, Your Grace. To think a hardened spy would cower from a step or two."

One of her eyebrows arched in a silent challenge that Percy knew before she uttered her next words, he'd rise to meet no matter how many quadrilles were involved.

"I *dare* you."

CHAPTER NINE

D ARE OR NO dare, Percy couldn't do this.

He ran a hand through his hair, feeling exposed without a wig or mustache to hide behind. There was no story this time, no façade or mission. Tonight, and every night here hence, he'd be the Duke of Grandfellow, vulnerable plucked fowl.

He had but two measly knives strapped to his person, the limit his skintight trousers and fitted vest and coat would allow. It was a joke to miss the itchy costumes and web of falsehoods to remember in company. But stumbling through half-formed accents and lying through his teeth were preferable to the spectacle he made now.

He'd slipped Lord Knight's majordomo a few pounds to keep from announcing him like a course at a dinner party, but it was no matter. As soon as his toe had crossed the ballroom threshold—an opulent and nauseatingly gilded room meant to display wealth and power—every eye turned to him, and then the whispers began.

Percy shuddered. Like insects skittering through bones. And he was the lucky corpse.

What the hell was he thinking?

"You showed up."

"Gah!" Percy scowled at his friend, the Duke of Camine, who leaned against the wall behind him, looking self-important in an elegant black coat and white gloves. Percy was in a sorry state if a damned duke could sneak up on him.

"I can't believe you came; I owe Charlotte five pounds." Hamish shook his head. "Why are you hiding?"

Percy indicated the potted plant he'd been using as a shield between himself and the rest of the flesh-eating maggots. "I was admiring Lady Knight's gardenias."

Hamish smirked. "That's a fern."

Percy straightened his cuffs. "I'd have sworn it was a gardenia bush."

Hamish's expression brightened with glee. "Good God, I can't wait for Charlotte to see you. All nerves and primed like a goose at Christmas." He glanced around, no doubt looking for his sharp-tongued duchess, who was currently chatting with her brother, the Duke of Lux, by the refreshment table.

"Your empathy is overwhelming," Percy muttered.

Hamish showed no remorse. "If our roles were reversed, you'd be selling tickets to my humiliation and using the proceeds to hire actors to immortalize the scene on stage."

True.

"Very well, have your fun. Ten more minutes and I'm gone."

"Why *did* you come?" Hamish cocked a brow. "We both know it wasn't for flower gazing."

For a woman. Percy nearly said the words aloud but didn't. A woman who was distinctly missing from said ball. The only reason a man like him would voluntarily enter this glittering hell. If Danny wasn't here, that meant she'd invited him and stayed home deliberately.

What a fool he was to believe her ill-conceived words. *"We could be friends."*

Even now, she must have been regretting what they'd done in her bedchambers.

Percy cursed. He'd told himself to go slow, to take his time. Instead, he'd jumped the gun like an idiot.

It wasn't until now, staring out at the sea of sharks and bottom dwellers, that Percy realized how great an offer friendship had been. Somewhere between last night and today, he'd mucked it all up. The thought made his insides twist, nerves having nothing to do with it.

Lady Charlotte Hurstfield, the Duchess of Camine, glided through the crowd and stopped before them, her wide smile matching the silver ribbon tied at her waist. She cast her husband a smug look. "You owe me five pounds."

Hamish wrapped an arm around her shoulders and pulled her close. "I don't appear to have anything on me at the moment. Would you be interested in a kiss as collateral?"

Her fingers spidered up his lapel, tickling the fabric. "I'll have to charge you interest, you understand?"

Hamish captured her fingers in his hand before raising them to his mouth and smiling. "That's just good business."

Percy rolled his eyes and stepped out from behind the *fern* and offered his place to the two. "A bit of privacy before you scandalize the unfortunate wallflowers? Or is your goal to be thrown out for indecency?"

"Ooo, thrown out of a ball." Charlotte glanced up at her husband. "That's something we've never done."

Hamish groaned. "No more lists, I beg you. We barely escaped a prison sentence with the last one."

Charlotte sniffed. "I didn't care for Egypt much, anyway."

"I was referring to Prussia."

She startled and frowned. "What laws did we break in Prussia?"

"*You* admonished the emperor for not having better tact in his public statements." The look he gave her was full of irony.

"It's a criminal offense to state the truth?" Charlotte sighed dramatically. "You men are such delicate creatures."

"You said it *to his face.*"

Percy admired how the Duchess of Camine didn't so much as blush at the accusation. How he wished he'd been there to watch her insult foreign royalty. He'd always known Lady Charlotte would do great things.

"Never mind me." Charlotte turned her sights on Percy. "Who's blackmailing you and how can I make their acquaint-ance?"

Percy missed his plant. "I came of my own free will," he said, and for extra effect, "I couldn't go a day longer without seeing you, my dear."

Charlotte ignored him and turned to her husband. "Did you force him?"

Hamish raised his hands in innocence.

Her gaze narrowed. "Is there a body cooling in one of the linen closets somewhere? No, don't tell me. I want to look surprised when the maids start screaming."

Percy scowled. Who needed enemies when one had friends? He straightened his cuffs again. "I'm leaving."

This was a waste of an evening. He could be at home, haunt-ing that drafty old mansion, or learning Mr. Brinkley's new names for the *six* parks on his property. Or anything else remotely less mind-numbing than standing here like an exotic animal on display.

"No time for that now," Charlotte said, glancing at a man over Percy's shoulder. "Mr. Richmund!"

A young man in a frightful, rose-patterned vest turned and made his excuses to his current party and made his way over, the frown between his brows not boding well.

Hamish offered the man a quick nod, whispering something in Charlotte's ear that sounded suspiciously like, "Do be kind."

Charlotte offered her hand to the new arrival and said, "Mr. Richmund, what a coincidence seeing you again."

Confusion flashed in the man's eyes, but he took her hand and bowed over it. When he stood, his gaze studied her face and seemed to find something familiar. "Lady Charlotte?" His eyes widened. "Has anyone ever told you you share a remarkable resemblance with your brother?"

Charlotte's smile, Percy knew, was one to fear.

"Never," she said. "What an odd thing to say. I suppose eyesight is the first to go after so many years of drinking. And it's *Your Grace* now. Do keep up."

At Mr. Richmund's baffled expression, Hamish steered his duchess towards the assembly floor, his face carefully blank, his eyes dancing.

"Come, wife. The next set is a waltz," he said, then he added quieter so only the two of them—and Percy—could hear, "When did you start lying?"

Charlotte's response was barely audible over the musician's tuning. "Lying? Dear me, was it not you who suggested I learn to pander to the masses?"

"God help us all."

Percy watched his friendly buoys bob away through the crowd, leaving him the easy decision to wade through the *un*pleasantries of chitchat with the fashion criminal beside him or drown in the scorn of improper societal etiquette.

Percy turned his back on Mr. Richmund, ready to be dragged into the inky depths, when a woman in green pulled his head firmly out of the water.

"Good evening, Your Grace," Danny said.

The way the candlelight made her skin glow, she looked heavenly, halo encircled. Her gown was of the same figure-hugging design as the navy one from the Leishires' ball, but this time the deep, evergreen color brought out the red undertones in her hair.

"You're lovely," he blurted out.

She blushed, twin splashes of pink on either cheek.

He stepped close, forgetting the man behind him, the gawking gazes of the others around them, the room itself, and pressed a kiss to her knuckles. "For a moment, I thought you'd left me at the mercy of the peerage."

Her lips tipped in a coy smile. "You'd have preferred the wild dogs."

She knew him so well.

He tucked her hand in the crook of his arm, feeling at once

comforted by her at his side and inanely foolish for the unfamiliar, gentlemanly action. "Dogs are far more interesting than people. They shred apart their prey for substance and survival." He glanced about the room. "Instead of these vultures that wait until one of their own has fallen and scavenge the ruin until there is nothing left."

She laughed. "Keep referencing the animal kingdom and my brother will dig *his* claws into you."

Percy envisioned a burly man with a taste for upholding sisterly honor. "Should I be concerned?"

"Only of long nights researching the flight patterns of the brown long-eared bat."

"Scholarly minded." Percy grimaced thinking of Gregori, Hamish's foreign inventor and their friend, and the man's terrifying focus. "I'll take the dogs and the vultures."

Danny's teasing tone was filled with amusement. "You fear book-laden lairs?"

"Any lair where neither survival nor malice are motivators."

"What, then?"

"Curiosity."

Danny laughed. "I have to disagree. Don is harmless compared to the other one."

Her smile was contagious. Other one? "Another brother?"

"Worse."

"Talking about me already?" someone said.

Percy turned to view their latest party addition, a woman who bore a striking resemblance to Danny with almond-colored hair and a full mouth, but where Danny's eyes filled with challenging fire, this younger woman's gaze was nothing but cold calculation.

Danny groaned beside him, and the sound seemed to spurn the other woman's smile.

"Come now, Danny," the woman said, the cold gaze giving way to mischief. "Won't you introduce me to your new friend?"

"WHERE IS MRS. Pebblestone?" Danny asked.

"I lost her around the punchbowl." Denise's gaze didn't leave the Duke of Grandfellow. "You're short for a man."

Danny sighed at her sister's thinly veiled insult. This was going to end in tears.

Danny thought she'd feel more over losing her virginity: regret, anxiety, fear. But being in the Duke of Grandfellow's presence again had diminished any lingering concern. Frankly, she didn't miss the society-coveted chastity, and the man had a way of putting her at ease—ridiculously—considering he offered no real information about himself without a fight. Fighting with him was electrifying.

A fight between him and her overreaching, brutally forthright sister, however . . .

Weighing the options of a doomed introduction or the future wrath of her mother, Danny reluctantly, albeit childishly, made a grand flourish of her hand to encompass all that was her troublesome sister. "Your Grace, may I present my sister, Lady Denise. Denise, this is Percival Cole, the new Duke of Grandfellow."

Denise's eyes widened over Percy's obligatory kiss to the hand. The look she threw Danny's way had her groaning a second time in as many minutes. "*You're* the handsome, interesting one?"

Percy glanced at Danny, brow raised. "Handsome?"

Danny gritted her teeth. Her sister's passion for inciting discourse was not what this evening needed. "Don't mind her. She's to be institutionalized as soon as I can forge Mama's signature."

Denise blew her a kiss and linked arms with Percy as if they were old friends, and something ugly settled in Danny's stomach.

"Such an eyesore, those gardens at Grandfellow. Unkempt, confusing." Denise pulled him along the edge of the dance floor, forcing Danny to take Percy's other side like an additional wheel on an already full axle. "Wouldn't you agree, Your Grace? The sculptures in the maze alone are positively gruesome."

"And she's off," Danny muttered.

Percy's mouth quirked, but his gaze captured Danny's on his other side when he replied, "I can't say I agree, Lady Denise. *Athena's Justice*, for instance, has become quite a favorite of mine after consideration. The figures alone are *stimulating*."

Danny's body heated at his silken tone. Yes, the sculpture was quickly becoming her favorite as well, but it had less to do with craftsmanship and more to do with the memory of fevered kisses and a threat to take her virginity on the fountain's edge.

"What a coincidence; Danny finds the sculptures more whimsical than savage as well."

Danny cut her sister a glare as if to say, *"You promised you wouldn't interfere."*

Denise's responding smile said, *"You wouldn't want me to be rude to our neighbor."*

"Yes, I would."

"Did you say something, dear sister?" Denise asked.

Having realized she'd said her last words out loud, Danny smiled sweetly at her sister and repeated, "I would love to find the refreshments with you, Denise." Extricating her sister's arm from Percy's, she offered him an apologetic look. "Excuse us, Your Grace."

Percy's lip twitched again, but he bowed his head. "Wouldn't want to overheat in this crowded room."

Denise tugged at her arm. "Actually, I—"

"Am famished?" Danny towed her sister away and out of earshot. "What is wrong with you?"

"What? He *is* handsome. *And* interesting."

Danny stopped them next to a table laden with tarts and sweetmeats, concern turning the sugary scent bitter. After her conversation with Percy last night, she now understood how dangerous it was to ask questions. "Forget whatever you learned." She'd need to take Don aside as well before someone took their family's inquiry as a liability. From what she'd surmised from her conversation with Percy in her bedchamber, his role as a man of the Crown didn't stop at the battlefield. Percy the agent wasn't out of the question. She believed the Home Office had their country's best interests at the forefront of policy, but the shadows in Percy's eyes weren't from patriotic pride.

The secrets he kept, whatever they were, ate at him.

Her own curiosity reared its cat-like head, but she pushed it away. Percy would tell her when he was ready if they could get a second alone. "Promise me, Denise. You will tell no one?"

Denise considered her in that maddening silent predator way she had, her gaze hard and focused, gauging how far she could manipulate the situation before her prey lashed out in self-defense.

"I'm serious, Denny," Danny said.

Denise's brow cocked at the childhood nickname. It had been years since the siblings had outgrown the trio of cute names: Donny, Danny, Denny. "Clearly." She waved her hand back and forth, dispensing with the posturing. "If that's what you want."

Far too easy. "I mean it."

Denise rolled her eyes. "Don't be so suspicious, sister. It will sour your complexion. Even I can acknowledge not every secret needs airing." Her gaze flicked to where Percy shook hands with the Duke of Lux across the room. "I like him. He's hard to read but composed."

Her sister's approval was strangely reassuring, though Denise's assessment was all wrong. It amazed her how no one else saw how Percy kept straightening his cuffs and running his hand through his hair, clearly uncomfortable with wearing his real face.

"You should marry him."

Danny startled at her sister's words. "What? He's a *friend*." Who happened to bring her to shattering orgasms with his tongue. Marrying would ruin everything. Gentlemen wanted docile and placating wives. *Innocent wives.* Not that Percy seemed the kind of man to turn his nose up at a woman with darker tastes.

Denise didn't miss her flushed cheeks. "You're attracted. Plus, he's rich, handsome." She shrugged. "Doesn't flinch when teased."

"Your ideas of what makes a man desirable baffles me." Danny crushed her racing heart. "Anything else?"

"Yes." Denise gave her a pointed look. "He makes you smile and blush and"—she scrunched her nose—"I don't know, glow, maybe."

"Glow?"

Denise mocked shielding her eyes. "I swear my eyes are watering. I may need to find relief behind a potted plant until you dim to acceptable vision standards."

"Be serious." Danny turned away from her sister's scandalous display, only to find the source of their conversation.

Danny cataloged the sensual tilt of Percy's mouth and the strong, square jaw and charming cleft in his chin.

As if feeling her gaze, he looked over and their gazes locked.

The couples on the floor slowed, the sound of the orchestra muffled. There was a stolen moment in time and then there was this; when time itself stole away, leaving everyone and everything in suspended animation.

Danny tried to blink but couldn't. Nor could she look away. Percy took up her whole view and more, as if she were looking at more than the present, but also a not-so-distant future.

A set of gloved fingers snapped in her face.

Danny blinked and turned her attention to her sister's smirking face.

"Go ask him to dance," Denise said.

Sound and reality crashed back in, along with a thrill at the bold idea. "I couldn't."

"Why not? Friends can't dance?"

Frankly, she had no idea. "What if he says 'no'?"

Denise's pitying set to her mouth filtered into her words.

"You are beautiful, strong, and clever, and you have the best cleavage in the room."

Danny blinked and glanced at her neckline. Her breasts *did* look rather well against the silk. "Thank you."

"You're welcome."

"What about you?" Danny wouldn't dwell on how she latched on to the need to accompany her sister as a means of cowardice.

Denise gave her a knowing look. "*I* will be fine. Perhaps I'll go in search of someone more fun to play with." Her gaze seemed to snag on someone across the room, her lips twitching up into a sly smile. "And I do believe I found the perfect partner, just returned home from finishing school."

Danny glanced at where Lady Kendra—fair haired, porcelain skinned and vile-tongued bully—had accepted a dance from the Duke of Wemberly. "Please don't engage the beast. She's nearly forgotten I exist, and I enjoy the lack of insults and glares."

Denise smirked, clearly not intending to listen. "Go on and dance." She nodded in Percy's direction. "He won't say 'no.' No man has ever said 'no' to you."

Percy isn't like other men, Danny couldn't help thinking.

"And if he does refuse . . ." Denise said, her gaze again lifting to the lady across the room.

Danny's stomach clenched. "Denise!"

Her sister's gaze returned, and she cocked a brow. "You're a Deime." Her smirk turned saucy. "Make sure he gives you a better offer."

CHAPTER TEN

"E NJOYING YOURSELF?" RENARD asked.

"Hardly." Percy considered the nearest terrace and how likely he'd break his neck from one story. Since Danny had escorted her delightfully exacting sister away—practically dragged by the hair—he'd absconded from no fewer than six matrons and their daughters of 'virtuous and obedient manner.' As if he were interested in keeping a woman like a dog to come when called and pant at his feet. He wished the mothers shared those morals.

"If anything, Hamish underplayed the boldness of marriageable ladies and their relations."

One such woman had cornered him as he'd exited the privy to inform him she had 'childbearing hips' and would permit dalliances on his part after the vows were made, discreetly of course.

Fingers curling into fists, Percy couldn't help his outrage. The lady's cheeks had bloomed the color of cooked beets, her hands had shaken at her sides, no doubt put up to such a humiliating conversation by a grasping mother.

If the lady had come of her own volition, he'd have welcomed the brash speech and flirted shamelessly, but no woman here had the confidence to speak as they wished and ask what they wanted without shame. None except one.

"That look spells trouble," Renard said.

Percy smirked. "Coming to a realization is all."

Renard's brow shot up. "Care to share?"

"Not with you."

Renard sighed and pinched the bridge of his nose. "Allow me to escort my sister from the premises before you set anything ablaze, please."

"Really, Ren, I'm offended to see you think so little of me."

"On the contrary," Renard said. "If half of what I know you to be capable of is accurate, I merely wish not to be a witness when the inspector comes later for questioning."

"You'd leave to undermine the implication?" Percy placed a hand on his chest. "I'm touched."

"That"—Renard smiled—"and Camille said I may return to the house if I bring my sister along."

Talk about a dog on a leash. The sooner the Duchess of Lux popped out an heir, the sooner Renard may regain a module of dignity.

Men in love remained the poorest of bastards.

"Take heed," Renard warned, nodding over Percy's shoulder. "Another lady approaches, and this one looks determined."

Never mind the dogs; it was the hounds out for the season's latest fox he needed to worry about.

"Run while you can," Percy said.

Renard didn't need to be told twice.

Percy put on his best glare and turned, ready to chew off his arm if need be, to get away from the latest hunter, only to find himself caught in a most welcome trap. "Lady Daniella."

She curtsied. "Your Grace."

"So formal." He smiled, his mood instantly lifting knowing the lady's other side wasn't nearly so. "Come to ask me to dance?" he teased.

"Yes."

He blinked at her serious expression. "A lady asking a gentleman." The woman never ceased to surprise. "Isn't that a social faux pas?"

"I wouldn't think you of all people would mind?"

The knowing look in her eye set his blood pumping. "Indeed." He dropped the elegant tone and reverted to the tongue of his childhood speech. "A rough-n-tumble boy likes a bonnie face with spirit."

"What you call 'spirit,' my mama would call ill-breeding."

"I've met your papa, remember? The man dotes on you but doesn't spoil," he said. "Your mama would be wrong." He indicated the occupants of the room with a wave of his hand. "If anyone here knew the real circumstances behind my title and fortune, the *ton* would know the true definition of illy bred."

Something like anger flashed across her face, and Percy felt his insides warm at the prospect the anger was in his defense.

"You must remember, Your Grace, I've met you." Her sudden smile was conspiratorial. "Everyone else would be wrong."

Percy's belly blazed with gratitude and something less respectable. How she looked at him without fear, how she defended his past without knowing but the smallest detail, it made Percy wish to throw her over his shoulder like the barbarian he truly was and take her away from all these sycophants and liars to a place that they could make entirely their own. A place where they could be but a man and a woman. A place where he wasn't the monster lurking in the dark. He'd be everything she believed him to be. Maybe one day he could believe it himself.

"Shilling for your thoughts," she said, smirking.

Friends, he reminded himself, releasing the fantasy. There was no place in existence where they could meet halfway. He could give her pleasure and intellectual company, but nothing more. Give a mule a bath and tie a bow around its neck and it was still an ass.

"I'm afraid I don't dance," he said truthfully, shocking himself. More shocking, he went into detail. "I was deemed a hopeless case by the officers in my regiment and by other coworkers later."

"I'm astounded." Danny gave him a onceover. "You, a man

who can leap from trees and cross a room in mere strides, cannot keep count with the music?"

"Afraid not." Percy waited for her reprimand. All gentlemen were expected to know the steps. A lady sitting down during the quadrille was a mark against a man of honor without a partner. One more tally on the books for his lack of breeding. And all men knew the sting of mouth-pie.

"That's marvelous!" Danny clapped her hands. "Positively titillating."

"I beg your pardon?" God, if only his brain would stop replaying the word 'titillating' in his head.

"You can't dance," she explained. "Here I was under the impression you were perfect. I do believe I like you all the better for it."

Percy would deign to acknowledge how the words 'I like you' made his heart pound or how a most appalling sound of surprise escaped his throat that sounded like a great swine in the throes of mud bathing.

"Perfect?" Absurd. "I am a liar, a thief, and a murderer—not to mention most lax in my correspondence."

"But you do all those things so infuriatingly well," she said. "Finally, something I can hang over your head."

"You're keeping score?"

"Absolutely." Her grin was radiant. "Isn't that what friends do? Tease each other and keep one another honest?"

And the swine was dispatched and fried into bacon. Somewhere, in the course of pulling a gun on him, a verbal sparring match that left him skewered, a hasty embrace, and a lust-filled encounter with his knife, the woman had indeed come to be a companion, trusted, desired.

They were friends.

Unbelievable.

"The next activity is yours," she said.

"Activity?" The only action he wanted to take right now was a long pull of a stiff drink.

"A ride in Hyde Park? A drive through Vauxhall?"

He grinned. "Pistols at dawn?"

"If you like."

He shook his head, still admiring the burns from his roasted hide. "Your list of items to hang over my head continues. You'll find I don't partake in many gentlemen's sports."

"I see." Her expression said she wasn't disappointed. "What does a rough-n-tumble boy do for amusement, then?"

He chuckled at her digression from aristocratic pomp to country lilt.

It was a bad habit of his, underestimating Lady Daniella. What would scare off most proper ladies didn't cause so much as a blink of trepidation. Which left the unfamiliar reaction of Percy wishing to show her everything.

Leaning close, he inhaled her rich scent of spices and whispered so only she could hear, "We play football."

"Really?" Her eyes lit up with instant curiosity.

Realizing their conversation had garnered more than a few eavesdroppers, Percy merely smiled in response. *Let the vultures circle.*

Noticing the attention, Danny shuffled towards that same fern he'd found himself acquainted with earlier in the evening and glanced over her shoulder to tell him to follow.

Percy was pulled forward by an invisible force, no more able to refuse her invitation than if a real strap of leather had tethered them together.

Like a leash, Percy thought absently.

But as he made his way to the quiet corner and sat next to Danny, sharing a quiet moment and organizing their next outing, Percy found he didn't mind one bit.

Woof.

CHAPTER ELEVEN

P ERCY WATCHED THE light filter through the glass panes of the Crystal Palace and send rainbows of color scattering over the heads of hundreds of people in worn moleskin and wool—and elegant frock coats and laced bustles—waiting for the doors to open for this monumental event.

Percy stared at the mix of bright colors and common browns, the clashing of fabrics and class hurting his head. What the devil were all these laced-up dandies doing here?

"I did not realize football was so popular," Danny said at his side, looking like a dream in a simple, rose-pink frock, not a laced ruffle in sight.

Denise and Mrs. Pebblestone—the lady's perpetually frowning chaperone—followed a step behind.

Denise scrunched her nose. "Or smelly."

"A workman's sport," Percy said, eyeing a better way into the building through the side garden than suffering the jostling crowd through the front doors. He tucked Danny's hand into the crook of his elbow and led their party towards the grassy lawn. "Come."

"Avoiding purchasing the tickets?" Danny asked, voice low and eyes dancing. "Be careful, Your Grace. Your criminal side is showing."

"Tease me all you like," he whispered back, tempering his desire to beg for more, "but these numbers are a perfect draw for pickpockets." Plus, he'd bought his tickets ahead of time. Being a worthless duke did have some advantages.

As luck had it, the garden doors led into the lower level of the palace, where the stairs to the upper levels were guarded by a big man in a dark coat.

"Tickets, sir?"

Percy withdrew the slips from his inner pocket and waited for the man to wave them ahead. Inside, he offered the sisters each an arm up the stairs—leaving Mrs. Pebblestone and her frown to walk unescorted—and around the full-surround balcony until they found their designated terrace labeled with a simple red patch of fabric on the glass wall behind.

Denise circled the semi-private terrace and the deserted second story. With a glint in her eye, she raised a hand to her head dramatically and stated, "How unfortunate. I do feel a nasty headache coming on. I believe I'll find the physician's terrace and see if they have a tonic and place for me to rest a moment."

Percy bit back a smile. "I shall escort—"

"I need to use the privy as well," Denise said unabashedly, already heading in the direction of the labeled area. "No need to concern yourself, Your Grace. Mrs. Pebblestone and I will manage."

Mrs. Pebblestone shot Danny a hard look before chasing after the youngest Deime.

Danny shook her head at her sister's retreat. "She's a terrible chaperone."

Percy couldn't disagree more. "I do hope she feels better."

Danny shot him a glare that had him pinching his thigh to keep him from laughing.

"Come." He beckoned her to the railing.

The two opposing teams were already afield—a sharp distinction where marble floor met trimmed grass—their jersey stripes a contrasting green versus blue, but with socks a myriad of colors, from nonsensical white to a distressing shade of chartreuse.

Hard to believe the field floor used to house some of the greatest treasures of the empire: cotton milling machinery, tapestries from India. Black-and-white photographs hung from the woven divider on either side, separating their private terrace from the next for some semblance of exclusivity. Percy glanced at the images, but his attention quickly shifted to the lady who watched the men stretch below with keen interest.

Noting his gaze, Danny asked, "What are the rules?"

Percy rested his elbows on the top of the railing, the seams of his coat pulling. "You don't know? I thought all good English families played lawn games."

"We do." Danny's grin was vicious. "But my siblings and I don't like reading rule books or following etiquette. We're a competitive lot."

"Then how do you know who wins?"

Danny blinked, as if he were missing the obvious. "Whoever comes up with the best insults, of course."

He chuckled and pointed to the sectioned-off areas at either end of the field, where a length of tape ran between two posts that would be measured exactly eight feet high.

"The ball must sail through that allotted goal for a point. Above the line or to either side doesn't count," he told her.

"And points are good?" she said.

"Only to win the game."

She smiled. "So, it *is* like insults."

He laughed. "Yes, but the ones made down there will be a matter of pride. You'll still see tempers fly on the field. Mark my words."

"The players get violent?"

Percy eyed her, certain he should have been concerned by how she sounded more intrigued than disturbed. "Blood runs hot in the heat of the game," he confirmed. "By fouls overlooked, mostly. A player besides the goalie touching the ball, players tripping their opponents, illegal use of equipment in the shoes or under the shirts." He shrugged. "Sometimes a player will throw a punch in frustration and the whole field will turn into a bare-fisted pugilism match."

She wrinkled her nose. "That's ridiculous. The players should conduct themselves with honor and play fairly."

He'd known from the start a strange thread of justice drove Danny. There was no other reason a clever woman would follow a suspicious man into a dark courtyard or have the balls to train a gun at him at point-blank range.

What it must have been like to see the world through black-and-white lenses. Percy wondered—grimly—which side he'd take if she turned her gaze his way.

"Fair is faux," he said. "Expecting life to adhere that way is a bit naive, don't you think?"

"Of course it is," Danny said, ever self-aware. She gazed at the field. "But wouldn't it be wonderful if we could know, at a glance, if someone or something was good or bad?"

There was something in her tone, or maybe it was the un-characteristic caving set to her shoulders, which had Percy believing Danny's mind was far from the players on the field.

"Is that what you really wish?" he asked carefully. "That right and wrong couldn't fall into shades of varying grey?"

"I do."

The way her gaze latched on to his, as if needing an anchor to hold, Percy had but one wish at the moment: To take her against the glass and wipe the look of defeat from her face and replace it with open-mouthed moans of ecstasy.

But the doors had opened, and the flood of bystanders poured inside, eager to find their seats.

Not so eagerly, Percy stood back as groups of tailored misters and polished misses strolled past, every one of them staring openly. After the tenth couple passed, their gazes not even touching the field, Percy cursed under his breath.

Had a caricaturist rendered his likeness to every blasted rag house in London?

Grumbling something unintelligible to Danny, Percy slumped back in the chair by the divider, the only seat that wouldn't be obvious to anyone passing on either side and would be impossible to see from the terraces directly across on the other side of the green. He hoped this infernal place didn't offer the looking glasses one would find at the theatre, or he'd be forced to sit here the entire match. And where was the grub? He hadn't eaten anything in over an hour and was properly famished.

Danny's amused chuckle sent desire straight to his groin. The laughter brightened her cheeks and drew attention to her lovely breasts as she pressed a hand to her stomach.

Leaning back, Percy crossed his ankles and decided anything going on around and below the field—or in his stomach—was nothing compared to watching the light from the glass above cast Danny in a halo of golden light. His hand went to his pulsing cock and imagined those lovely breasts where his fingers squeezed him at the base. While everyone else foolishly watched the men below tackle and wrestle in the dirt, he'd focus on a livelier and more worthwhile player, the one who made him at once wish to spectate and compete.

Danny's breathless laugh faded as she noted his silent stare.

Her gaze dropped to where he stroked himself through his trousers and the fingers splayed across her stomach skimmed upwards as if to draw away a sudden tightening in her bodice. Breaths turning labored, she bit her lip, her other hand coming to clench the skirts between her legs.

Percy groaned, his willpower threadbare. Friends. They were supposed to be friends. If he truly wished to be on equal and respectable terms with her, this growing obsession with her and those luscious breasts must desist at once.

"Percy."

Percy closed his eyes. His name on those sweet lips; it was torture.

Even here, where the normal privacy of walls and floors were illusions of translucent glass, where her sister could happen upon them any moment, she responded, undeterred by their public surroundings, not caring about their positions. It would take nothing to send her over the edge. A few licks over her skin, a well-placed finger against her folds and she'd come.

Fuck it. He could respect her just as well with her coming on his cock.

Eyes snapping open, his gaze locked on hers. "Come here."

She came without hesitation, at once displaying a hunger for scandalous danger and unquestioning trust that left Percy swelling with a need to prove both her desires right.

When she stood before him, her eyes were heavy lidded and glazed with lust, looking down at him as if he were the culmination of everything she'd ever wanted.

Percy swallowed his growl and told her huskily, "Turn around."

Gathering her hem, he lifted the back of her skirts with one hand—the divider at their side hiding his actions from view and her standing form further hiding his seated person—and meaning no one who walked by would be any the wiser as his fingers danced along the silk fabric that went to mid-thigh and . . . stopped.

He couldn't temper his growl this time. "You're not wearing drawers."

Fingers gliding up to find the wet curls between her legs, she gasped at his light touch and ground against his hand, her pants coming faster. "I liked the feel of nothing."

He rewarded her brazen admission with a quick thrust of his finger between her folds, shocking her body.

With her fist coming to her mouth, anyone passing by would believe she was delicately suppressing a sneeze. From Percy's angle, he saw she'd all but broken her knuckle's skin biting back her first orgasm.

He could have dropped her skirts then and considered a job well done, but this was a place of sport and pushing one's limits. The perfect place to beat one's record.

"Spread your legs, darling," he whispered.

"My legs are trembling."

He smiled. "I know." He opened his trousers with his free

hand, and his rigid cock sprang free. The hand against her skin snaked around to grasp her bare hip. Easing her over his lap so her skirts bunched between them and continued to hide him from view, he raked both hands up her thighs, letting his nails scrape the satin soft skin up, up.

He worked her against him, catching her cleft against the crown of his erection until the moisture pouring from her made the motion as smooth as silk against butter.

She threw back her head, her breathing ragged.

Angling her hips back so there was room for his hand, he rubbed quick circles around her bud, forcing her climax to go on and on as he continued to thrust her folds against his entire length.

A record four-minute climax was a respectable goal a man could live with.

She collapsed back against him, the edge of her corset digging into them both, but Percy was no more capable of movement at the moment than she. One last brush of skin and he'd erupt like a geyser.

Chest heaving, the hair at the back of her neck was wet and smelled of an erotic blend of sweat and cloves. Percy pressed a kiss where her gown met skin and breathed her scent into his soul.

She sighed. "Football is my new favorite sport."

Percy laughed and aided her to her feet, tugging her skirts back into place before wrestling his rock-hard erection back into his stays.

When he'd finished buttoning his trousers, he looked up to find her nibbling her bottom lip, her gaze trained on the evidence he hadn't released.

"Should I do something for"—she waved her hand in his direction, her cheeks reddening—"you?" she finished.

How he loved her attempt to sound anything but proper. "Unnecessary, my dear. Your pleasure is all that matters."

"But . . ." She needed to stop worrying her lip before he

soothed her mouth with his own teeth and tongue. "I want to give you pleasure too."

If they hadn't been in a palace of glass, if there hadn't been others sitting inches away, he'd have bent her over the railing and taken her so hard and fast, their violent coupling would have shattered the walls around them.

Cock jerking, he grimaced and rubbed a quick circle to ease the ache building in his sac. "Another time, I promise." God, he was randier than a schoolboy promised his first suck. He was a man of seven and twenty, for fuck's sake.

"Do you need a minute?" she asked, cheeks flushed.

She needed to stop blushing too, especially now that he knew the dusty pink it brought to her cheeks was the same color of her folds when rubbed to completion.

He cleared his throat. "Thank you, yes."

She walked to the railing and watched the players on the field, the sounds of cheers and displeasure meaning the match was well underway.

Percy made quick work to flag his arousal. Two quick pumps and he spent over the rim of his trousers into a handkerchief. If he hadn't withstood Danny's erotic little sounds of climax for those four minutes of torture, he'd have been ashamed. But he'd given her all his attention, using his skills and nimble fingers to tip her over the edge and hold her there without a care.

He'd known she was special after he'd stolen into her bedchamber and made her come with the barest touch of his blade, but this . . . Her nestling herself over his cock and working into a frenzy despite the overcrowded stadium, there wasn't a single more erotic fantasy his twisted mind could conjure. She was enchanting, fantasy-inducing.

Perfect.

"Now this is a surprise," someone said.

Noting how Danny stiffened and whirled to face the source of the cold tone, Percy peered around the divider to see a woman in a white dress.

Porcelain-skinned and with ringlets of blonde hair dangling under a wide, feathered hat, she'd have been considered the highest standard of beauty in society's circle, but the overly large skirts and rose-embroidered bodice made Percy think of a child's doll.

Danny offered a civil bob and said with uncharacteristic reservedness, "Lady Kendra."

There was no civility in Lady Kendra's sneer. "Lady Daniella." Her gaze searched the couples on the closest balconies. "Isn't your sister with you?"

"Denise wasn't feeling well."

"A pity." Her gaze turned smug. "Couldn't find another escort with those lackluster charms? It's hard to imagine men still fighting over someone so *popular*."

Percy reeled back at the vulgar connotation. Expecting Danny to give this bitch her due, he watched angrily as she said nothing.

Lady Kendra lifted the fan attached to her wrist and snapped it open in an act one could only describe as aggressive. "But I guess you're used to losing respectable men's favors. Any man of caliber would see the disgrace of an alliance with the biggest tease in London."

Danny flinched, and Percy's vision flashed with a single, blood-dripped word: Enemy.

Whether from residual passion from their secret touching or the easy camaraderie growing between them, his desire to protect her came as naturally as the hand that found the knife at his ankle on reflex.

Whoever this person was—he wouldn't attach a descriptor as kind as 'lady' to this creature—she needed a deep cut and a lengthy death.

It amazed him how no one shouted the injustice of such blatant lies. The occupants of the closest terraces must have heard Lady Kendra's insults, and yet there was no call to arms, not even a stern look of disapproval from the couples walking past.

And the way Danny stood there and took the assault.

He'd had enough.

Sliding behind the divider, he startled a trio of smartly dressed ladies—offered a devious wink for their silence—and came around the other side to give the appearance he'd just arrived back from mingling with others on a separate balcony.

"I do apologize for taking so long, Lady Daniella." He kept his gaze on her startled face and conveyed his support with a quick brush of his thumb on her wrist as he came to her side.

"Oh, my." Lady Kendra's fan came up and flitted wildly.

Jaw gritted, Danny offered introductions. At least *someone* had manners. "Your Grace, this is Lady Kendra Fairchild. Lady Kendra, this is the Duke of Grandfellow."

Recovered, Lady Kendra smiled coyly over her fan with eyes the color of envy. "The Duke of Grandfellow. Charmed."

Minding his own manners, Percy took the lady's proffered hand but didn't offer a kiss. "A pleasure."

"How strange to see you here." Her gaze bounced between the two. "I did not know you were acquainted."

"Bromley and Grandfellow reside in the same countryside," Danny said quietly.

Percy didn't feign his admonishment. "Don't be so cold, Lady Daniella. What would your papa say if he heard you speaking of our family's close friendship so callously?"

Lady Kendra's gaze narrowed at Danny, seeming to reassess her opponent's threat of connection. With a cry more moan than squeak of surprise, Lady Kendra appeared to trip while standing completely still, and Percy had no choice but to catch her before she barreled into Danny.

"Forgive me." Lady Kendra pressed a hand to her cheek, all innocence. "I'm horrified."

Percy set her on her feet and retracted his hands, else they be tainted by the woman's growing pile of spewed manure. "Think nothing of it, Lady Kender."

"*Kendra*, and you are too kind." Lips pouting, she sided up to him, pressing her bosom against his arm and putting herself directly where Danny had been. "Are you a fan of sporting events, Your Grace? The players can become so rough when invigorated."

Percy refrained from sneering. Calling Danny a tease was laughable in the face of such a pathetic attempt at flirting.

His gaze flicked to Danny and her downcast gaze and the simmering rage in his blood boiled over, but not past reason. No, his blood was comprised of dry ice, cold and far-reaching. He need not finger a single blade on his person. He was a duke now, titled and powerful. And he was nothing if not an adaptable killer.

There were many kinds of death he could administer.

Ignoring Lady Kendra's furrowed brows, he walked around her—his cut visible to all the gawking eyes trained on them—answering her question while lifting Danny's hand and kissing her knuckles. "Only those players who respect their opposition are worth mentioning."

Danny was a force of nature, proud and perfect. Anyone could suffer doubt in the face of such hostility, but he'd make her remember she was a queen. He'd force everyone to see.

He raised his voice to be heard clearly from three terraces on either side. "Of course, any amusement is stellar in the right company. Don't you agree, Lady Daniella?"

There were unshed tears in her eyes, but her smile lit up her entire face. Her words, when she responded, were full of spirit.

"That goes without saying, Your Grace. But I have yet to determine if current company is worth the praise."

Percy wanted to roar his approval. Not just for Danny reassembling a teasing tone, but for how Lady Kendra sputtered her disbelief behind them.

Let the doll bleed out with the knowledge no one wished to play with her.

Now to twist the blade home.

Glancing over his shoulder, he feigned a look of embarrassment. "Oh, apologies, Lady Kinra. I forgot you were there." His laugh was cold. His whisper more so. "But I assume you're used to losing men's favors, what with being a judgmental pig."

Someone should really fix the doll's jaw. It appeared to be unable to close.

When Lady Kendra's mouth did close, it was with a teeth-grinding *snap*! Even her curtsy looked like a toy with rusty bolts. "Good day, Your Grace." Her gaze promised retribution as they settled on Danny. "Lady Daniella."

She didn't wait for their returning farewell. Skirts whirling, Lady Kendra turned on her heel and proceeded around the balcony, down the steps, and out of the palace as every eye from the second level followed.

Percy resisted crowing their victory from atop the railing, not wishing to scuff his boots.

"That was unwise," Danny said, gaze on Lady Kendra's blurry figure through the glass as she walked towards the line of carriages on the street outside. "She'll go to all her friends and twist what you said so she is the victim."

"Then the lady is an idiot." Percy hated how Danny worried about his reputation when she should have been fuming about the insult to her own. "She should not have spoken to you in such a way. The lady is lucky I don't spread her own words to the masses." His eyes narrowed at her silence, a sneaking suspicion bringing his anger back to the boiling point. "Do people always speak to you in such a way?"

Her wince said 'yes,' though her mouth lifted sardonically. "Do you plan to cut every last person who gives insult?"

"Haven't you heard? I'm a rake. A libertine. Beyond reform, I'm afraid."

"A carefully crafted mask."

"You doubt my less-than-noble intentions?"

"Don't take it personally, my lord. I doubt *every* man's intentions."

Her line had been made in jest, but to heart it reached, specifically *his* blackened heart. Danny was beautiful, clever, and perceptive. Others had clearly noticed and left a bad taste in her mouth.

Percy contemplated that lovely mouth, complete with full lips and wicked tongue, and a profound anger overtook him. "Who was it?"

"Pardon me?"

"You're pardoned," he quipped. He stepped close and tilted her chin up. He'd eviscerate the slandering bastards. "Give me the names of the idiots whose intentions made you question the others. I'd like them; in writing preferably."

"Contemplating homicide so openly, Your Grace?" Danny didn't appear concerned. "Lower your voice, for I'm not sure even a duke can recover from that scandal."

Percy leaned down, his lips skimming her ear, and said, "Let them talk, Danny. I know true worth when I see it." He pulled back, enjoying her wide eyes, and plucked a non-existent speck from her shoulder, as if his closeness had been nothing improper. "There now, Lady Daniella. Your dress is fine. Though the dust in here must be addressed." He glanced around, his charade believed by those closest who turned away with disinterest.

"Thank you," she whispered.

Percy offered Danny his chair by the divider and took the seat opposite, the soft gratitude in her voice unsteadying.

Not for the first time, Percy seriously envisaged poisoning the entirety of the *ton* at the next social function. Aside from a handful of redeemable mavericks, the world would be better off.

"Lady Kendra poured her drink down the back of my dress during my second season," Danny said suddenly. "I spent the entire evening sitting in the corner, refusing offers to dance by feigning a hurt ankle. Mama was livid." Her smile was self-deprecating. "But I know she would suffer my silent presence over the image of me trailing red punch all through the twirls of a waltz."

Percy's plans for mass murder abated. "That's horrific!" Barbaric. "What could you possibly have done to deserve such savagery?"

"She fancied Lord Roswell."

"And the man sweated gold?"

"The earl proposed to me my first season."

"Doesn't the man prefer men?" Frankly, it was well known.

Danny blushed. "As far as I know."

Danny had refused him, obviously, and still Lady Kendra held a grudge. Women. Were. Terrifying.

"There were others," Danny continued.

"Other suitors?"

She nodded. "That's why many of the ladies call me *London's Greatest Tease.*"

Percy's brain recalled the look on her face when he'd accused her of something similar in her bedchamber.

He cursed. "Jealousy and cruelty." He'd take a straightforward knife fight over society's version of 'civility' any day.

She deserved better.

"Was that Lady Kendra I saw barreling for the door?" Denise said, coming into view with Mrs. Pebblestone, though her gaze lingered on the carriage that pulled away from the curb outside.

"It was," Danny said.

"And she didn't stay to say 'hello'?" Denise sniffed. "Looks like someone finally put her in her place. I must find them and congratulate them on a job well done."

Percy stood and smiled. "It was, wasn't it?"

Danny rose herself and elbowed him before asking her sister, "Feeling better?"

Denise's hawk-like gaze tracked Danny's moves, no doubt noting the little space between them. Gaze softening, her mouth pulled down at the corners, and Percy readied for another stellar performance.

"Unfortunately, I don't believe the physician was of any help. I think it best if I return home."

Percy nodded. "I will call the carriage."

"Good." Denise said. "And I will send it back as soon as I

arrive at the Deime family townhouse."

Danny shook her head. "You cannot go by yourself—"

"Of course not," Denise said. "Which is why Mrs. Pebblestone will accompany me."

To this, Mrs. Pebblestone shook her head. "Absolutely not, Lady Denise. I could not leave Lady Daniella here unchaperoned. Think of what society would say. You will simply have to grin and bear your pain like any proper lady would."

Denise's mouth curled upwards, and even Percy knew to be scared.

"I see," Denise said. "It will be an interesting discovery which society finds more offensive: My sister being escorted by a duke alone, in full view of *hundreds* of onlookers, or the youngest daughter of the Earl of Bromley, noisily losing my breakfast all over the field." She glanced at the party as a whole as if to gauge their opinions. "Time will tell."

Mrs. Pebblestone's lips pursed. The poor woman looked a bit green herself at the dilemma. Glancing around at the packed space, no doubt realizing how many titled and well-connected families were present at the spectacle, she seemed to come to a decision. "I will take Lady Denise home."

Danny nodded. "We will come—"

"Later," Denise said with a pointed look. "The Bromley Townhouse is but a few short blocks from here. When the match is finished, we can meet there, though I daresay we may need to take one of the family carriages back to the country." Denise bobbed her head to Percy. "Thank you for your offer, Your Grace, but your coach is far too small for all four of us to travel again for such a journey, and I do fear what may come of your upholstery if I must endure another trip without proper ventilation and space."

Percy wondered if Lady Denise truly did suffer a touch of motion sickness when her complexion paled slightly at her own words. She'd certainly been uncharacteristically silent throughout the drive into London.

"My apologies, my lady." Percy bowed over her hand. "I will escort Lady Daniella to the townhouse upon the conclusion of the match, none the worse for wear, have no fear."

No doubt noting her charge's sickly complexion herself, Mrs. Pebblestone turned to make for the stairs.

Denise inclined her head at Percy's promise, but her words were given with such quiet force, there was no question of her next statement's sincerity. "If I feared you would not treat my sister with all dignity, Your Grace, I'd have pushed you off the balcony.

CHAPTER TWELVE

A N HOUR LATER, the crush of carriages in the street was enough to block traffic for two straight days.

Percy spied a disgruntled coachman waving from the top of a lion-crested carriage—*his* coach and man, he reminded himself— and Percy returned the man's hand signals with a clipped, *"Move when you can. We will walk."*

The man's eyes widened, surprised, no doubt, that the new Duke of Grandfellow was versed in the common language of servicemen. He tipped his hat in understanding.

Danny, of course, missed nothing.

"Always a surprise," she said as they skirted the traffic and crossed the road to a quieter side street. "Any other hidden talents, Your Grace?"

Oh, what he could do with hot wax and a splattering of whipped milk.

"It wouldn't be any fun if I told you," he said. *Showing* her, on the other hand . . .

A playful finger traced his bicep, and Percy felt the light touch down to his groin.

"I couldn't persuade you to reconsider?"

God blast it all, the sound of her husky voice was worse than torture.

"Put that smart mouth to good use, and I'll divulge every last secret I know," he challenged, not caring if national security could handle the breach when he sang like a bird.

Those flirting eyes widened. Licking her lips, she glanced at the quiet alley, the cramped layout of the buildings casting long shadows even in the middle of the day. "Here?"

"Why not?"

Her curiosity got the better of her. "What do I do?"

Jesus, she couldn't be serious? "Get on your knees."

He made the command in jest.

Despite knowing her fearlessness, he *had* been teasing. The alleys at the edge of St. Giles Rookery—a route his distracted mind had taken by rote—*were* deserted this time of day with most residents working their shifts at the local mills. They were *also* invested with filth and prostitutes on a good day, pickpockets and cutthroats on a bad.

A heightened sense of danger taking hold because of the woman at his side or old paranoia out of self-preservation rising to the surface, Percy's gaze swept the dark alcoves and the nearby roofs for unwelcome eyes.

It wouldn't be prudent or safe to linger here. He'd whisk Danny somewhere safe and *then* they could resume their fun.

But Danny had no intention of waiting. She dropped down in front of him, her clever fingers working open the fly to his trousers without a word of instruction or encouragement. He had to stop this.

"Danny—"

"Shh. I'm concentrating."

Percy was mesmerized by the lovely V between her brows until the last button slid through its hole and his cock sprang free, pointing due north with confidence.

Her shocked gasp was quickly followed up with the exclamation, "My, you're large."

Percy gritted his teeth as her compliment brushed hot air across his crown. "Thank you, my dear. I do try."

Her fingers tickled his length in a querying touch.

Cock jumping, Percy pulled back. He'd taken this too far. The woman was magic and mayhem. Instead of disgust and outrage at his tasteless teasing, she was compliant. Interested. *Innocent.*

Her hands were instantly there, stopping him from wrestling himself back into his stays. "I'm not done."

"Trust me, darling." He restrained her with a light circling of her wrists. "What I had in mind isn't for a lady, and I'm a rutty scumbag for suggesting it."

Her struggles stopped, but the stubborn glint in her eye said she wasn't done. "Would it bring you pleasure?"

Fucking over the clouds. He wouldn't admit it.

But the woman was a bloodhound and wouldn't accept less than all his secrets. "Your ear wiggled."

Damn it!

"Yes." He dropped her hands and ran his own through his hair. "Men like getting their cock in a willing woman's mouth. It's crude and undignified and feels like having your personal demons sucked out of your body by an angel. But the mere thought of *you* putting your mouth on me . . ." He grasped himself in hand and rubbed the white that beaded out around his crown with his thumb. "God, I don't think I'd survive."

His words registered in her eyes, and the answering call of desire pushed his back to the alley wall.

She didn't beg or flirt. Without looking away, she slid her hand down his length and pressed pursed lips to his tip.

Percy knocked his head against the wall, the last of his will-power fading in a last effort whisper of reason. "Danny, I was *teasing.*"

She smiled, that sunlit halo behind her head setting off a predatory glow in her eyes. "Then you challenged the wrong lady, sir."

And she dragged him up to heaven.

THE WANTON LADY on her knees was another woman. Danny had

no idea where she'd come from or how she knew how to drag her tongue along the velvet of him before drawing him inside, but she reveled in the feeling, in the sense of control.

He tasted like salt and unfettered lust. The very length and solid feel of him against her tongue was like a blunt blade, at any moment ready to twist and cut her innocence in two.

Danny dug her nails into his hips, needing him deeper, needing all of him inside.

The tip of him hit the back of her throat and liquid heat slipped down her thighs.

She sighed.

"Danny."

His hands fisted in her hair, ruining her coif and shooting sensation to her toes.

"Danny," he said again. "Stop this."

Never.

But she heard his reservations and shame, so much like her own buried where no one was supposed to see, and she wouldn't deny him his consent.

She slipped him out of her mouth, sucking the full length of him until the suction on his tip dropped more of that salty white onto her tongue. With effort, she looked away from the sword she desperately wanted to sheathe, and asked, "Shall I stop, Percy?"

She dared him to lie. Dared *him* to deny what they both wanted. She'd leave it to him to decide. He was a worldly man who'd been through unspeakable things. If he meant what he'd said about his tastes being demonic, then she wanted to sink into hell to meet his needs, needs she was quickly coming to realize matched hers.

There was no fear, no shame. Whoever this man brought out in her was the real her. She'd wasted three long years pretending.

No longer.

She willed her desires to show on her face. Willed her fantasies not to send her over the edge even as her legs grew slippery with arousal for him, for this.

He saw it all. Gaze going wild, he twisted his fingers in her hair and growled, "Saints above, forgive me."

Grip tightening, he impaled himself into her waiting mouth and all other prayers and coherent thoughts were lost in a tight rhythm that left them both panting.

In, out, in, out. Each brush of that saltiness on the back of her throat drove her to rush his pace, needing more. Apple scones were nothing compared to the all-male, all savory, and hot taste of him. She only hoped there was more; the inconsistent trickle of moisture he gave her wasn't enough.

He took over the rhythm, pumping into her mouth with inhuman grunts. His loss of control was too much.

The wet friction had her clenching her knees together. She tumbled over that edge, sucking him inside to his root when her climax dragged a moan from the very core of her being.

The fingers in her hair clutched her to him. "Danny, I can't—"

He moved back.

Her teeth stayed him; her hand went instinctively to cup the heavy sac at his base.

A violent shudder racked his body, and then at last that salty taste poured across her tongue.

This went beyond friendship, certainly beyond mere lust. Neither had looked away as the other came. Their gazes had locked, the feelings shared. Danny would swear they'd been of one mind and body in that moment of lost pleasure.

When his climax ended, he pulled free of her mouth and dropped to his knees in front of her. With gentle hands, he cupped her face, his expression open and achingly soft.

They stared at one another. No words were spoken. Their bodies had done the talking, a conversation of soul-searing magnitude.

What were words but precursors to action?

Danny didn't speak. Leaning forward, she pressed a kiss to his mouth and smiled at his huffed laugh.

He didn't let her pull away. Breaking the kiss, he pressed his forehead to hers. "I've seen heaven."

Danny's smile grew. "If heaven feels like that, I may join my mama in church from now on."

"Blasphemy!"

She loved his quick wit and the ease of his company. They'd urged each other to come in a public space, in broad daylight, in the most vulnerable of positions, and nothing about it felt awkward.

Being with him was as natural as breathing.

"Can you stand?" he asked softly.

"If I can't, will you carry me?"

That laughter again. The sound was rough and beautiful. "I'll carry you to the nearest inn and spread you on the bed for my evening meal."

She shivered at his silky threat. "Oh, no! It looks as if my legs won't work, sir."

He helped her up and dropped a kiss on her brow, his grin positively feline as he buttoned his trousers. "Minx." The humor faded. "If I don't return you home soon, not even your sister will be able to keep up the ruse we silently agreed to attend."

"And what ruse would that be?"

"That I'm an honorable man who won't sully your virtue at the first available opportunity."

She pursed her lips together to keep in a smile and said with all the seriousness she could muster, "This was hardly the first sullying."

"Good point." He dragged her to him and made quick work of her lips, tongue, and knowledge of the English language.

Danny contained her squeal of delight when that expert tongue flicked out and tasted the delicate spot on her jawline right beside her ear.

Her core went liquid, sending slick want down her still-damp thighs.

"What we 'ave here, Freddy?"

Pleasure turned to ice in her veins.

They tore apart as two figures stepped into the shadows, each carrying a knife as long as her forearm. But it was the wicked gleam in their eyes that had Danny's fluttering stomach dropping out.

Both were broad, young. They were wearing long coats too big for their frames and had the same ruddy-cheeked faces.

Danny rubbed at her eyes, sure she was seeing double.

The twin on the right laughed, a hoarse, ugly sound. "Bloke was telling the truth. I'll be damned."

Percy tensed at her side. "What do you want?"

"Payment."

"What payment?" Percy glanced at the rooftops, his jaw tight. He mumbled something that sounded like, "There *had* been eyes on us." Louder, he said, "Who told you we were here?"

"What's this? A talkative mark?" The man elbowed his brother. "Freddy, the bastard wants to talk."

"No time for that." Freddy's gaze raked over Danny's body. "I'm eager for payment."

Danny shuddered as Percy placed her behind him.

"When I tell you to," he whispered, "run."

Panic pitched her words high. "There are two of them!"

"And more on the way." Freddy sidestepped, placing himself in her path of escape with a triumphant smile. "No use running, chicken."

"Not in those fine skirts." The brother laughed.

"Go on, George." Freddy nodded towards Percy. "But don't be too quick." His slimy gaze landed on Danny once again. "I want to take my time."

Danny's hand went to her reticule and to her pistol safely tucked inside, but Percy's hand stayed her.

His head shake was infinitesimal.

She heard his unspoken words: *I'll take care of them. Run.*

Running solved nothing, she knew firsthand. The clawed fingers of memory snagged at her calm, but Danny wouldn't let herself fall apart. Not here and not now.

Gaze flicking to the glint of blades and hearing the man's words *more on the way*, Danny took stock of her limited weapons—a single bullet in her pistol's chamber with two bodies to stop—and swallowed her frustration down to do the only thing she could.

She screamed.

All three men cringed.

In between one scream and the next, Freddy spat at his brother, "Shut 'er up before we 'ave the bobbies chasin' us down."

Percy shook off his shock as the other twin stalked forward and sent him to the ground with a kick to the knee and a nasty crack to the face.

George went down, cradling his leg and spitting curses.

While Freddy skirted back, using his brother's body as an obstacle, Percy had no choice but to step over in the narrow alley.

Danny drew the gun from her reticule and trained it on George, who froze coming to his feet. "Don't move," she said.

Percy wrestled with his opponent, but Freddy got in a lucky shot to his shoulder. He went down and the twin beelined straight for her.

Danny whirled to face him head on, shifting the gun to retrain the scope.

Fingers wrapped around her ankle and pulled the legs out from under her. She went down in a heap of skirts, her hip smarting as it struck the cobblestones.

The gun went off with a loud *crack* and fell out of her hands, now useless.

Percy's shout of warning came too late.

George staggered to his feet and Danny yelped as his hand fisted in her hair and dragged her against him.

"It's over, bitch," he spat in her ear. To Percy, he said, "One more step and girly 'ere gets jabbed."

Percy released his fresh hold on Freddy, his gaze fastening on the knife George tapped against his leg.

Freddy came to stand at his brother's side, his teeth stained with blood when he smiled.

"That's better now." George wiped a meaty hand across his face, blood from his nose smearing. "You're a tough bastard, I'll give you that," he said to Percy. "Now, drop that knife and put your 'ands on the wall so my brother here can settle this quiet."

Percy didn't move. "Let her go, and I'll do as you say."

"Percy, no—"

George's fingers yanked at her hair, successfully cutting off her plea. "Keep your mouth shut, girly." His other hand ran down her arm suggestively. "You'll 'ave your turn, don't you worry."

Danny shuddered and cold sweat plastered her dress to her back. Not for fear for herself. The idea of Percy hurt . . .

"Do. Not. Touch. Her."

Danny noticed the noise from the alleys nearby had gone alarmingly silent at Percy's growl.

George chuckled. "Listen to 'im, Freddy. No need for the bobbies. We got a 'ero on our 'ands."

They laughed.

But Danny wasn't looking at the twins. Her gaze stayed fixed on *him*, watching those smiling eyes turn cold, as if humor had never touched them.

Her neck hairs bristled.

Before her eyes, Percy changed from the teasing man of mystery to a creature of the dark. A man who haunted the steps of those deserving punishment. For the first time, Danny questioned her unfailing gut.

Percy tipped forward, his hands crossing in front of him to snake inside his coat pockets, but he didn't straighten, even when two knives slid into his hands and dropped to his sides like two bodies hung from the rafters.

From the darkness, a voice said, "There are no heroes here, gents."

Danny felt a chill settle over the alley at the eerie voice, *Percy's* voice.

She swore his next words were whispered in her ear.

"Only a demon."

Danny gasped.

How he'd gotten behind them was a trick of the shadows. One second he'd been in front of them, his eyes dark, his body slumped over like a puppet with loose strings, and then he'd been at their backs, knives in hand.

A flash and Freddy went down, blood spattering the alley wall.

George spun, taking Danny with him. His eyes widened in spooked recognition until a ring of white hugged his pupils. He whispered a name everyone knew to fear. "Butcher."

In his panic, he stepped back, twisting Danny too far to one side and slicing a gash in her arm.

The sting dulled almost immediately, and Danny was transported back eleven years to a different night and the cold feeling of hands on her person. Her pain churned into fear, shifted, coiled deeper and hot in her belly.

The thug's knife tapped the underside of her chin.

And the fear shifted again, until the intimacy of the blade scraping against her neck felt scorching, pleasing, even with the wrongness of her reaction sprouting cold sweat over her body.

A small moan burst through her lips before she clamped her teeth together.

George hesitated at the sound, relaxing his grip on her shoulders and turning away from Percy's looming presence.

His mistake.

Percy slipped between them and rammed the hilt of his knife into George's temple.

The man dropped, knife clattering to the cobblestones.

Danny willed her racing heart to slow, prayed the boiling heat in her veins to lessen. But the man's blade had skidded to a stop at the toe of her slipper, the tip piercing the satin. The visual of penetration, the knowledge that the smallest shift of her foot and the bite of the steel would catch her toes . . . Danny grabbed at the skirts between her legs and fought another moan.

"Danny?"

She glanced up from the knife to see Percy, his face a mask of horror.

Oh, God.

There was no relief at the thug's disarmament. Danny kicked the knife away and dropped to the freezing cobblestones, the pleasure draining away to leave behind waves of sick.

It was over. There was no use hiding it anymore.

The demon inside her had been released and no amount of praying would keep the world from seeing. From *him* seeing.

And condemning her like the broken woman she was.

CHAPTER THIRTEEN

DANNY PRESSED THE heels of her palms into her eyes, wishing to erase the wanton images of her arousal from Percy's mind, and more than that, destroy her instinctual reaction to life-threatening danger.

The cobblestones had bruised her tailbone, and the smell of waste churned her stomach, but the pain was nothing compared to the knowledge she belonged here in the gutter.

Percy crouched beside her, his knives back to whatever hidden pockets lined his coat. His voice was soft, his touch gentle when he said, "Danny."

"Don't look at me!" She curled her knees to her chest and buried her face into her hands. Dismissing her disgusting obsession when it was another layer of desire between the two of them was one thing. But he must know now, Percy had *seen* how broken she was to moan and find pleasure at the hands of such miserable men.

"I'm so sorry, Danny. I didn't mean to frighten you."

The antipathy in his voice pulled her rioting emotions into line. She looked up, not caring about the tears staining her cheeks when his eyes held nothing but shame. Did he not realize what had happened? He thought she was appalled at his heroism?

"You saved me, Percy. Saved us both. *I* am the creature to fear here. I stood there like a useless doll, a victim of my own . . ." *perversion*, she almost finished.

The waves of humiliation crashed down upon her over and over, washing the past week's joy away. Her mama scorned her for denying so many marriage proposals, but who would want a wife who didn't work properly? That night at the Leishires' ball, cornering Percy in the courtyard, she'd felt a connection, a similar darkness swirling in him. How naive she'd been to think she'd found the place she belonged.

"You should have let them take me."

"Don't say that!" He dragged her to her feet, his face a thundercloud of rage. His mouth worked, but nothing came out. Emotion flashed across his face, a lightning storm of hurt, anger, sadness, and confusion.

He crushed her to him, and his pounding heart matched her own.

"I should never have let this happen," he said, voice unsteady. "But . . . damn it! I don't know how to fix this."

She couldn't be fixed. Everything—therapies, laudanum, unrelenting prayer—and nothing had worked.

There was more to her taste for knives, too much to explain. If the effect of the break was unforgivable, the cause was unmentionable. Percy may have believed he was uncouth and unworthy of love and loyalty because of a past he found distasteful, but he'd fought for his country and for survival.

She was nothing but a coward. Worse, her reasons for pleasure were the greatest betrayal of decency. No man would agree to a wife like her.

"You're shaking," he whispered against her hair as he tightened his arms around her.

His hard chest felt like a wall, protecting her from the world outside and the ugliness from within. "How can you touch me?"

The man should have been backing away slowly and hoping her corruption wasn't catching.

He stiffened. "Do you want me to let go?"

Never.

She wouldn't voice the desperate plea in her mind. Pressing

her profile into his shoulder, she shook her head and felt him relax.

They stayed like that, wrapped in each other's arms, completely different from their embrace ten minutes ago, but still intimate, though things between them had changed again, in a way Danny wasn't yet ready to face.

"Fucking quims! Look at this mess."

Percy swung around, knives already in hand at the new arrivals.

Two more men stood in the alley: one, a giant with a bald head. The other, a whip of a man with his hood up, securely hiding his face from sight.

The hooded man toed one of the twins, a derisive snort coming from the depths of the shadows. "Freddy," he said to the bigger man. "That other must be George. Fucking Greens overstepping their lines again."

"Not just the Greens," the big man said, gaze falling on Danny and Percy.

The hooded man turned, lightless eyes seeming to flash. "Percy." He shook his head. "Of course it's you. This is your doing, I take it?"

Percy swallowed. "Just out for a stroll. A fine day for it, don't you think?"

The other man wasn't interested in pleasantries. "This isn't your turf anymore, *Vengeance*. Pops banned you from the rookeries after your last rampage."

"Hardly a rampage." Percy sniffed and jerked his chin in the direction of the two unconscious men. "They'll live." His gaze narrowed on the cut on Danny's arm like two slits in the curtain to hell. "Though I may remove a few appendages before their bodies arrive at the clinic."

"Gonna chop up the bodies this time? The coroner will be thrilled," the hooded man said mockingly. "Are you the one pilfering from the docks too?"

Percy quirked a brow, though the easy expression looked

strained. "Someone steal the board up your arse, Syd?"

"Barrels of sand, stolen right off the ships." Syd crossed his arms over his chest, the moleskin tightening over lean arm muscles. "Whatever agreement the Duke of Camine has with the harbormaster, it won't be long before the captains take action to protect what's theirs. Might want to remind your master of that."

Danny's head was spinning, attempting to keep up with the conversation. The Duke of Camine was stealing cargo? And Percy was part of it? But what would anyone want with a bunch of sand?

"It wasn't us," Percy said. "We can look into the situation if the Merrys are spread too thin?"

"'We'?" Syd regarded Danny. "Quite a fine partner you've found." Danny could feel those hidden eyes assessing. "She's injured."

"She'll be fine," Percy said too brightly. "Nothing my friend and I can't handle."

"Does your friend have a name?"

"Untitled, I'm afraid." Percy shifted to block Danny's view, and her from the others. "Call her whatever you will. Only fifty-fifty she'll answer, anyway." He glanced at her over his shoulder, his expression tight. "Isn't that right, Betty? Belinda?"

Rampage, huh? She gratefully latched on to a spark of anger, anything to wash away the residual shame swirling inside. "Are you sure it's not *Butcher*?" Danny asked.

Percy winced and lowered his voice so only she could hear. "It's a long story. Now is not the time."

Jack the Ripper, the Demon of Whitechapel, Leather Apron, the Duke of Grandfellow: If terrorizing London was what he meant by following orders... "You killed prostitutes?" she whispered back. "What did they do, spit on the army?"

"Your lack of faith in me is insulting." He threw a grin towards the two other figures before answering quietly, "They were foreign agents and quite skilled, I'll have you know."

"That's . . ." Danny had nothing to say to that. "Unexpected."

Percy clapped his hands together and maneuvered them towards the mouth of the alley without turning his back. "Thank you for your rescue efforts, lads, but as you see, we are well and should be going."

Syd didn't need to move to stop them in their tracks. "You shouldn't bring proper ladies 'round these parts, Percy. Anything might happen to them when you're not looking."

The hulking man at Syd's side cracked his knuckles and smiled viciously.

As Percy's entire back muscles flexed, hard enough to break walnuts against, Danny came to the horrifying realization that Percy was afraid of these two and was doing his best to keep them from learning her name.

"I don't know what you mean," Percy said, never taking his eyes off the two men.

Syd snorted. "With that bustle and those earrings, every criminal from here to West End could pick her as an easy mark."

Percy stepped forward, friendliness gone. "I'm a messenger for the duke, a man Markus respects. If it's compensation you want for setting foot back on your turf, fine, but the girl stays out of this."

"The Merrys don't want your blunt. And the understanding between Pops and the duke is for him, and him alone." Syd glanced the big man's way, and a silent message passed between them. He turned on his heel, the big man in tow.

As they passed, Danny held herself perfectly still, taking her cue from Percy. When Syd spoke again from behind them, his voice was harder than steel.

"Stay out of St. Giles, Percy. Next time, we won't hesitate to take you out like the rest of the trash. This is your last warning."

Not ten seconds after the two men turned out of sight, Percy said, "Let's get out of here."

Danny didn't argue. Pulling her fallen hair back into a rushed coif, she followed Percy through a maze of decreasingly dirty and narrow streets, saying nothing until they'd left the acidic smell and uneasy feelings behind and stepped onto a main thoroughfare teeming with carriages and the more familiar scent of soap and horse.

Her mind was abuzz. Those men in the alley were gang members; it was the only explanation. She was not so sheltered she was unaware of the rampant brawls over imagined territory in the worst of the slums, but to think they'd stumble upon not one gang but two, in the middle of the day, the last being a couple Percy knew, and more alarming, the two knew Percy.

"Say something," Percy said at her side.

What was there to say? *I knew you had ties to criminals for your job, but those two men have me trembling through three layers of linen.* He'd mentioned 'foreign agents,' which meant her suspicions about the Home Office were spot on. Dealing with unsavory characters must have been a hazard of the job, but no one should grow familiar with those icy stares and committed threats.

Danny had a most irrational desire to wrap Percy in her arms like a child and hold him until he remembered what it was to feel safe.

"The smaller man didn't like you much." Nor the big, for that matter.

Percy winced. "Syd doesn't like anybody. Can't afford to when you run the best gang in the rookeries."

Danny didn't hide her surprise. "Syd is the leader? He's so slight." When the two had passed, Danny had been shocked to realize she was a solid three inches taller.

"Never go by appearances, Daniella." There was no teasing in Percy's voice. "Underestimate the smallest man and you will die."

Danny wouldn't make light, not when the spark in his eyes had gone out. "I'll remember."

"Good."

He offered her his arm and they kept pace on the left side of the sidewalk, passing costermongers and piemen selling everything from fruits and vegetables to mutton and eel.

The reality of danger, not two alleys over, had Danny itching beneath her skin, but she wouldn't give in to fear, nor let it claim her optimism. Today's outing and conversation would not tarnish under the light of realization.

What had transpired between her and Percy had been carnal, inevitable, like two strikes of lightning clashing in the dark. She wouldn't hope that he'd see past her demons, not when he struggled with his own so viscerally. All she could do was express how little that mattered to her now.

The shame still clawed at her, tearing at her mind to drag her into a dark mental space too horrifying to return to reality. But Percy hadn't run away. He'd stayed, held her while she'd fallen into that bottomless pit, and then pulled her back into the light.

She'd come to care for him. The man who teased her and laughed at the prim and proper. The man who taunted her body into the most delirious sensations of eroticism. And the man who fought enemies in the dark to protect her from harm, even when she could see how much the violence ate at him.

The world could be ugly, people more so, but in the end, everyone was surviving the only way they knew how.

He was one of them, and she was too.

As far as commonalities went, she prayed it would be enough.

PERCY'S BODY RELAXED as they moved farther away from the slums, though the hard set to his jaw remained.

He was lamentable. He should never have brought Danny within spitting distance of the rookeries. Syd had been right, the savage bastard. They were both far too well dressed to remain unnoticed, and even dirt smeared and wearing a sack, no one could mistake Danny's rigid spine and fine speech as anything but elite.

If he'd been thinking at all, he would never have agreed to a friendship between them. But the woman's presence ripped all rational thought to shreds. Not that their friendship would remain intact. Silent and gaze distant, she was probably concentrating all her fierce will on keeping from hysterics.

He'd been a fool all along thinking he could rescue her in the Crystal Palace from two-faced ladies and all past regressions would be wiped away. And that look of worthlessness on her face after the two thugs had been disarmed, he knew the feeling well.

"So . . ."

Percy admonished himself for how he held on to her one word with bated breath. When she said nothing else, he prompted, "Yes?"

She cocked her head, her lips tilted in unfathomable humor. "Vengeance? Butcher? How many names have you had in your career?"

Percy's shocked laugh was a release he needed, and a painful reminder setting expectations for Lady Daniella made him that much more a fool.

"I gained a new name every time I reinvented myself. First, to sound tough as a child, then as a man of rank in the army, and much later, as an evil shadow in the dark." He winked. "I told you I was famous."

His good humor vanished, remembering how close she'd come to harm. Gaze zeroing in on the wound on her arm, his chest tightened past the point of pain and went straight to unbearable. "Your arm needs bandaging."

She covered the cut with her hand. "The bleeding stopped. I'll be fine." Her small smile squeezed the heart in his chest. "Good thing your talents include disarming thugs." At his continued silence, she said, "I *am* fine, Percy."

Be *he* wasn't!

This was what he got for thinking he could keep something so innocent and beautiful close. Had he really been so naive as to think a monster like him could keep her safe?

"What I've done is deplorable, even in the name of serving

my country," he said.

"Your actions were sanctioned. If you hadn't done what was asked, someone else would have, and probably with less skill and mercy."

Mercy? She couldn't be so blind. "I'm no better than those thugs in the alley, threatening your life on a whim to commiserate with my past."

Danny stopped, right there in the open street, and said with passion, "You don't scare me, Percy. I pray I never understand what it is to take a life, but I can imagine the types of people who do it leisurely.

"I know you. I know who you are. Whoever those men were, you don't hide in the shadows anymore. The lives you've taken were necessary, even I can see that. You aren't a man to go blindly into anything. You were given orders."

"The bloodied hands are mine, Danny."

She gripped his face, refusing to let him look away. "Which makes you the strongest man I've ever known."

He shook his head, successfully extracting himself from her warm hands. He focused on the bustling street vendors and customers perusing the stalls, and he envied their simple lives. "Don't make me out to be a hero. Killing is easy when you're used to it."

"Lie to someone else, Percy. I see the deaths haunt you."

Percy stilled. His body reflexively made to flee from the attack, dive out of harm's way, but there was no escaping her words. She'd always seen him, even when he couldn't see himself.

Haunt him? He *was* haunted. He could laugh and lie and carry on like a man without a care in the daylight, but at night, when the shadows wrapped themselves around him, he remembered the faces, the screams, worse: The silence when his victims weren't given even a last cry of torment and outrage at what he'd taken from them for simply being on the opposite side of politics.

"Wherever you've gone," her soft voice called. "Come back

to me."

Percy's visions of blood and darkness wavered, then brightened, until all he saw was her shining face.

"I'm here," she said, lightly cupping his face with her hands. "You're safe with me."

There was that feeling again—the same warming and aching in his chest from the night in her bedchamber—a most pleasing pain Percy didn't know what to make of.

Trust. Compassion. She gave so much without realizing and asked only for his honest, vile self, like she saw the person beneath the monstrous exterior.

She hadn't earlier, he reminded himself. She'd collapsed and shook with the terror of his true face. But then she'd accepted his embrace and Percy swore in that moment she'd accepted all of him come what may. Trust. Compassion. *Loyalty.*

For a street urchin turned assassin, who'd never stayed in one place long enough to grow attached to anywhere, never felt safe enough to sleep with both eyes closed, the hand of connection she offered him in camaraderie and comfort had a distinct feeling of coming home.

And if the woman who wished to see the world in black and white—evil versus good—didn't see him as a dweller of the former, perhaps he'd try his hand at being worthy of the latter.

CHAPTER FOURTEEN

"HERE AGAIN?" DON set his journals and unlit lantern on the grass and sat, long legs out in front of him.

"Not here specifically." Danny pointed to a place farther down the hill by the water's edge. "Last time, I sat there."

"Arguing semantics? You are in dire straits."

"Yes, indeed," she said mockingly. "And a smart man would leave me to my contemplation."

"Hmm," he said. "What are you reading this time?" He tilted up her book to read the title. "*Poisons and How to Tell the Difference Between Fatal and Life Threatening.*" He chuckled. "Your outing went well yesterday, I take it?"

Danny groaned. "Don't start." Her hip was bruised, her scalp stung. Somewhere along the way home, she'd lost her favorite pistol. And that was all before she'd walked through her front door.

Upon returning to the townhouse, Denise had swooped down from whatever perch she'd been sitting in wait on and demanded every detail of the extra activities at the match, her ills mysteriously cured with insatiable curiosity.

Danny had obeyed, though she'd omitted their detour into the slums and the more sensual sport she and Percy had played on the terrace. Denise had relented after a solid two-hour interrogation on the carriage ride back to their country home, but not even the darkened carriage could've hidden the heat in

Danny's cheeks. Luckily, Denise could only persist so far with Mrs. Pebblestone within earshot.

Danny was lucky she didn't combust thinking about Percy's fingers against her thighs, and that hot length against her bruised folds. How she wished she could've lifted her skirts and seen him. Even the alley had been too dark to make out more than shapes and the feel of satin skin and steel.

If any of Uncle Jack's statues in the Fellow Pleasure Garden were an indication of average size, Percy was a monster. Less than a day since she'd seen him last and she missed his presence, his calming tone. How she hated not knowing if it would be the last time he'd darken her door.

There'd been so much left unsaid when he'd departed.

"Are you unwell?" Don's dark brows pinched in concern. "Your face is pale."

Danny nodded. "How is your research going?"

"How was your outing?"

"You're starting," she accused.

"And you're evading."

"You won't relent on this, will you?" Danny sighed and stared out at the water, the surface rippling with a chilled breeze. "Confusing." Confounded. Befuddled. Out of her mind.

Through the ups and downs of the day, Danny's feelings had remained constant. No, she wouldn't lie to herself. Her feelings had *deepened* with every flirting glance, every scandalous brush of skin against skin. And when Percy had revealed the depth of self-loathing he housed, her feelings had changed altogether. Friendship wouldn't be enough.

Percy needed loyalty and comfort, though he would never admit it. And Danny couldn't escape the fact that she wanted to be the person to give him those things. But she knew nothing of his darkness. Hearing details didn't equal understanding. As much as she wished it, the ghosts in his past may be more than even she could overcome. She knew from personal experience. But she wanted to try to be more for him and for herself.

She'd explain her own past and pray he could look past her rougher edges. And if he decided after hearing everything that he never wished to see her again, she'd have no regrets.

And if he condemned her . . .

Danny buried her face in her hands, her heart a mushed rag in her chest. "What should I do?"

"I'm astounded, Danny!"

Her head shot up at her brother's affronted tone.

"You already know the answer," he said. "You decided days ago what he meant to you."

Danny startled. There was no way her brother knew what she'd been thinking. She hadn't mentioned Percy at all, had she? "What do you mean?"

Don thumbed his nose and gathered his trade tools as if he'd turn tail and run after such cryptic words.

"Donald!"

Shaking his head, he rose to his feet, journals tucked underarm and lantern swinging from the other. "Stop asking what others think, sister. One thing Father and I agree on: You have a mind and ideals—and are mercifully not as impetuous as Denise—so use them. No one knows your mind better than you. Or your heart."

Danny gaped. "I've never heard you so outspoken."

"Unimaginable that a gentleman besides Father wishes for a mind to be put before the sex?" Don's expression was grim but fierce. "I was there that horrible day when the inspector returned you to us, remember? Seeing how strong you were then made me strive to be stronger myself."

Danny's heart squeezed. Her brother was the first of her family to see her that night, and the first who'd offered comfort the only way a scientific twelve-year-old boy knew how. He'd brought her to his personal library and spent hours sitting beside her while she'd forgotten the scars and fears in the details of the world.

He thought she was strong. The truth was, she'd grown

strong because he'd shared his strength.

"Don—"

"Prepare yourself, sister." Don smiled, bypassing the gratitude. "I believe a being's worth resides in nothing of physical substance. I can't. You know, you've *seen* where I go every night." His gaze went to the line of spruces at the other end of the lake, where the first signs of nocturnal life rustled in the needled limbs. "I learn more about myself by watching animals go about their lives, predictable but adaptive, relentlessly pursuing that which they need to survive.

"As people, we forget how much we've been given. Observing animal behaviors, cataloguing their struggles and triumphs, my greatest hope is one day others will read my notes and think on how they may better the world for more than their own pursuits, so we may all survive."

What an unforgiving speech. Only her brother could turn the eating habits of a flying mouse into a campaign to save humanity.

"That"—Danny found her throat was tight—"should be your speech to the House."

He laughed. "Think anyone would listen?"

"*I* would."

"You are a rarity, dear sister." Don tapped the front of his journal with a concluding rap of knuckles. "Now go win your duke."

Danny's heart clenched even as her cheeks hurt from smiling. "So much for not telling me what to do."

"I'm your older brother." He grinned, tapping his journal a second time. "I can't go completely against my nature."

PERCY BOLTED TO his feet and left his seat by the fire to cross to the window, feeling her presence before she threw the first stone.

Chest tight, he opened the window and looked down at an

apparition in dark skirts and whispered her name.

"Danny."

The smile she offered him was guarded. "I didn't mean to wake you."

"You didn't." God, she was beautiful with her hair unbound, her cheeks flushed from exertion. "What are you doing here?" In the middle of the night, after traversing miles alone through the woods.

"I . . ." She shook her head. The tip of her boot made circles in the grass. "I only meant to check how you were feeling."

"Me?" It would serve him right to be bleeding out in a gutter while rats gnawed on his entrails. "*You* were the one injured." He ran a hand through his hair, willing his brain to come up with something comforting to say. "I assume you couldn't sleep?"

Fuck, he sucked at this.

"I mean," he tried again. "I am here if you wish to talk?"

"Because I was cornered by two armed men?" she said, with a wry twist of her lips Percy didn't understand. "Not to worry. Happens to me on a regular basis."

He dropped his hand, only to realize it was shaking in anger. "Don't joke about this. You could've been hurt. You could've . . ." *He* couldn't say the word. The thought of her death enraged him, broke him. Only seeing her now, standing outside his window with bright eyes, dimmed the chaos building inside.

If she was here, did that mean she hadn't decided to abandon him? Their benign parting words at her family's townhouse had left much unsaid, including her wishes going forward.

Percy cursed himself again. He was not a bloody house pet that could be left out in the cold. He was a proper stray, unwanted except for when a kindhearted person offered a scrap of affection before returning home.

As she should do now, for her own good.

"Stay there. I'll be down in a moment." He didn't wait to see if she listened. Being two stories up and having no mighty oak tree to shimmy down, Percy made his way to the back of the house and out into the yard via the servants' entrance, each second with her out of sight a second more for his gut to twist into knots.

Feet eating up the lawn, he stopped an arm's length away, the sight of her tentative smile loosening the worst of the tangles.

The breeze caught a wisp of her hair where it fell softly against a rosy cheek.

"Hello," he said.

She laughed, that hair catching the corner of her mouth.

Damn it, now he couldn't stop staring at her lips.

"Hello," she said back.

He fought to keep his hands to himself. Why must she be so distracting? "That's not what I meant to say."

"It wasn't?"

"I meant to walk you home."

"That's an action, not a phrase," she teased as she tucked her hair behind her ear. "Unless you meant to say, 'May I escort you home?'"

Percy's chest—and groin—went tight watching her slender fingers play with her hair. "I would never be so well-mannered."

"Would you say, 'I *shall* escort you home'? Because I like a man who takes initiative."

"Danny."

"The mere fact you would bring me home at all negates your call to ungentlemanliness."

Percy lost his fight and reached for her, running a knuckle down her cheek and across those lips, refusing to hope. "What are you really doing here?"

"You didn't come to me." Miss Composure fiddled with her fingers, the action innocent and self-conscious and entirely charming. "I waited, you see, and I don't like waiting. I won't be one of those women who sit around waiting for a man to call. I've had man after man call, and I sat there like I am supposed to, but I won't do it anymore. Er—what I'm supposed to, I mean. Not that I have men parading through my drawing room . . . I'm saying this all wrong."

Percy couldn't believe his ears. "You're babbling."

She nodded. "I'm aware, and it's embarrassing, but I have something to say, and I refuse to stop until I say it."

"I'm listening." Percy strained not to miss a single, rushed word.

"I want you. *I* came to call on *you*. And I must tell you, I don't envy men the anxiety of it all." She dropped her hands and nodded with satisfaction. "Now that I've said my piece, I'll be going."

She turned on her heel.

She made it to the treeline before Percy took off after her, his heart pounding.

"Wait!" Percy tripped over a root in the dark, the moonlight not extending to the forest floor.

Danny marched on as if night vision was among her many talents.

Percy struggled along, his brain racing. "Would you stop?"

"Leave your audience wanting more," she said, *not* stopping.

"This isn't theatre." Percy cursed at another tree root. "I'm not wearing the right shoes to chase you."

"Exactly!"

Percy glanced up at her triumphant expression, seeing she'd mercifully stopped, and he took a moment to catch his breath.

"Now you see," she said, "I am the chase-e . . . chaser?"

Percy shook his head at their ridiculous farce. Must have been the lack of oxygen to his lungs because he matched her lunacy. "Well, I refuse to be the *chas-te*. We both know I'd never play it credibly."

"I thought this wasn't the theatre."

"I don't know what this is!" Percy threw his arms wide. "It's the middle of the night, I'm not wearing boots, and you just confessed your dishonorable intentions if I'm not hallucinating. What am I supposed to think?" How could he stop from hoping?

She huffed, her arms crossing over her chest. "That you can't wait to see me again tomorrow."

Percy rubbed his temple. He'd lost feeling in his toes five minutes ago and neither of them seemed coherent enough to talk plainly. She was overly tired too. That must be the reason she was here. A good night's sleep and she'd regret reaching out her hand.

He turned on his heel, suddenly not sure he could manage the next twelve hours. "I'm going to bed." There was little concern for her wellbeing on the way home. The madwoman could take on hungry animals, unfortunate poachers, and blasted tree roots in her current state.

"You can't go *now*." She traversed the root-lined floor with little trouble—proving him right—and came nose to chest with him. "I'll have your answer, sir."

"What answer?" He glanced around, certain he'd suffered food poisoning from dinner and was even now in his bed in the throes of fever. "You didn't ask any bloody questions."

She shook her head. "The question was implied."

This must have been why Hamish and Renard had turned to politics and charity. Nothing seemed complicated after standing toe to toe with a woman.

"Take mercy on me," he said. "What question am I to answer?"

"Will I see you tomorrow?"

"Do you want to see me tomorrow?"

"Don't answer a question with a question."

"Yes, fine. I'll see you tomorrow." He paused. "If you wish?"

"When?"

"What?"

"When will I see you?"

Percy held his head. "Dawn. Before the rooster crows. Before the dairyman." Now *he* was babbling.

"Don't use that tone. No one is forcing you to visit."

Percy dropped the charade. "Danny, you don't need to do this." The mere fact she was here to mend their friendship after what he'd subjected her to was too much. "You needn't play the martyr. I can never make up for what happened today, and you should feel no obligation to continue our acquaintance based on the circumstances. We are neighbors. Obviously, avoiding each other is out of the question, but we can limit our exposure. Take turns excusing ourselves from the obligatory events."

The words burned, and the burn lingered, leaving Percy's insides little better than a melting pot of revulsion and regret.

"You don't wish to be friends any longer?" she asked.

Percy studied her in the dark, convinced the shadows were the reason her expression looked fallen. "I didn't say that."

Her gaze lifted and the moonlight caressed her face. "Which is it, Percy? You're either so disgusted with my reaction in the alley that you wish to be rid of me, or you can overlook my behavior this afternoon and we may continue as we have been."

What the hell was she talking about? Percy blinked down at her, and because it bore vocalizing . . . "What the hell are you talking about?" She couldn't think *she'd* done anything wrong? "If you mean your screaming, I thought it ingenious."

Her brows furrowed. "Screaming? Who said anything about screaming?"

"You did."

"No, I didn't."

"Woman!" Percy grabbed her by the shoulders and forced her gaze to meet his. "Speak plainly, Danny. What am I to find so heinous that I would walk away?" The idea was laughable.

"My . . . reaction to that man's knife." Her jaw tightened and her eyes went blank, hollow. "Don't bother denying you didn't notice."

Of course he'd noticed. Percy still couldn't quell his surging hatred for the man who'd elicited such a perfect sound from her mouth. "What of it?"

Her mouth gaped. Closed. Opened. "You're repulsed by it." She frowned. "Aren't you?"

"I told you days ago I wasn't." How many times must he

repeat himself?

Danny stared up at him.

Apparently once more.

Percy tipped up her chin and enunciated his words. "You. Are. Perfect."

She sniffed and wiped her cheek.

And now she was bloody crying.

Heaving, really. Good God, how much water could pour from a woman's face?

Percy patted his shirt and trousers helplessly in search of a scrap of fabric to offer her.

"You—" Her voice broke. "You don't know what that means to me. I feel . . ."

Percy offered his sleeve, willing her to finish her thought before he went mad.

When she'd delicately dabbed at her wet cheeks, she smiled up at him, eyes bright. "I feel better, thank you."

Percy knew that wasn't what she'd set out to say, but he wouldn't press her now that she'd found her composure. Since this seemed as good a time as any, he offered his own damning statement. "I thought you'd never wish to see me again after what I did to those men." Remembering, Percy gritted his teeth. How easy it was to shut off his mind and let his body do the work even now, like a devil pulling his willing strings.

Danny cocked a brow. "You disarmed them expertly and with little bloodshed. What on Earth would I find disagreeable about that?"

Percy rubbed his neck. Surely, he didn't need to explain this to a proper lady? "Because I hurt them without thought or remorse. I may have finished the job if you hadn't been there."

"The men were going to *kill* us," Danny said.

How was she not understanding? "But my past—"

"We all have a past. Pasts we must face and accept. There are things in mine that are abhorrent, things I would never wish to share with another living soul."

Percy shook his head. Even now, she downplayed his demons and willed him to condemn her for having her own. "Nothing you could say would change how I see you. Nothing."

"Percy, you can't say that until you know the truth."

"Enough!" How could she not see how perfect she was? "I don't bloody care about your past."

She threw her hands in the air. "I don't care about yours, either!"

"Good!"

"We'll never speak of this again, then."

"Great!" *Thank God.* "I'm going to kiss you now."

"You should."

"Fine!"

Their mouths came together, more teeth than lips, and their bodies seemed to mutually sigh at the contact.

Percy ran his fingers through her hair, and the moan that escaped her throat was a match to the one drawn from his own lips. The tension between them bypassed simple lust. This was the sealing of a contract, an unspoken agreement that nothing of the last few hours changed anything. Though confusion ricocheted through Percy's mind like a loose rubber ball, their friendship remained intact, possibly stronger than before.

Percy vowed it would stay that way.

He broke their kiss to press his lips to her temple.

"This friendship between us, I tell you I won't abuse it again," he vowed. "You'll be safe with me. I'll *keep* you safe." God damn, he was begging, but he'd do far more humiliating prostration to keep her in his life. "Danny, I will—"

She stopped his words with a finger to his lips. "You talk too much, Percy. Kiss me if you need to move your lips."

Everything she said was so agreeable.

He growled low in his chest, taking her command as commandment. "As you wish, my lady."

Temperaments compatible, bodily chemistry more so, there was no use dissecting the connection between them. Self-reflection was for scholars and men with too much free time to preoccupy themselves. So, Percy did as he was told and kissed her with oblivious pleasure. *Only* kissing tonight. There was no need to rush. This time, he'd do this right.

He captured her mouth again, dipping his tongue between her inviting lips, and promised there'd be no more silly missteps.

CHAPTER FIFTEEN

THERE WAS SOMETHING new and different from the ever-present thread of desire between him and Danny today. A sense of quiet contentment Percy hadn't expected.

With Denise somewhere on the grounds preoccupying the displeased Mrs. Pebblestone with some new malady, Percy leaned back against a low-lying stone wall, one of dozens in Grandfellow's topiary park. Eating sandwiches layered with varied thin slices of meat and cucumber and taking in the filtered rays of the warm sun, Percy concluded revealing one's true nature to another person was a freeing exercise that left a kind of peace to one's constitution.

Taking another bite of salted pork between two healthy slices of rye bread, Percy found he didn't mind the peace or quiet one bit, or the sandwiches.

"Teach me one of your cons," Danny said beside him.

Percy choked on his bite and pounded his chest with a fist. The blanket they were using for Danny's activity choice of a picnic twisted around his boot. An activity Percy had assumed was less likely to end with them in some dire situation. Now he had second thoughts.

"Cons?" He set down his food in hopes of further harm and cast a frown her way. "I told you I was an officer."

Her returning expression was stubborn. "Not *always* an officer."

He tilted his head to get a better angle to look at her face. This should be good. "And what other occupation do you believe I held?"

"A spy and a conman."

"Obviously," he muttered. No use denying the allegations. There must have been a smell men like him carried around, something the nose of a buttoned-up lady of the *ton* could sniff out like old trout. Though he'd wager Danny was a rare breed that far surpassed all others. What other woman could sniff out *his* secrets while wearing the most fetching sunflower gold frock, all with the expression of a general staring down her enemy until they cracked?

Not seeing a way out of answering, Percy relented. "We prefer the term *prestidigitator*."

"Prestidigitators are illusionists that entertain the masses," she pushed back immediately. "I doubt your prestiditeg-es are amused once they realize they've been conned."

Percy ran a hand over his face. She was a freaking dog with a bone. And as stubborn as a bull in the pen. There was no getting out of it, then.

He sat up and pointed to one of the gardeners across the park currently moving potted topiaries to one side of the walk, standing back and apparently finding fault, and then returning them to their original position, only to repeat the process a minute later.

English servants were touched in the head. There must have been something more productive for a grown man to do than play board-less chess in the middle of the afternoon?

"Imagine you want that topiary," he said.

Danny laughed. "Why would I want a bush cut to resemble a bear?"

He raised his brows at her lack of imagination. "Perhaps it's the only remaining record of the animal. Maybe the late Thomas Woolner cut it during his last hours of life. A collector would pay handsomely to have such a rare piece from the artist they admired, wouldn't they?"

"That bear was cut by Mr. Stonebrook, a most prestigious *gardener.*" She frowned at the bush. "I'm not even sure that's actually meant to be a bear." She squinted. "A boar on its hind legs?" Her head tilted to look from a different angle. "A pregnant goat rearing in a fit of apoplexy?"

Percy rolled his eyes. This coming from the woman who couldn't imagine a priceless tree worth pinching. "Work with me, woman."

She sighed and tucked a stray curl behind her ear. "You were saying the topiary is the last precious piece by a famous, dead artist."

Percy nodded. "And you want to steal it."

Her eyes widened. "I do?"

He leaned close, enjoying her quick intake of breath. "*We* do."

She licked her lips. "Where do we start?"

Her eagerness was so damn charming. Percy cleared his throat and mentally slugged himself. *Focus, damn it.*

Percy cleared away a spot on the blanket and used what remained in their basket to indicate each position.

He set a ham sandwich down. "This here represents the gardener. What we call the 'mark.' As in—"

"The person you wish to con." Danny waved her hand for him to glance over the obvious.

Next, the chicken sandwich on a buttery, toasted, wheat roll he set at a spot behind the ham. "You will work in Mr. Stoneybrook's blind spot."

"Stonebrook," Danny corrected.

Of course she knew the name of his gardener. No doubt along with the man's wife and three children's names and how many seedlings they kept in pots by their window over the winter.

"Do you wish to learn or not?" he asked.

Danny mimed buttoning her lips, silently promising to hold

her tongue . . . until she mimed unbuttoning her lips and said, "Must I be the chicken sandwich? It feels wrong."

"The chicken feels wrong?" He spoke the words carefully, making sure it sounded as crazy when he said it as when she did.

She nodded. "Couldn't I be the roast lamb? Or the garnished eggplant?"

Percy blinked. "There's an eggplant sandwich?" He searched for the remaining items in the basket and, indeed, found a telling purple layered sandwich, the bread soaked through to wet paste. He dropped the thing and grimaced as it made an unappealing *splat*. "Why on Earth would you wish to be the eggplant?"

"It's unexpected, isn't it?" Her brow wrinkled. "I was under the impression I am charged with seeming unthreatening, so the mark underestimates my threat."

Jesus. "You got all of that out of two sandwich placements?"

Percy reflected on if he truly wished to continue the woman's education in criminal sport, realizing he may have been feeding a monster in the making.

It was a credit to his own monstrous nature that he found the idea of Lady Danny's shift to underhanded tactics wildly arousing.

"You're correct," he said. "Except it's *my* job, as the distraction, to play the unassuming."

He saw the wheels turning in her mind as she tapped her chin. "So . . . you're the eggplant?"

Percy sighed. "Yes, I'm the stupid eggplant." How had he gotten roped into these ridiculous conversations?

"What am I to do, then?" she asked.

He grinned, pulling the last sandwich from the basket: a five-layered beauty of salami, ham, roast beef, cheddar, and some kind of pickled beet. Upon reflection, a much better substitute for the complicated woman at his side.

Replacing the chicken sandwich, he set the new indicator down. "You are the real star. While I distract Mr. Stoney, you will pinch the topiary."

She didn't correct the name-butchering a second time. No,

her head was firmly in the game.

"Won't he notice right away the topiary is missing and catch us?" she asked.

He tapped his nose. "Not if we put a fake in its place."

Her mouth dipped into a disbelieving curve on one side. "And where, pray tell, are we to magically acquire a perfect fake in the next few minutes?"

He shook his head. "It doesn't need to be a perfect match. Only close enough of a resemblance to pass a glancing inspection so when the gardener moves on, if he happens to glance back, he'll see what he expects to see."

Danny's eyes lit with understanding. "And by the time he realizes the tailless sow is missing, we'll be long gone."

He leaned back and took a bite of the five-layered heaven, speaking around his bite. "It's called a 'Frenchman's Switch.' Used to play the trick on unsuspecting tourists all the time as a boy."

Danny laughed. "I bet you were good at it?"

"Not at first," he said lightly, though the words conjured childhood memories weighted like boulders.

Finishing the sandwich, Percy brushed the crumbs from his hands. "Do you think you understand the play?"

"I believe so."

"Good." Percy smiled and gave her a nudge. "Because now we're going to do it."

She startled. "You want us to *literally* steal that maybe-a-bear-probably-a-bloated-rabbit topiary?"

"No better way to learn than by doing."

"We shouldn't," she started.

But as her little, white teeth came out to worry her bottom lip, with her distinctly using the word 'shouldn't' instead of 'couldn't,' Percy knew he had her.

Pointing to a field down the hill running alongside the treeline, where an overgrown but clearly marked path led around the park and out into the other side of the topiary gardens, Percy told her, "Use the path and keep low. Pick up stray sticks that will be the right height and freshly dropped leaves that are still green." He pinched a half a dozen pins from her coif and handed them to her, resisting the urge to run his fingers through the curtain of chocolate-rich hair that fell.

"When you've found enough material, stick them together."

He felt the excitement building in her through her shaking hands and increased breaths.

She licked her lips again, clearly one hundred percent in her role because she murmured low, "When will I know to exchange the pots?"

"I'll give you this signal." He made a high-pitched whistle, though quiet enough not to draw Mr. Stonebrook's attention. After he'd repeated the sound twice more, he asked, "Think you're ready for this, partner?"

It wasn't as if they were caught, Scotland Yard would be hauling them off to the pen, but there was still a risk of gossip by the servants if Lady Daniella Deime and the new Duke of Grandfellow were found stealing topiaries and sneaking around in a most unbecoming fashion.

All this Danny had to be painfully aware of, being the daughter of an earl and previously familiar with the ugliness of the *ton*'s chatter and ridicule. But Danny showed no nerves at all as those lovely lips curled upwards in a conspiratorial smile that had Percy reaching for that godforsaken mushed excuse for a sandwich and stuffing it in his mouth to keep from kissing her senseless.

"Let's do it," she said, the spark in her eyes contagious. "Let's con Stoney."

Percy's smile stretched until he was sure he could pose for a dentifrice campaign. He swallowed the eggplant and waved her on. "After you."

"No, no." She shook her head. "I'm not here, remember? Go on as if I'm but a cricket in the grass and unworthy of note."

Percy continued smiling at the beautiful creature in front of him, looking as harmless and innocent as the wisps of clouds in the sky. No one would suspect beneath that simple frock, a storm of a woman was brewing to blow the years of elitist rules far to the sea.

He couldn't wait.

ARMS FULL OF her bounty, Danny picked her way through the path and stopped in the shelter of the waist-high wall that separated park from garden to construct her patchwork counterfeit.

With shaky hands and a racing heart, she did her best to put together a passing likeness of the topiary, while listening for Percy's signal.

Deep down, she knew the feeling of excitement was wrong. A person who enjoyed taking other's things was halfway gone to criminal, weren't they? Rationally, she knew what they were doing was technically not a crime. Seeing as how the topiary already belonged to Percy and it was with his explicit tutelage and encouragement that she 'pinch' it.

The way he'd sketched out the plan, his deep voice painting the movements and paths with such a dramatic buildup, Danny could see how the romance and the payoff would tempt an otherwise honest person into a life of crime.

Especially if one's partner was a silver-tongued devil.

Mentally stepping back to criticize her substitute, Danny deemed the likeness passing. And not a moment off, since the next thing she heard was a pair of male voices discussing the other gardens on the estate.

"Is there room for a shipment of statues in one of the other gardens?" Percy asked.

"There's already the Pleasure Garden, Your Grace. Decked out with more than forty pieces." Mr. Stonebrook sounded surprised. "Are you interested in collecting more?"

"Er—yes," Percy said, recovering well. "But those are all

nudes, you see? What I'm planning is a celebration of the *animal* kingdom."

"Animals, Your Grace?"

"Of course!" Percy said. Danny heard a slight *slap*, imagining him clapping the gardener on the back and making the older man highly uncomfortable. "Naturally, I came to you for recommendations, Mr. Stoney. Just look at the exceptional work you've done on these topiaries. A man who could design such a magnificent bear out of nothing but wood and leaf, why, who else would I come to but you?"

"That is a cow, Your Grace."

At the outrageous claim, Danny risked the entire operation to peer over the wall and examine the topiary. She frowned at the four-footed blob and the smaller mounds atop. If that was a cow, she feared for the heifer's constitution.

"Exceptional cow," Percy went on, as if he'd meant the right animal the whole time. "I want animals of all varieties showcased, in their real sizes, but I want them to complement each other."

He directed Mr. Stonebrook's attention towards the trees, and Danny ducked back behind the wall to avoid detection.

"Wouldn't want a cricket next to an elephant, for example," Percy said.

"Indeed not, Your Grace! Why, the idea is preposterous."

Percy sounded too enthusiastic to Danny's ears to be sincere. "I knew you'd understand. Now, we must think about this carefully. Do you have any birds currently in the garden?"

"Birds? No, Your Grace."

"Not even a spotted raven?"

"Never heard of it, Your Grace."

Neither had Danny. She groaned. Poor Mr. Stonebrook. If her gut was correct, Percy was about to send the lovely old gardener on quite the merry goose chase.

"Unique creatures, the SRs. Rarely sighted this far south," Percy said. "Small heads, large wingspans. Come, I'll draw you a picture. Strangest bird you've ever seen. There must be a recording of the beast in the library here."

Danny readied, listening as the men's voices grew quieter as they moved towards the house.

"And their call!" Percy embellished loud enough for Danny to hear even beneath the water in the middle of the lake. "Think a mix between a sparrow and an ostrich. Like this . . ."

Danny didn't hesitate. As soon as that high-pitched whistle hit her ears, she moved. Keeping low, she beelined straight for the *cow* topiary. Glancing around and seeing no one, Danny placed her counterfeit in a nearby empty pot and set it beside the real one, feeling a surge of triumph taking hold.

Only for it to sink into frustrated failure.

No matter how hard she pushed or pulled, the real topiary had the weight of a grown miniature bush with a full root system, a load of dirt, and a ceramic pot to boot. The only way that topiary was getting stolen was if the thing sprouted legs to walk away on.

Danny bit her lip and racked her brain. There must have been something she could use around here. If Mr. Stonebrook, a middle-aged man, could lift this thing half a dozen times in a matter of minutes, surely, all she needed was a bit of a start?

But as Danny found neither tool nor barrel—and the shed where the main tools were kept would take far too long—her frustration mounted. Not only frustration.

A part of her also acknowledged a sliver of pride in the undertaking, pride and skill she felt in need to prove to Percy. He'd always challenged her to work through her questions and come to her own conclusions at the speed and power of her own mind.

Somehow, she didn't believe the detail of the bush's weight had slipped Percy's notice. Not an officer and an agent whose very life depended on calculating to the smallest degree. There must be a way for her to move the bush.

Think, she told herself. If pushing the pot was out of the question and dragging was beyond her capabilities, what was left?

The answer came to her like a knock to the head.

Shaking off the daze, Danny sprang into action. Using all her weight, this time instead of pulling the base, she carefully weaved her hands through the leaves and smaller branches to grasp the main system in the middle and pulled until she felt the pot tip onto its side.

Once the pot lay safely on its side and ledge, Danny had little trouble rolling the thing off the path and into the field, where no one would see the tree in the tall grass.

Hearing the sound of voices emerging from the house, Danny put shin to bush and hand to stem to get as far from the garden—and possible detection—as quick as her weary legs and waning arms would allow.

When she hit the safety of the trees, Danny tucked the pot behind a thick oak and sank to the forest floor, her muscles twitching, her breath ragged, and her skin flushed with exhilaration.

She marveled at the breeze, the mogshade, the trees themselves. She'd done it! She'd stolen a bush. Clipped and made all the more an achievement by its incredible weight and shaped like a regal cow . . .

Danny glanced at her trophy. All right, the bush was rather worthless and the rendering of the animal awful, but sitting here, ruining her best frock in the dirt, she felt the adventure and partnership as real as if she'd stolen the Crown Jewels.

And that was priceless to her.

Snap!

Danny's head swung around hearing twigs snap under approaching boots. She sagged against the pot when Percy walked into view, his grin dashing.

"Well done, partner." He shook his head, his admiration clear. "And that fake you put up wasn't half-bad, either."

Danny's chest swelled with the compliments, as much as possible when her entire body felt like undercooked blancmange. She slapped the side of the pot with the palm of her hand, feeling giddy now that the theft was over.

"Why that was nothing, good sir. I could have taken the lot, but I didn't wish for poor Mr. Stoney to lose his position. I hear the aristocrat who lives here is fond of his animal collections. Especially his *spotted raven*."

Percy smiled as he took a seat beside her, using his half of the pot to rest his back. "You're a natural. You even figured out how to move the pot." He nudged her shoulder with his own. "Clever girl."

Clever she may have been, but sore she was now.

She grabbed her shoulder and winced. Conmen must be the most athletic people in the world. "I may have to crawl through the woods to get home."

"Growing pains of the criminal life," Percy said. "You should stick to cornering villains instead of joining their ranks."

It was her turn to smile, the only movement that didn't hurt. "That sounds highly dangerous. A lady would flirt with ruin if she listened to your advice."

She rolled her head to set him down with her fiercest imitation of Xanithippe, but the action left them facing each other, their bodies and mouths but inches apart.

Suddenly, her aches and pent-up energy transformed into a flood of awareness.

Here they were again, in a most compromising position, not a servant in sight.

Judging by the glazed look in his eyes, he felt the tension mounting between them too. His voice was rough when he said, "It's all right to admit you enjoy it."

His gravelly tone shot bolts of want to her toes. Leaning forward, she didn't know to which she referred—to the criminal behavior or him—when she confessed against his lips, "I like it."

The kiss was no more than a wing's brush of lips, but the contact felt like it carried with it an emotional pressure Danny couldn't decipher. Pulling back a breath, their gazes locked. No one had ever looked at her like him: full of hunger and intensity . . . and pride and respect.

A correlating feeling of connection clicked into place somewhere in the vicinity of her chest.

She reached out, her fingers whispering across his mouth, eager to grasp the feeling before it vanished. "Percy—"

"What in tarnation?!"

Danny gasped at the distant yell. She and Percy broke apart to poke their heads around the great oak in time to see Mr. Stonebrook scratching his head at the stand-in bush, his mouth working and his gaze searching the area.

"What in tarnation?" the gardener repeated. He stood back from Danny's poor excuse for a trimmed bush and peered around the pot as if the original were hidden behind.

Danny watched in rapt horror, fearing the man to stand on his head next, until the man beside her snickered.

No, it was worse than a snicker. Percy snorted.

"Oh, no." Danny arranged her face into a severe expression, holding back the beginning of her own mirth.

Percy snorted again, wiping the laughter from his eyes.

"Don't, Percy—"

He snorted a third time, followed by a whoosh of breath that sounded like a great *"UHHHYUK."*

Danny lost the battle. Her laughter burst out, as sporadic and unchecked as his.

Children's laughter.

They laughed until the tears ran. They laughed until their sides pinched and their chests heaved.

When at last Danny released a final hiccup, she found herself on her back, staring up at the canopy, pressed side to side with Percy.

"I haven't laughed like that since before I was fresh out of stay bands," Danny said.

"Now, *that* is criminal."

She laughed again, her sore cheeks now matching the rest of her body.

She glanced at the pot resting comfortably above their heads.

"Whatever shall we do with this? If we bring it back now, Mr. Stonebrook will genuinely believe he's lost his faculties."

"It doesn't matter what we do with it. Its purpose has already been served," Percy said flippantly. "No topiary has ever been so well desired."

At the word *desired*, Danny felt a resurgence of those troubling feelings from earlier. Lingering excitement from the theft? A delayed case of hay fever? Partial possession of a long-dead spirit reliving the thrill of a merry jaunt through the woods?

What on Earth was the matter with her?

Oblivious to her internal turmoil, Percy rolled onto his side and offered her a wide smile. "Congratulations, partner." He extended a hand across his body. "To your first successful con."

Danny slid her hand into his and prayed those new emotions swirling inside weren't the beginning of a long con she played on herself: Desiring more than the agreed-upon friendship that was quickly becoming the most rewarding relationship in her life.

CHAPTER SIXTEEN

"Y ou're whistling," Renard accused from across the poker table.

Percy glanced at the two men playing cards from his seat by the window. Having found himself a hot cup of tea, a plate of biscuits, and a soft cushion, he'd been lost in his thoughts while he waited for them to finish their game. Thoughts of a dark-haired woman who came with his name on her lips and his finger between her thighs. A woman who kissed like a wild nymph in the dark embrace of the woods and stole topiaries from unsuspecting gardeners like a pro.

"Am I?"

Hamish placed his cards on the table. "Been doing it since you walked in."

Renard cursed and threw his losing straight down before leaning back in his chair and eyeing Percy. "A bit peculiar."

Hamish shook his head. "Downright unpleasant."

"And smiling. Do you see that smile?" Renard said.

Hamish looked alarmed. His won pot forgotten, he too turned to study Percy, brows drawn. "Is that what that was? I thought he was holding in a bodily complaint."

They were like nattering magpies. "Did you summon me here for a reason," Percy said, "or merely for your ill-witted sport?"

"Sport, I should think." Renard glanced at Hamish. "Was

there something we needed?"

"Not I," Hamish said.

"You didn't summon me?"

Hamish shook his head.

"Perhaps Charlotte sent the missive?" Renard offered.

Percy inclined his head to the garden out the drawing room doors, eager to finish this errand so he might make other, far more agreeable, calls to a neighboring estate. "Is the duchess outside?"

Renard nodded. "Camille is with her and my daughter." The last word he said with male pride.

Percy would enjoy reminding the smug man how two days ago, he'd paced the floors of his country estate so long, he'd left a permanent line in the carpet, while his duchess had lain upstairs, screaming bloody murder the entire twenty hours of labor.

Starting for the door, Percy found a good place to set his cup and saucer as he bid the two adieus.

Hamish thumped the table. "Good gracious! He's gone and found her."

Renard stretched his arms over his head before picking up his own cup of tea. "Found whom?"

"His duchess."

Percy froze.

Renard startled. "What makes you say that?"

"His attendance at the ball, willingly going off to the firing squad. The whistling, the smiling, what does that make you think of?"

Renard set down his cup, rattling the china in his surprise. "I hadn't thought of that. You think it's a woman?"

Percy gritted his teeth, his reply too quick. "No."

"That's a yes," Renard said. "Who do you think it is?"

"Some barmaid, perhaps?" Hamish said.

Renard wrinkled his nose. "Too common. What about a governess?"

"Enough!" Percy shouted.

"Oh, my," Hamish said. "It's worse than we thought."

"Indeed."

"What the bloody hell are you two talking about?"

"Should we tell him?" Renard asked.

Hamish shrugged. "He's not smart enough to figure it out on his own."

No one would find their bodies in the Thames if he weighed the corpses down. "I'm going to kill you both."

Hamish cocked a brow. "You're in love, idiot."

Percy sputtered. "That's . . . That's . . ."

"True?" Renard said.

"Honest?" Hamish offered.

"Impossible."

The men weren't listening. They continued to prattle on over the likelihood the woman was a seamstress from London, or a Scottish lass, or something akin to a bullfighter from Spain.

Percy would have sliced them open with his tea plate if the word hadn't shaken him badly enough he had to sit back down on the divan.

Love. Such a meaningless word men spouted whenever it suited the need to disarm a woman. But, hearing it now, annoyance and indifference weren't the first emotions that sprang to the surface. This time, there was a warmth, a kind of contentment, and a face.

Did he love Danny?

It was true she was clever and disarming. He relished her company when able and thought of her constantly when apart. He'd chalked his single-minded thoughts to the rarity of their friendship and pent-up desire, but he didn't crave her body—well, he *did*, but not physical connection alone. He ached for her mind and easy company, the sound of her laugh, and the unmitigated certainty with which she saw the world in an optimistic light.

Good God, he was in love.

"Damn it!"

"Ah, see? He's figured it out." Hamish shook his head, his

expression pitying.

"This is terrible." Percy stared at his hands. This couldn't happen. Affection and connection were risky, but love . . . Nothing good would come of losing his heart. "She'll get hurt."

"Confident, isn't he?" Renard crossed one leg over the other and leaned back in his chair. "No certainty she'll say 'yes.' Women are unexpected like that, especially if she's a lady."

Percy heard the Duke of Lux's words and hope flared. "That's right! She'd refuse me." Of course she would. He may have had a fancy title and fortune now, but Danny knew what kind of man he really was. Her own fortune and standing in society were greatly coveted. She'd have no shortage of suitable offers. Hadn't she hinted as much? She enjoyed their friendship. Mutual pleasure wasn't the same as true affection.

"No luck there," Hamish said. "If it's the lady I think it is, she'll have him. *Only* him, if Charlotte's insight is correct, which it always is."

Percy turned to him sharply. "What do you mean?"

"If the gossip rags are to be believed, you've been spending an inordinate amount of time with Lady Daniella Deime." Hamish nodded when Percy frowned. "Charlotte and Daniella struck up a friendship after meeting at the Leishires' ball. I overheard one of their conversations in which the lady asked after a mysterious man she'd met at that same ball, a man she was convinced was an acquaintance of ours."

Percy reined in the desire to cut his friend's tongue from his mouth hearing Danny's name on his lips, and the unspoken closeness of their acquaintance. "Get to the point, Hamish."

Hamish's brows rose in a maddening expression of superiority. "The lady has turned down nine proposals since then, I hear. It doesn't take my wife's sharp mind to make the connection." He gave Percy a pointed look. "I wonder if her refusals have anything to do with a certain mysterious man?"

Nine proposals? The number *was* scandalous. And yet, the number wasn't near staggering enough for a woman as fine as

Danny. The men of England were morons.

"She turned them all down?"

"Earls, barons," Hamish said. "A viscount or two."

"Wasn't there a duke in there as well?" Renard asked.

"You're right. Duke of Wembley."

It's not possible.

She'd been waiting for him. The idea was ludicrous, as unimaginable as a lady who demanded a kiss in payment for silence. Or a lady who walked miles in the dark to check and see if a black-hearted devil was all right.

Would she say 'yes' if he asked?

Ties of any kind led to death. That had been the first rule drilled into him by his superiors.

But he wasn't an officer in Her Majesty's army anymore, nor an agent sanctioned by the Home Office. If he avoided the rookeries, his enemy list comprised of a single name.

Nic, that evil bastard, hadn't shown himself in over three years—very possibly a rotting corpse at the bottom of the Thames. And if he was gone . . .

Danny was wild and sensual, clever and competitive, beautiful, charming . . . and she made the most erotic sounds when she came. Why couldn't Percy beg her to take him?

He threw his cup and saucer on the table and went for the door. He bloody well was going to find out.

"Where are you going?" Hamish asked.

"To get my duchess."

His friend waved him off with a knowing smile. "I'll send your regrets to Charlotte."

PERCY'S HANDS WERE clammy as he was shown to the second-floor drawing room. He'd practiced what he'd say, even memorized one of those insipid poems of Byron's the ladies all twittered about. Over and over, he recited some benign description of a beautiful woman until the door opened and his mushed brain called out in greeting, "Of cloudless climes!"

Frankly, the young man who'd walked in was just as surprised as he was.

Taking in the split tailcoat and an unfortunate mismatch of polka dots and stripes all in the same ensemble, Percy assumed he'd just professed his affections to a half-blind footman.

But if the servant found Percy's outburst odd, the man matched the insanity by saying, "I prefer Wheatley's poem: 'To Maecenas.'"

Percy blinked. "You prefer verses of inadequacy to lamentations of love?"

"Is that what you got out of it?" The man rubbed his chin, where a peppering of whiskers would have any housekeeper descending from the rafters in a rage. "I took the words as more of a hopeful prayer. An interesting perspective, Mr. . . .?"

"Percy." He grimaced, remembering he was a titled man and here on a formal visit. "Er—Grandfellow."

The man's dark brows arched. "The Duke of Grandfellow. How fortunate." He plopped down on the divan opposite Percy's seat and crossed his legs at the ankles, revealing a glaringly obvious mismatch of stockings. "Now we may speak."

"Speak?"

"Size you up, to be frank." The man's dark gaze gave him a onceover in a way that felt familiar. "I have concerns about your worth."

Were all footmen this blunt and patronizing? Percy reconsidered his distaste for English servants.

"How do you feel about fox hunting?" the man asked.

Percy had no idea the protocol in such an impromptu interrogation, but the man seemed sincere and unbiddable, and Percy could use a verbal match to calm his nerves.

"No prelude, sir? No pleasantries?" he asked. "No introduction?"

The man threw Percy a smirk. "Were you not the one who

confessed your intentions upon my arrival, not even a formal kiss on the hand?"

Oh, but the man was impossible not to like. Perhaps he could steal the cheeky man away from the household and bring him back to Fellow Hall.

"Fox hunting is barbaric," Percy said truthfully. "Any man who wishes to boast of skill should reserve his claims to the day after a ball. The patience required is just short of saintly and the maneuvering of social etiquette far more dangerous."

"I see you've attended your fair share of balls."

"Three, and it was four too many."

The man chuckled. "And what are your thoughts on trees?"

"Trees?"

"I'm a purveyor of nightly reports. Most evenings, I walk the grounds in search of interesting creatures found in trees." Leaning back, the man leveled Percy a gaze that had him itching under the collar. "You wouldn't believe the things one finds high up at night."

Percy cursed himself for not waiting for a moonless sky. There was little doubt the man had found a most interesting sight over a week ago, when a man had found himself knocking on the window of a lady of the house in the dead of night.

Keeping his voice steady, Percy met the man's stare head on. "Most men would raise the alarm at a predator sighting."

"I'm not most men, Your Grace," he said.

There was a long pause, but the silence was not empty. Percy forced himself to not look away, feeling if he did so, he'd lose whatever test he'd stumbled into. A minute passed. Two.

With a warm smile, the man stood, all traces of hostility gone. "Very good. You pass."

Percy tracked his movements to the door, feeling oddly disappointed and more than a little relieved. "That's it? No more wooing? I feel positively used, sir."

"Seeing as I was not the person you came to visit, I leave the rest of the wooing up to you." The man gave Percy an inscrutable wink and nodded in the direction of the window. "You'll find Danny practicing archery in the side lawn."

Percy didn't ask how the man knew whom he'd come to visit. Nor why he referred to her so familiarly. His gaze went to the view outside and the three-ringed target in the distance where two arrows were seated in the inner ring. Of course the Goddess of War was a superior shot, and she was currently armed when Percy found himself in need of discussing an overly emotional subject.

"A word of advice, friend," the man said, drawing Percy's attention. "Stave off the poetry. Your delivery is horrible and will make no impression on her."

Percy's gaze narrowed. "You're not a footman, are you?"

The man bowed. "Merely a concerned party and at your service, Your Grace." Before the door shut behind him, the man called over his shoulder with every pompous air of a gentleman, "I'm rooting for you, Byron. We all are. Don't screw it up."

CHAPTER SEVENTEEN

PERCY STEPPED ONTO the lawn, taking in the distant targets and the table laden with bows and arrows, their mistress nowhere in sight.

"Danny—Lady Daniella!"

"By the trees!"

Percy followed the muffled voice to the treeline at the far end of the field and stared up at a scraggly spruce in horror. "What the devil are you doing?!"

Reaching for a higher branch, Danny glanced down between her arms, her cheeks flushed and wisps of hair curling around her chin. "Percy, good. I'll need you to catch her."

"Catch her?" Seeing nothing in the immediate vicinity, Percy could only surmise she'd struck her head while climbing and was now hallucinating. His chest squeezed with panic. "You mustn't move after a bump to the head." He slouched off his coat and unbuttoned his cuffs to roll up his sleeves. "Wait there. I will come get you."

"No time for that," Danny called, stepping onto a higher branch. "If Lord Pickles is startled, we may lose our footing. I'll reach up and guide her down to you."

Her injury was worse than he feared. Lifting his hands, he approached her at the base of the tree as if she were a frightened animal. "I understand, Danny. Whoever this Lord Pickles is, I will see to his care."

One of the branches rustled and Danny's face appeared in a hole in the foliage. "Can you *be* more condescending? I am not out of my head. Lord Pickles is real and currently attached to my sleeve."

Her face disappeared and a pained cry sounded before the ugliest cat Percy had ever seen made a blurred beeline for the trunk; indeed lost its gnarled, clawed footing, and dove out of the tree like a hawk on a mouse.

Percy caught the fuzz ball upside down—appalled at the missing tufts of orange fur along its spine—and proceeded to get his best shirt shredded by a pair of ungrateful hindquarters. Extricating himself, Percy held the wretched thing at arm's length and deduced the puss was no worse for the wear, though the mentioned sleeve had taken damage if the long strip of blue linen in its mouth was any indication.

"Did you catch her?" she asked from somewhere above.

"Yes."

"Is she unharmed?"

"I thought you said the cat was a lord?"

"Why can't a woman hold a man's title?" Her voice was growing closer. "You haven't answered my question."

Percy saw a muddied slipper peek out from a lower branch, along with a beautiful, bare ankle. Setting the feline down, he went to the tree's base and harangued the influence of stupid poets.

Beautiful ankles, ha! Next, he'd croon over an exposed wrist. No, wait! What hark, a loose curl. Someone call the vicar because he was a besotted fool.

The woman was more than mad, rescuing cats from trees, groundskeepers from shoulder injuries. One of these days, she'd break her neck looking out for everyone else but herself.

A fact he'd change today if he had any say in the matter.

"Percy!"

He focused on the hem of her skirt that followed her exasperated voice. "Aside from an unfortunate shearing by the tree, your

Lord Pickles is discomposed but whole."

"Oh, she always looks like that. She wrestled with a vulture a few years ago and the fur never grew back when the cuts healed."

Percy bowed his head to the cat at his feet with new appreciation. "My apologies, Lord Pickles. I had no idea you were a veteran."

The cat's tail flicked superiorly.

"She likes you," Danny said.

Percy eyed her hemline as it made a slow descent onto the next lowest branch. "You can't even see us."

"I can tell."

Of course she could. "May I assist you down?"

"No need."

Percy gritted his teeth watching her satin slipper skid down the bark of the trunk. Not only was the woman risking neck and life falling out of a tree, but she couldn't even be bothered to wear the proper footwear when doing it. "Really—"

She dropped down to the ground in an elegant crouch and stood, eyes bright and stunning. Brushing off her hands, she peered around him and smiled at Lord Pickles, who eyed their exchange with a grand show of pomposity.

"Troublemaker," she said.

Percy's blood heated at the purr in her voice. He'd climb a tree and mewl for rescue if this was the outcome. He picked a twig from her mushed coif—berating himself for being jealous of a damn cat—and silently surveyed her for any injury. Aside from a long tear in her sleeve, the remains of which were still clamped between Lord Pickles's teeth, she looked fit and radiant from the exercise.

"You shoot, climb trees, play nurse to servants, steal bushes from unsuspecting gardeners." Percy shook his head. "What's next? Carriage races at twilight?"

"I haven't the time, what with late-night rendezvous with a certain gentleman."

"If the gentleman isn't me, there's a dead man walking

somewhere."

She rolled her eyes at his serious threat and nodded towards the targets. "Care to practice your shot, Your Grace?"

How he'd like to deliver the arrow in his pants straight to her center. Percy sighed. He'd never get through this afternoon.

"That bad?" Danny laughed. "You must be the shame of the Home Office."

Percy smirked, a sudden idea lending to his growing good humor. "Care to make a wager on who's the better shot?"

She tilted her head, her smile coy. "I'm not bad. Even the rough-and-tumble boys would be hard-pressed to take the lead."

There wasn't a possibility the woman was bad at anything. "Is that a yes?"

Coyness turned to confidence. "What are your terms of surrender, sir?"

God, he liked her aplomb more than her eyes and ankles and wrists put together. And grandiose arrogance must be rewarded in kind. "I'm a trained assassin by Her Majesty's service. You may set your own terms of defeat."

Teeth flashing, Danny trekked back up the hill and took her place opposite the targets. "*When* I win, Your Grace, you are to do as you once claimed and import a grove of coconut trees here and attempt to grow them for no less than a year."

Percy guffawed. "That's insane." He could worship at her feet for merely suggesting the grueling endeavor.

"Good thing you're so confident in your winning."

He smiled. He was going to enjoy taking the egg too. "And when you *lose*, my lady, you will acquiesce to any question I ask at the conclusion of our wager."

Curiosity lit her eyes, but she didn't ask for specifics. Confident, indeed.

Nerves had Percy narrowing the terms further. "Two chances, no more."

She laughed. "Feel free to take a practice shot. One will be enough for me."

Dear God, he was going to marry her if he had to offer up his soul to the goddess of archery. "Agreed." He waved a hand over the table with the equipment. "After you."

There was no hesitation in her choices. Picking up a medium bow, she placed a quail-feathered arrow on the string and pulled back until her thumb rested against the corner of her mouth, the action displaying toned muscles in her arms.

Percy felt a moment of apprehension seeing her perfect form. He held his breath as she released.

The shot went wide, missing the target altogether.

Percy crushed his cry of victory and took up his place where she'd stood, using a longbow and an arrow that ended in a decorative raven wing. Leveling his gaze at the top of the arrowhead, he inhaled and released.

His arrow struck the inner ring, just shy of the dead center where he'd intended. There was no need to rub his victory in her face.

Composing his expression, he returned his bow to the table and offered Danny his hand.

"Better luck next time." He should feel guilty for baiting her, knowing the difference in their skill levels. He didn't. Not if it gave him even the slightest advantage she'd agree to his proposal.

"Condolences *are* in order, Your Grace." Her triumphant smile gave him pause. "For you."

He dropped his hand she'd refused to shake and frowned at the target. "I wouldn't have taken you for a sore loser . . ." He trailed off as she crooked her finger. Following her order, he leaned over . . . over, around the target until a second target—a good fifty feet farther back—stood hidden in the trees.

And in the dead center was her arrow.

Percy froze.

There were snipers who couldn't make that shot.

Danny smiled sweetly. "I call that one 'Baiting the Duke.'"

Percy stared.

She'd fucking conned him.

"There's a perfect plot of land on the south side of the Grand-fellow property for a green house," she said. "By the time you break ground in the spring, the trees could be shipped and have arrived in plenty of time. The Duke of Camine will assist if you have questions, I'm sure. His peach tree grove is sublime, from what the duchess implies."

If he wasn't already a smitten fool, her sound thrashing of his ego would have done the trick admirably.

But she wasn't done.

"I know as an ex-assassin in Her Majesty's service, you have quite the reputation of superior skill, but if you need any assistance defending your grove until the trees take root, I am but a stroll through the woods away."

Percy applauded her technique. That knife twist would have gutted a man with even a modicum of pride.

"Watching you wield that bow, I find myself doubting my male prowess to protect anything," he said.

Her smile never wavered. "I could feign hysterics if it would lend you to feeling less impotent."

She was marvelous.

"I do believe the sharp insult to my male pride has reaffirmed our roles aptly, but thank you for the offer."

"You are most welcome."

That grin of hers—forget marvelous, she was devious, lovely. He'd been right in his assumption of her success as a force of nature. Give the woman a weapon and she'd hold the world at arrow point. Give her a worthy title and she'd rule like a gods' damn queen.

Now to offer her the world.

"Nothing else to add?" she asked with a tipped lip.

If bland poetry—and *superior* skill—was out, it would be best to be direct. "I do believe I'm in love with you."

Her sudden parted lips and stunned silence vanished with a smile. She set down her bow and crossed her arms over her chest. "It's about time you came to your senses. Or is this merely self-preservation? Truly, Your Grace, I'm nowhere near as proficient with a moving target."

Her teasing brought bright hope to the dark uncertainty in his chest. "Does that mean you approve of my affections?"

"Not only do I approve, sir . . ." Her gaze was hot and honest. "It seems you've ruined me for every other man."

Her silken words, like fingers brushed across his groin, had his feet eating up the scant distance between them.

She was ruined? He pulled her into his arms, his hands digging into her hair to guide her head closer, her lips a hair's breadth from his. He growled against her mouth, "You ruined me the moment you put that wicked tongue on my knife."

Her eyes danced with amusement. "A quick lick is all it takes? Men are far easier to snare than I anticipated."

"There's that wicked tongue again."

And he kissed her, soft and slow, letting the ease and skill of his lips and tongue do the talking. She didn't return his affections, *yet*, but there was no doubt about their chemistry. She was a lady with dark appetites, and he was a would-be duke who wielded them as second nature. She was intrigued by him and comfortable. For now, that would have to be enough. He'd use that connection to deepen their relationship. He'd do his damnedest to make sure she wouldn't regret ending her impressive refusal streak for the likes of him.

He ended the kiss with a scrape of teeth against her lower lip and groaned when she shuddered in his arms.

"You'll marry me, won't you?" He rested his forehead against hers, a wave of nerves making him unable to face her. "I can't promise the stuffy and distant life of an aristocrat. I won't tolerate separate beds or holidays away. If you agree to become my duchess, you are to be my partner, for always." He flinched at the ultimatum. Danny had been raised by typical English peers. Their customs and expectations so unlike that of a working man. Though they were considered superior in their manners and outlooks, he'd never settle for half a life. Better she know now, then agree to his proposal and be miserable later at his modern ideals of marriage.

But when he glanced down to gauge her level of reluctance, it was to find her smiling.

"Did you truly believe asking me to be your equal would in any way dissuade me?" she asked.

"Some women would find the idea peculiar and frightening."

"*Some* women," she admitted.

"But not you?"

"I think you know that answer already, sir. I don't steal bushes with just anyone."

His heart was flying. Cradling her face in his hands, he soaked up that smile, that knowing glint in her eye, and the silent challenge in her voice. "I need to hear the word, Danny. I need to know you're serious. Once you decide, I won't let you go."

She scrunched her nose, her eyes dancing. "When you put it that way, perhaps I *will* reconsider. I've heard Mr. Pendor is amiable and still on the market."

"Minx!" Percy kissed her, long and hot, until all the games and banter were stripped away and replaced with sincere sensation.

"Yes," Danny said against his lips when they'd become breathless. "I accept your proposal . . . on one condition."

He didn't hesitate. "Cats to rescue? Dogs to tend? I'll hire two dozen servants for you to fuss over and proclaim you their saint."

Expression amused, her gaze flicked up to a window on the southern side of the house. Her smile turned guilty. "There's one thing I need us to do first."

Us. How lovely and *un*-singular that sounded. "Name it."

"Convince my father."

He kissed the tip of her nose, his heart light. "An easy ask."

THIS WAS GOING to be harder than the teeth-chipping biscuits they served in the workhouses.

Percy had faced warriors, soldiers, having his toenails ripped off by a lovely Frenchman named Sweetling, but standing in Lord Bromley's study, waiting for the man to announce his fate, Percy decided he missed the croissant-loving torture man and his affinity for pain.

Gone was the informal man who'd wolfed down biscuits like a child before dinner. Gone was the same man who'd clapped Mr. Brinkley on the back and shook his hand when the old groundskeeper had joined them on the terrace at Fellow Hall. Lord Bromley sat back in his chair behind his desk, fingers steepled so only his eyes were visible—eyes that hadn't blinked since Danny and he had entered the man's haven hand-in-hand ten minutes ago and announced their engagement.

"Am I to understand, you formed an attachment after but a few outings?" he asked finally.

Danny smiled and shook her head. Thankfully, she'd taken the time to change out of her ruined dress and re-pin her hair. "No, Papa. The truth is, Percy and I met my first season at the Leishires' ball."

The older man's unblinking eyes turned some color that reminded Percy of brimstone. "You've been carrying on a secret engagement this entire time?"

"No!" Danny exclaimed. "Goodness, Papa. I would never keep—"

"Lord Bromley." Percy stepped forward, dropping Danny's hand to look the man in the eye—and do what he should've done in the first place and asked, "May I speak to you in private, sir?"

Danny frowned. "I will not leave. This discussion is my future as well."

"Please, Danny." Percy willed her to understand her father's fears and the parental instinct to posture. *Trust me as you've always done.*

She understood the unspoken words, his perfect lady. Give

her a month, and she'd have no need for conversation. A look and she'd know his mind better than he did.

Expression softening, she nodded. "I'll check on tea and biscuits for after."

Percy watched her leave, waiting until the latch clicked closed before he addressed Lord Bromley. "I'm in love with your daughter."

Lord Bromley wasn't impressed. "Near a dozen men have claimed the same."

What a tough old bastard. No quarter, no mercy: If the remaining two Deime family members he had yet to meet were half so callous, it'd be hard not to fall for the whole family. Though he suspected he'd informally met one of the two earlier. The Deime family coloring and inability to keep to manners was startlingly similar.

Percy could be just as uncivil. "Your daughter did nothing but insult me at the Leishires' ball, berated me, threw suspicion at me."

Lord Bromley's surprise didn't stop at his expression. Apparently, no other man had claimed *that* before. "And you've come to admit you've grown to love her despite all that?"

Percy laughed. "I love her *because* of it. A woman who isn't afraid of title or prestige, a woman who speaks her mind and calls a man's bluffs is rare. I couldn't help but fall for her."

"And what of your background? I find it inconceivable that Jack would never mention you."

"My father and his family were estranged," Percy said. "I never knew my grandfather's cousin except as a passing memory from my childhood. His title and fortune were never mentioned, and I never asked."

Lord Bromley nodded, as if he'd suspected as much. "When did your father pass?"

"I was young, sir."

Lord Bromley recovered with a frown. "What of your living? How did you support yourself?"

"I took a commission in the army, sir." Percy wouldn't mention the years in between when his father had passed away and how he'd managed to pay for such a thing. "I was recruited early to work for the Home Office." He quickly added, "Though I am now retired from the work."

Lord Bromley's eyes widened. "The Home Office?" He went back to that contemplative steepling of fingers, knowing not to ask further inquiry on the subject. The truth would be easy enough to verify with the right connections. Connections an earl in the House of Lords would have. "I see."

Lord Bromley was quiet for some time, five minutes twenty seconds. Wielding silence like a weapon, another thing the family had in common. Then, "I won't claim to understand the hardships of your youth, nor will I denounce what courage and will it takes to raise yourself up to the position you acquired in Her Majesty's forces.

"Nor am I blind. I can see your affection goes deeper than my daughter's fine features and fortune. Knowing how Jack ran the estate, I know you are in a better position than even I to provide for my Danny." Lord Bromley's gaze was unyielding. "But I would not give my blessing for such worthless reasons."

Percy's insides twisted. "Sir—"

The other man held up his hand for his silence. "I *would* give my blessing to a man who shows my daughter respect, a man whom she in turn respects. A man who finds worth in a woman's opinion. If you'd demanded she leave this room to secure my cooperation, I would have shot you between the eyes before the door finished closing."

Percy swallowed. He had a suspicion Danny's expert marksmanship was hereditary. "But?"

"But you asked, and she left." He stood and walked around his desk to offer his hand. "I trust my daughter's decisions, Your Grace, and so I will put my trust in you as well." His hand was a vise around Percy's fingers. The smile on the older man's face was tighter. "Don't turn my daughter into a liar."

Percy returned the bone-crushing grip and found his insides warming to the idea of a typical family. He couldn't resist poking at the other man's hostility. "Shall I call you 'Papa' too?"

Lord Bromley's smile was all teeth. "Not if you wish to avoid that bullet."

Percy took it back: The ambushes and teasing, the thinly veiled threats—having a family far exceeded all expectations.

CHAPTER EIGHTEEN

A STRING OF harsh storms and incessant rain made the whole
wedding a muddy, undignified affair. Carriages lay
abandoned in the road—wheels stuck in six inches of mud—a
quarter of a mile from the church, hems were ruined, coifs were
matted messes, and Danny couldn't have been happier.

Three weeks of waiting for the bans to be read was four
weeks too long. She'd offered to elope on more than one
occasion, but in this Percy would not budge, on the formal
wedding or on spending the night together until after the
contracts were signed.

Every night Danny sat up in bed, listening for a telling knock
on her window in hopes Percy would relent in his ridiculous
notions of chastity. And every night she fell asleep disappointed
and unbearably aroused at the thought of him sneaking in and
laying his naked body atop hers. Not even Charlotte's early
wedding present—a scandalous book of erotic positions—made
any difference.

If there was any question of Danny's impatience, there could
be no misconstructions when she'd grabbed Percy by the lapels
and planted one on him in front of her family, friends, and a red-
faced vicar as they were presented as the Duke and Duchess of
Grandfellow.

Danny had felt no shame rushing through the courses of their
wedding dinner, and even less shame shoving her grin-faced

siblings out the door before the moon had reached its apex in the sky.

And there had been no question of a lady's maid tonight.

Percy had laughed the entire way up two flights of stairs and into the master's wing when she'd taken his hand and dragged him behind her.

Danny tapped her foot, waiting for him to unlock the door, shaking with need. He'd dressed in a non-formal suit of grey moleskin that showed off his thighs and rear. Curls brushed back to reveal sharp cheekbones and piercing eyes. The man was a walking god. And he knew it.

She crossed her arms over her chest, not giving a fig for wrinkling the starched, white linen that came up to her neck, and refrained from snarling at him to forget the room. He could push her up against the wall and have her in the hallway.

His eyes danced in the low light. "In a hurry, love?"

How was he not ready to shred off her dress? All blasted day had been torture to remain civil and clothed. She snarled this time. "To get the awful 'consummation' portion of this evening finished, yes."

All he did was smile: straight, white, dashing. Damn the man!

"Fine!" She ripped the veil off her head and threw it to the floor. "I want to be in bed with you, or on a rug, or on a chair." The way her stomach fluttered, and her legs trembled, she didn't care which.

His gaze darkened. "We've done the last two. My vote is for the bed this time."

At the word 'bed,' Danny's core clenched. Swallowing a moan, she touched her breast through her dress and confessed, "I may not make it that far."

His fingers laced through her wandering hand, and he pressed a kiss to the inside of her wrist, his eyes full of heat and humor. "Then come, my dear."

A *click* sound of the lock unlatching and the door opened.

And she attacked him.

Fabric ripping, buttons flung across the floor, Danny took weeks of sexual frustration out on the innocent wedding ensembles, not relenting until they were both down to their last articles of clothing and their ragged panting filled the silence.

Thankfully, Percy's maddening composure seemed to have finally snapped.

He cupped the back of her head and tilted her lips up for access, his grey eyes black in the low firelight. "I meant to be gentle this first time."

She nipped at his hand, not caring how she'd digressed into a rutting animal. "When I want gentle, I'll ask." She pulled back and released the clever drawstring at the back of her neck, holding the two ends closed with one hand.

Eyebrow cocked, he asked, "And?"

"I didn't ask."

She let go of the strings and her slip fell in a pool of satin at her feet, leaving her completely naked.

Percy muttered a foul oath and grasped the straining rod through his trousers like he'd done at the Crystal Palace.

But there'd be no teasing this time around.

She inclined her head, making herself clear. "That's mine."

He huffed a laugh and shook his head. "Now and always, my lady."

"Good." She wet her lips, remembering the velvety feel of him in her mouth, and somehow knew he'd feel even silkier inside. Wet need slipped down her thighs.

He watched her, his gaze raking hotly down her body, as if he could see the evidence of her body's desires.

She rolled her eyes. "*Now* would be nice." But she didn't wait for him to come for her.

Replacing his fingers with her own, she ran her thumb up his length, flicking open the snaps of his underwear as she went until the garment fell away, and he was full and hot and bare in her hand.

He hissed as she dropped to her knees and licked him root to crown.

Hand fisting in her hair, he guided her back to her feet and pressed a kiss to her shoulder, mimicking her earlier licking along the column of her neck. "Not tonight, darling. Tonight, I give you *everything*."

Her legs quaked at his wicked promise. "You sure like taking your time."

"Anticipation heightens the arousal," he whispered in her ear.

Melting. She was actually melting. "I'm aroused already."

His fingers danced across her bare thigh, dipping into her soaked folds. He moaned and his Adam's apple bobbed as he swallowed. Those sinful lips spread a line of kisses across her jaw until they found the corner of her lips where he said, "Then follow me."

Shucking off his loose undergarment, Danny's attention went to the sculpted muscles of his backside as he led her to the bed in the corner, the top covered in black silk sheets.

He crawled atop the bed with predatory grace and rolled onto his back, his gaze expectant.

A moment of self-doubt took hold as Danny followed, her frame dwarfed by her virile husband, but Percy stopped her from lying down at his side.

"Straddle me," he said.

Danny's core tingled at the invitation, though her eyes and brain couldn't help interjecting upon seeing his wide torso. "My legs won't reach."

His smile was wolf-like as he grasped her by the hips and placed her legs on either side of his flat stomach.

The hot length of him pressed urgently against her back, delicious and demanding. Danny licked her lips again, but her mouth had gone dry. "Oh, look," she said, fighting a giggle of nerves. "They reach."

His cock jumped at her back and her giggle burst out. Mortified, she pressed a hand over her mouth.

Chuckling, Percy reached out and laced his fingers with hers.

"You have complete control. Nothing will happen if you don't wish it."

Easy for him to say. "I don't know what to do." Her mother's talk over 'a wife's duty' had been little better than a fish in a burrow reference, which Danny knew from all her reading was not habitually accurate.

Percy didn't laugh this time. Kissing her fingertips one by one, when he reached her thumb, he explained liberally, "My cock angles upwards like the curve of your finger. When you are ready, my cock fits inside and that curve will help stimulate muscles that will give you pleasure. When you are more comfortable and accustomed to me, different angles and positions will give you the same if not more pleasure."

Oh. Danny blinked at where his mouth currently demonstrated, taking her finger between his lips while his other hand played with the curls between her legs, leaving no question where those 'muscles' that would be so pleasurable were located.

She'd never look at her thumb the same way again.

She nodded. "Okay, I'm ready."

He smiled gently and drew her down on top of him to press a kiss to her lips. "Guide me in, love."

Reaching between them, she grasped his cock and brought him to the juncture of her thighs. She shifted on instinct to find that angle he'd mentioned, ending up sitting upright and lowering herself instead of pushing back.

His tip stretched her wide.

The position left her legs trembling and her head light.

"Take your time." Percy's jaw clenched so hard, a muscle ticked in his cheek. "The first time will hurt."

Danny wouldn't voice how his warning egged her on.

She took in another inch or so of him, and the sensation was maddening. The anticipation left her hazy.

"Is this one of your illusions, Percy?" she asked, her body grasping and eager for more.

"Yes, my dear." Her eyes opened and fixed on his dark gaze.

His fingers danced up her thighs, the rough skin adding another layer of sensation. "This is the greatest of illusions," he confirmed. "One that never need end."

And it felt that way.

She pushed down, down, endlessly down until she sat against his root. Pulling, pinching, the pain intensified, like a pinpoint blade buried in the depths of her body.

She came with a gasp, the power of it rendering her speechless.

And then he cupped her bottom in his hands and rolled his hips beneath her, hitting a spot that sent her over a second time, and a third.

The rolls turned to bucks, wilder and wilder until Danny lost count and consciousness of the movements and rode his powerful body through instinctual pleasure alone.

And she refused to ever stop.

THE WOMAN WAS so damn receptive.

Six orgasms. Percy knew he was an accomplished lover, but the sounds Danny made when she came . . . If there was a competition in the new Games of the I Olympiad for making one's wife come, he'd be a fucking medalist.

She was perfect lying in his arms, soft and warm and smiling a satisfied smile that had Percy's groin stirring. Noticing, she bit her lip and trailed her nails down his growing length.

Receptive *and* relentless, and he had the scratch marks to prove it.

He was a lucky, fucking bastard.

"Care to share another *position*, husband?" she asked, her nails scraping down to his sack. "That last one is my favorite so far."

Bent over the mattress, her tight rump in the air, her sheath had choked his cock with a grasp that could very well become addicting. Of the four positions they'd done, it was his second favorite. "Did you not care for your first ride?"

She bit her lip, and the sweetest blush spread over her cheeks. "I did."

"You can ride backwards as well."

If he'd hoped to darken that blush until her entire body flushed pink, he succeeded. What he hadn't expected was the glint of anticipation in her eye.

"Shall we do it now?"

Percy groaned. The woman was a warrior, of that there was no doubt, but even she had to have a limit. He kissed her nose and shook his head. "You should rest."

She glanced about the room. "Here? You meant it when you said we wouldn't sleep apart?"

"Yes." Percy swallowed, unsure why the thought of her retiring back to the duchess's chambers made him feel hollow inside. "If you want."

Her smile cast aside all doubts. Snuggling into the crook of his shoulder, she grabbed a handful of blankets and threw them over their naked bodies.

Noticing a chill in the room, Percy frowned. He hadn't thought to build a fire, or even shut the blasted door. They'd see how disciplined a duke's staff was in the morning and if any of the maids could look their master or mistress in the eye.

Danny didn't seem to mind any of it.

"This is cozy." She lifted his arm and draped it across her midsection as if he were yet another layer necessary for her comfort.

The thought had Percy warming from the inside.

"Be careful," she said, glancing up at him. "Smiling like that, your carefully honed mask of disdain will be ruined."

It wasn't all a mask, he thought, and the truth of it leached the growing heat from his body. His arm tightened around her body, drawing her close until they lay side by side, heart to heart.

But the distance between them would remain until he offered

up everything.

"There are some things you should know about me before you decide to stay," he said quietly, despising how hard the words were to get out.

She laughed. "A little late now, Your Grace. What more must I know? You have a secret passion for tennis? You want a whole household of cats? Lord Pickles is still young. We'll find her a worthy tom and have kittens before spring."

He smiled at her light tone, praying the weight of his past wouldn't take that from her. His duchess didn't balk at his bed sport or his skills to fell a man in a dark alley. It was a leap of faith for him—a miracle in and of itself—to believe she wouldn't recoil at the rest of his unsavory life. "I lived on the streets before I went into the army."

Danny's expression turned serious, no doubt remembering their brief and unwelcome reception in St. Giles. "I meant what I said, Percy. You don't need to speak of it if you don't wish to."

He ran a hand through his hair. He'd never told anyone of the years after his father had died. They were ugly and unfit for innocent ears. But she had never scoffed at his admissions, never admonished his actions—after determining he wasn't a hardened criminal—and if she could offer unfailing loyalty to a fiend like him, then he'd return it in kind without cowardice. He *wanted* to tell her.

"I went to public school until I was eight," he said, unable to keep the nostalgia from his voice. Aside from the normal teasing between boys, the time spent trading off between school and his shifts at the local cotton mill was the happiest of his life, until now.

"My school in Southwark was behind the times, still using the old system to teach the younger kids with assignments from the older, but I knew my letters and numbers when I started at age five, and when the headmaster made me a monitor, I took pride in teaching my peers." He smiled, remembering. "But the best was when we'd be allowed time outside to play. The idea was ridiculous. Time to play? What did the school expect us to do? Of course, it wasn't long before the boys figured out increasingly hard games for us all to play."

Danny tilted her head up at him. "You learned football from the schoolyard?"

Percy nodded. "Those of us who'd only known work embraced the time to stretch our newfound brains and bodies. Some of the older boys had transferred from private schools, their families suffering setbacks. But they brought all kinds of games. Things for the older boys to try and the younger ones to imitate." He'd thrived on teamwork and strategy, easily showcasing his skills and earning a spot on the bigger boys' teams. It was in those few glorious years of youth Percy had known he'd been destined for something bigger than himself.

"Then my father died." His gut clenched, that same sinking feeling he had when he'd been told the fire had trapped dozens of workers in the factory. There'd been no more time for games or learning. It was all he could do to pass as an older boy and work longer shifts. But the fire that had taken his father and destroyed the textile mill had also displaced near a hundred other able-bodied workmen, men who'd been worth more to a cotton mill than a child half their size.

He skipped over the weeks of cold and hunger when he'd been dumped into the streets, unable to remember much except agonizing pain and fear. "I fell into a gang soon after, one that taught the skills I needed to survive."

The scars across his palms from where the other members had struck him with a switch until he could pick a pocket without a single brush of fabric was a reminder of how surviving didn't equate to living. But it was a lesson he'd taken to heart.

"I had a tough time. My father had raised me to know the difference between right and wrong. Those same older boys who'd been like brothers to me at school were now my targets."

"Oh, Percy." Danny clutched his hands, her expression a mixture of sadness and anger. "Did no one look out for you?"

Percy nodded, coldness creeping into his chest. "There was another boy my age, Nic. He'd been there a good year before me. He showed me how to use my size and brains to corner a mark without them realizing how the clever could outmatch the stronger.

"When the other members got frustrated with my conscience, that same boy stood up for me. He was my only friend." He paused, collected himself. "As soon as were able to pass as young men, we enlisted, stealing the stash the gang kept and buying ourselves commissions and setting off to camp before the rest were any the wiser."

Percy's fingers clenched into fists, the knuckles turning white. "What fools we were. We'd traded one battlefield for another. The things we saw, things we did, the blood of my enemies was in my hair, my eyes, my soul. That sense of wrong and right I clutched so diligently was lost in the trenches. We distinguished ourselves with the hard missions, taking the ones no one else wanted for bigger rations." His smile was self-deprecating. "A kid from the streets always appreciated food, if nothing else.

"We were recruited after the second Anglo-Marri War by a man who claimed he worked in the Home Office. He offered food, training, prestige, shelter. At first, we couldn't believe our luck." Percy shook his head. How naive they were. "They knew exactly what to use to make us comply." The only person he'd ever truly trusted besides Nic had been his handler.

Agents were asked to do unspeakable things, horrible acts necessary for the safety of their country in the name of patriotic loyalty. Percy had killed in the name of that loyalty: women and countless men. With every death on his hands, his soul had slipped farther and farther away until he had no longer been the one wielding the blade, gun, garrote, his bare hands. The method didn't matter. Only the body. He'd forgotten so many of the faces.

"I did what I was asked: murder, espionage, arson. We were an unstoppable force, but that didn't stop me from questioning.

When I had doubts, I was commended. When I returned from a particularly bloodthirsty mission, I was given a medal. Now, I see the manipulation for what it was. But he—"

Remembering hurt like a knife to the gut. His friend, his comrade, his partner, with whom he'd shared hardship, fear, triumph, and valor. If Percy clung to the remnants of his rotting soul, Nic had lost his completely.

"Nic became a liability to the Office. He stopped caring about collateral damage, leaving a trail of bodies wherever he was sent. I castigated him repeatedly to take care. I wouldn't believe he was unreachable."

But it hadn't been up to him.

Percy had sunken so deep by that time, he hadn't blinked when the order had come. The coldness in his chest spread, leaving him numb. "His termination came down from the highest order. At the end of our current mission, I was to dispose of my partner."

Danny gasped. "Those bastards!"

The overwhelming chill thawed just enough for her outrage on his behalf to warm his heart. But the heat vanished upon his next statement. "We were in enemy territory when the missive arrived via our contact."

Deep in France, lying in wait to assassinate a local government official. Assassinations like those were not uncommon, but Percy had felt a nagging sense of misplacement even then. The Home Office didn't encroach on the Foreign Office's missions without explicit communication and designation of duties, all of which had been absent.

The politician hadn't been their usual type of target, and their vantage point at the Hotel Saint-Jacques had been far too conspicuous. But Percy hadn't questioned it. Preparing to kill his best friend, they'd settled in for their usual surveillance and Percy had acted, pulling his knife and sinking it into Nic's back.

The Second Bureau of the General Staff had interrupted. To this day, Percy had no idea if someone had slipped their location to the authorities, or if their luck had been rot that night.

"We were caught in the middle of our tussle, separated, and taken to a place with no light. I knew Nic would die without medical attention, and I was glad of it. Even my blackened conscience could be lightened by the idea I'd saved him from my fate."

How Percy wished Nic had died by his hand. For the monster that had risen back out of his friend's grave was a monster of his making. All the terror and bloodshed spilt since that night was on his hands.

"He wants my head," he finished simply. If the monster still lived, he longed for blood, Percy's most of all.

And Percy could not blame him. He'd deserved death many times over.

Even more reason Percy prayed Nic had found peace at the bottom of the river.

"Is he gone?" Danny asked, her expression open and achingly beautiful in the face of all his ugly truth.

There was no need to worry her. There'd been no sign of the bastard in three years. "He is."

Danny's fingers intertwined with his, her silent support overwhelming. "I'm sorry you lost your friend."

Percy laughed, though the humor was dark. "I stabbed him in the back, and you're sorry for me?"

"For what he meant to you." Danny lifted his hand and rubbed her cheek across his knuckles. "But you are not like him, Percy. No matter how much you wish to believe you're a lost cause, I've seen your kindness and passion. I've seen your sins eat at you. You're no more a monster than he was an angel."

Percy's heart gave a pang. She was a miracle, his wife, able to soothe the sharpest pains of his past with her indomitable spirit and goodness.

And he needed to be inside her now.

Rolling her on top of him, he grasped her hips and grinded into her core, feeling wetness slip against his cock.

Her eyes widened, but her smile was inviting.

She didn't object when he twisted her around so he could lightly spank her backside.

She moaned and grasped him at the root but held back.

"Mount me," he commanded.

He felt her shudder with her own need. "I thought you said to rest?"

He spanked her again, and her body shuddered in completion. He guided her down and sat up to tighten their position, whispering in her ear, "I'll rest when I'm dead."

CHAPTER NINETEEN

ONE COULD ONLY put off a summons from the Duchess of Camine for so long.

Percy normally found Charlotte's commanding and insulting presence refreshing, but being pulled away from his lovely wife—where a week's worth of carnal depravity in his bedchambers left him none too eager to return to polite society, or pants—had him less than pleased.

He was shown to a secondary drawing room, the one that wasn't used for normal callers, and proceeded to wait in the ungodly bright room with its gold, filigreed wallpaper and eastern-facing windows. The only thing acceptable in this torture chamber were the plush rugs underfoot in a most agreeable almond brown, a perfect match to his wife's eyes.

Percy's irritation came back with violent vengeance. By the time the door had opened and the Duke of Camine had entered, he was half-blind and spitting for a fight.

"What the hell is this? I came, so where is your wife?" If this was a stupid social formality to reinstate their acquaintances after his marriage, he was going to break something.

Hamish leaned an arm on the mantel and grinned. "The honeymoon is going well, I take it?"

"Bugger off. I could be there still if it weren't for this unwelcome interruption."

Hamish took pity on him. "There's a man here. Called this

morning. Charlotte is with him now, interrogating him."

That was what had happened to the main receiving room. As much fun as watching another man crack under the scrutiny of a relentless duchess sounded, Percy doubted he'd been called here like a dog to admire Charlotte's ability to render a man to ash.

"What has that to do with me?"

Percy didn't like how his friend's smirk slipped. "The caller is uniformed and in possession of official orders."

Percy froze, something like dread fighting its way to the surface. After he'd revealed his past to Danny . . . It had to be a coincidence. "Have you seen these orders?"

Hamish shook his head. "Confidential."

The men shared a knowing look. Hamish didn't know the extent of Percy's past, but he knew enough to know 'confidential' was a blanket term for 'covert,' especially when it came to agents not *officially* on any public record.

"Charlotte will keep him entertained, or *restrained*, until you make a decision one way or another," Hamish said.

Gratitude never came easily to Percy, but he offered it now sincerely. "My thanks, Hamish." Whatever the 'orders,' they couldn't be good. But despite his book length of skills and talents, he wasn't a soothsayer. "I'll see him."

Hamish nodded and went to the bell pull.

Two minutes later, the door to the drawing room opened and the Duchess of Camine entered, expression severe—a byproduct of a one-sided conversation with an unwilling partner—while the uniformed man in question followed, his buttons and boots polished to a high shine that would pass any inspection, and a crown on his shoulder that indicated an officer of years and rank.

Strait-laced, confident: Percy took stock of the man's personality by his airs alone. The fact the major had served at least eight years didn't bode well either. Since when did ranked officers make recruit calls?

When the major's gaze landed on Percy, recognition evident

in his hard stare, Percy knew he was fucked.

Expression wooden, Charlotte offered introductions, her displeasure at being thwarted unmistakable when she announced the officer's name and rank first against protocol. "Your Grace, this is Major Wallace with Her Majesty's Army. Major, this is Percy Cole, Duke of Grandfellow."

Wallace stepped forward, his feathered bonnet giving the man's highland station away. "I apologize for not approaching you sooner." His gaze cut to the duchess. "I was waylaid by outside forces who assured me you were indisposed."

Not just the force of a duchess, Percy thought. His gaze narrowed. "You had me followed." It wasn't a question. Those trained eyes he'd felt on him hadn't been his imagination. A Highland soldier would know how to keep himself hidden during surveillance.

Wallace nodded. "My orders were to keep you in sight until your orders were received."

"Orders from whom?"

Wallace didn't respond but had the good mind to step back at the feral grin curling Percy's mouth.

It was always easy to hold one's tongue . . . until someone skilled threatened to slice it open.

Percy sighed at the need for restraint. He had few reservations the Duchess of Camine would stop him from bleeding the man dry, but the carpets in this room really were exquisite.

"What do you want with me, then?"

Wallace cleared his throat and leveled Charlotte with a superior stare, the dismissal clear.

"If you'll excuse me," Charlotte said, glaring at the major. "I have embroidery to tend to." She swept from the room, a decided chill left in her wake.

Percy flinched at the loud *snitch* as the door closed. Major Straitlaced better pray he never found himself in a dark alley with the duchess. He'd learn exactly how comfortable the woman was with needles . . . and a bloodied man.

Hamish did a fine job not strangling the man for the insult to his wife, but that didn't stop the Duke of Camine from growling, "Get on with it."

Wallace extracted a sealed roll from inside his coat and handed it to Percy.

Breaking the wax, Percy opened the orders and his stomach bottomed out.

Percival Cole, Captain in Her Majesty's Army, is reinstated to active duty as of the twelfth day of the month.

Percy scoured paragraphs of government bullshit, ending at a list of names signed at the bottom, more than one ranked signature present, including the new Home Office Secretary—a man Percy knew well.

The orders *were* official.

"Fuck."

Hamish took the paper from his hand and read over the information, his scowl pinching his brows into a deep V. "This is preposterous," he scoffed. "Percy is a duke."

Wallace nodded but spoke directly to Percy. "Your changed circumstances were noted. You are to deliver yourself to Her Majesty's army headquarters in Whitehall, rank intact." He nodded to Hamish and marched to the door, throwing over his shoulder, "Welcome back, Captain."

Upon the major's exit, the room, and the two men, were left in suspended silence.

He must have been dreaming. The entire production was ridiculous. Him, go back into the army? He'd been assured by his superiors that his transfer from squadron to the Home Office would be dealt with. Just as the conniving government sycophants had said Percy's last mission had been a sanctioned one with minimal risks.

The same mission that had left him and his partner exposed and at the mercy of French intelligence and pitted two childhood friends to fight to the death. Which made this command all the more puzzling. As far as Percy knew, everyone from his old life believed he was dead.

Everyone except Nic.

Percy felt the joy and hope that had sprouted up in the last few weeks shrivel and die in his chest. "The bastard has made his move." Damn, he was a fool! He'd let his guard down. Deep down, he'd actually believed Nic had died in the Thames.

Hamish didn't need to ask to whom he referred. "You think this is Nic's doing?"

Percy couldn't help but pace as he thought. Movement always helped when one was used to action. "Who else? It's the kind of delay tactic he'd use while preparing his next move." And if the army was made aware of his non-dead person, it was a matter of time before the Home Office came calling.

"Why give himself away like this?" Hamish asked.

"I don't know." The lack of knowledge was unhinging.

"Nic is dead," Hamish said firmly.

Percy stopped, a moment of hope stopping his running thoughts. "Did the Merry Men find the body?" He'd send Syd a bloody basket of flowers if they did.

Hamish sighed. "No." He returned to the pressing matter. "Are there any grounds they can re-conscript you?"

Percy nodded. "I was never officially discharged."

"But commissions were abolished."

"My contract was bought before the law was passed."

"That was twenty years ago. You can't join the army as a child."

His voice was dead when he said, "You can if you lie about your age."

Hamish's whistle sounded like an incoming cannonball. He clapped Percy on the shoulder. "Let this be a lesson in deceit, old boy." He sighed. "We'll go to the Home Office in the morning. And if they won't see reason, we'll take this directly to St. James Place."

Percy wouldn't acknowledge his relief at the other man's

offer, though it was unnecessary. His connections in the Home Office would be of far more value. The reception, however, might prove tricky. "You mean to aid me in shirking my duties to the Crown? You *have* turned into a revolutionary."

Hamish grinned. "On the contrary. You're a useless duke now, remember? Your duty lies with your land and tenants. Ledgers and accounts won't see to themselves."

Percy shook his head, the idea of active duty not sounding so bad after all. "Nic will have foreseen the argument and made contingency plans."

"The man isn't God, Percy. He may outdo us all in evil machinations and ridiculous hair, but he remains unequal in the face of our forces."

"Since when can dukes outmaneuver anyone who can't be bought or intimidated?"

"Since never."

Percy rolled his eyes. "Markus and his merry band have proven they can't catch a cold. You shouldn't put your faith in them, either."

"I don't." Hamish smiled. "I *do*, however, know a group of women to whom Death Himself would beg for mercy."

Percy grasped his meaning and his own mouth quirked to one side. Hope wasn't dead yet. "No force like it on Earth," he agreed.

Dukes may be no match for his former partner—who could read Percy's actions like chapters in a book—but Nic Brandt stood no chance against the collective and unexpected force of duchesses.

"Think they'll agree to intervene?" Percy said.

"Save us poor menfolk through cleverness and grit?" Hamish snorted. "I pity the man who tries to stop them. Make sure to grovel accordingly."

The door opened and the Duchess of Camine entered as if she'd been waiting on the other side for this exact moment. Expression eager, she said, "We'll do it."

Percy gave Hamish a grin. "I didn't even need to grovel."

The humor faded quickly, spurned by the certainty that his greatest enemy still breathed. If Nic knew about his commission, then he'd know about his rise in pedigree. Striking now of all times, when Percy had just made his official appearance in society, he must've been watching him for some time, choosing this exact moment to reveal himself.

But why now?

Charlotte clapped her hands together, already preparing. "First we clear up this army matter, then we see to disposing of that miserable cur."

Percy snorted. And women said men were bloodthirsty. "You could've warned me I was walking into a formal reinstatement."

Charlotte skewered him with a sharp look. "If you had come when I'd asked weeks ago, I would have. I made it a point that the man must take his business here in front of witnesses so no mistakes would be made. I had no idea the man had official orders, only that he thought to impose on you."

Ah. He bowed over her hand, his contrition sincere. "You are a goddess, and I am unworthy."

She sniffed. "Apology accepted." Obviously feeling a rare sense of empathy for him, she advised, "Make sure to discuss it with Daniella. Wives like to be informed when their idiotic husbands decide to do foolish things."

Percy froze, something cold and unsettling churning in his stomach. Her words played inside his head. And again. He slowly released Charlotte's hand. "I should inform my wife."

She rolled her eyes. "That's what I said. I'm sure your duchess will have something to say about this whole business."

"My wife." The bans were posted, but the papers had been late due to the weather. Much of the country would just now be hearing about the nuptials of the Duke of Grandfellow to Lady Daniella Deime.

Hamish materialized at his side. "You've gone as white as a sheet. What is it?"

Percy felt his legs buckle. He half-sat, half-crouched on the edge of the divan, all his strength going to formulate a strategy.

Charlotte glanced at her husband. "Is he all right?"

Hamish shook his head.

"Is he faint? Shall I call for biscuits?"

"No biscuits," Percy said. "No tea, no tarts, no cake. No food." Not when his stomach was a somersaulting mess.

"No food?" Hamish dropped beside him, eyes wide. "Good God, man. What the devil is the matter?"

This couldn't be happening. But everything lined up. The timing, the delay. He was a married man, with a precious wife at home. If he got called away now, there'd be no one to protect her. Not even a lord could sluff off his duties to present himself when the demand came straight from the Crown.

The game was ending, forced by a man who'd lost too many battles but who was determined to come out the victor. Nic wouldn't show mercy or restraint. What transpired between Hamish and Charlotte, and even Renard and Camille, had been nothing but petulant tantrums by a man bored with too many skills to remain inactive. But what lay between him and Percy, that was personal.

"He will kill her." Nic was going after Daniella. The reinstatement was a way to tie Percy's hands. He lifted his gaze and saw his own horror reflected in his best friend's face. "He's going after my wife."

⇢⟫⟫⟫✕⟪⟪⟪⇠

AFTER VETTING THE runners he'd hired and confirming with Hamish that Danny was safe and guarded at Fellow Hall, Percy made his move.

He had no need for an escort. The floors may have been polished, the walls painted a new coat of the same slate grey. Agents may have come and gone, internal promotions switching figureheads like stacking dolls all with the same empty heads, but one thing the Home Office never did was change.

Entering the private entrance by way of a false pillar, Percy fought his stealth training and walked confidentially down the hall, his hat tipped back. Up a secret staircase to the second-floor offices, he opened the third door on the right.

Percy defended on instinct.

The blade came a second later. He caught the knife between his middle and pointer finger, a mere inch from his open left eye. Grinning, Percy lowered the weapon and regarded his former handler as he sat behind his desk, looking the same—if not a bit tired around the eyes—as always in a dark suit, bored expression, and a curled wig. "Nice to see you too, Ridley."

If David Ridley was surprised to see Percy's handsome mug, he gave nothing away. The man had always had the most unnerving poker face. "You haven't lost your touch, Percy."

One eye on Ridley, Percy used his other to admire the room with its golden inlaid mantel and burgundy drapes, and finally landing on the woodblock at the edge of the man's wide, mahogany desk. "Congratulations on your promotion, Home Secretary."

"Not nearly as impressive as *your* new title."

Percy laughed and crossed the room to toss the blade onto the stack of papers on the desk. "You know why I'm here?"

Ridley leaned back in his chair. "I cannot go against official commands."

Percy's fingers itched for his own blade concealed in his sleeve. They'd been friends once, a rare description Percy had handed out to a smaller number of people than the fingers on one hand. They both knew a single letter and Percy's service would be dissolved and his person free. But nothing about the Home Office was truly that easy, or free.

"I might, however, be able to request termination of your orders if you were to show good faith in your continued loyalty to the Crown," Ridley said.

Percy waited.

The man shifted through some papers, looking both busy and inconvenienced, a demonstration of his power over the situation. "There's a matter of your last mission."

"The French ambassador is dead," Percy said. The only thing that had gone right that night.

"Yes, a job well done," Ridley said. "Since you managed it while being in French custody at the time. We've missed having a man of your caliber."

Percy shrugged. It wouldn't do to give the man all the gory details. Ridley would know them all by now, anyway. "You plan to blackmail me into reinstatement of a different kind, then?" He shook his head, infinitely disappointed. "Poor show, old man."

"A single mission," Ridley said. "For a man of your talents."

Meaning subterfuge, espionage, and murder. "There's a mouse in the works?"

"More like a rat."

"And you need a snake." Because the last chase hadn't ended with him in a French prison. Percy cursed. "A fine metaphor, but I left for a reason. What's catching rats when there's a mongoose holding your tail?"

"Your capture was never part of the plan." Ridley's expression hardened. "But it happened, and you escaped, as expected. The reason you are here remains, to clean up the mess you made."

Then HO knew.

Percy ignored the fingers of dread trailing his spine. A rogue agent was a blemish on any service, but one who kept their head down and their nose clean was of little consequence when there were other, more pressing men who needed killing, the reason Percy imagined he hadn't been hunted down like a fox in the woods. But an agent who attacked the peerage and left bodies lying in the street . . .

"You knew of Officer Brandt's recent activities," he accused. And the HO hadn't lifted a finger to stop it. Rage burned his insides, but Percy's mask remained cold. "Your complacency nearly cost two dukes their lives."

Ridley sneered. "None of his actions can be laid at our feet. Drawing unwanted attention, conspiring with political factions who are no better than mercenaries, Brandt relinquished his position the moment he stopped following orders and made a mockery of this establishment."

The factions' involvement was new. Percy tucked the information away. "You mean the moment *you* lost control of *him*."

"Some in this office would claim you are the same liability." Ridley studied him thoughtfully. "You've made some powerful friends in the past years: dukes, duchesses, brothel madams."

Now they came to it. "How well informed you are."

"And now a duke yourself. What a turn of events."

Percy snorted at the other man's derisive tone. "Had I known my lineage was so well titled, things would have been different, trust me."

"Then you knew nothing?"

Percy's gaze narrowed. "Did you?"

"No." Ridley's displeased tone assuaged Percy's suspicions. His greatest skill had always been anonymity.

Ridley confirmed as much when he said, "We don't make a habit of recruiting men too easily identified by the populace."

"But that doesn't make me without use."

Ridley smiled. "You were always quick to the take." The older man rubbed his face, and the calculating gleam in his eyes faded. "The truth is I've known of your voluntary retirement for some time and chose to keep it to myself. You were a fine officer and a sublime aide-de-camp for our headquarters, and I wouldn't ask for your assistance if I believed there was anyone else who stood a chance at silencing Brandt."

As far as compliments went, it was gushing.

"Your recent rise to notoriety complicates the situation, but not egregiously," he went on. "I could have torn up your orders for recommission as soon as they passed by my desk, but to put it plainly, I knew you would not darken my door for anything less than a command from the Crown itself. So I took advantage."

"You didn't send the orders yourself?" Percy didn't like that one bit.

Ridley shared his displeasure. "I tracked the informant as far as the Birmingham East Office, where the name and sighting were lost in a contained fire too convenient to be anything but intentional."

Nic's signature.

Percy fought a shudder. "Then you're desperate?"

Ridley stood and went to the window that looked out onto the busy thoroughfare. "I'm not a young man anymore. I've scraped and worked my way up the ladder for a legacy I can leave my sons, and security I can leave my family. More so than any viscountcy." He rubbed his face again, the action leaving years behind in the creases around his eyes and mouth. "Decades of intrigue and death, conspiracies and cover-ups. I've done my best to act with honor and make decisions that are in the best interests of England."

He turned to face Percy, his once-broad shoulders weighed down with responsibility. "I'm tired, Percy. In the coming years, I have every intention of enjoying my own retirement. I've cleaned house, tied up missions, and trained my new protegees to a degree near criminal. Everything is finished, except this."

He took the papers from his desk—what Percy now saw were his official orders of reinstatement—and tore them in half before tossing them into the fire, where they curled into a smoky promise.

"Do this for me, old friend," Ridley said, all manner of antics absent from his tone and face. "You'll have the full cooperation of the Home Office and any agents at your disposal. Do this, and you will be redacted from every letter, every memory in every mission, and be free to the life of luxury you deserve. I promise you."

The offer was generous, but the consequences if the mission failed were long reaching. Nothing was that simple. There was more than one rat in the hen house it seemed, which made contacts and resources restricted regardless of old Ridley's best intentions. But as Percy knew, the HO wasn't without its use, either.

"And if I don't succeed?" Percy asked.

Ridley's expression was nothing short of disparaging. "For all our sakes, pray you do."

Percy nodded, a haphazard strategy forming to encapsulate the resources now at his fingertips that weren't tainted. Things like hermit inventors, government pardons, and incinerators to hide the bodies. With some luck, he may be able to mend fences and recruit an army at the same time. It would take a horde of demons to take on the Devil. Nic's inability to control his collateral damage would be the death of him.

"I have a plan," Percy said, calculating the players in this final game. "But you may need to compromise some of those honorable intentions."

Ridley's relieved expression turned to one of business and resignation. "Tell me."

"You admonish the mercenary." Percy smiled, knowing there was a good chance they'd all be dead by week's end. "But how do you feel about loveable rookery gangs?"

CHAPTER TWENTY

PERCY STOOD IN the open doorway of his bed chambers, watching Danny brush her long hair in front of the vanity. He swallowed a lump in his throat and memorized the varying brown tones in her hair—rich chocolate underneath silky almond—not knowing the next time he'd have the privilege to drink in the sight of her.

Noticing his presence, her eyes met his in the mirror, and her slow smile had Percy's groin filling with hot need.

"I've been waiting for you for hours," she said, setting her brush down.

I've been waiting for you my whole life. Percy's nails dug into the doorframe to stop from going to her. This wasn't a time for emotion to take over.

At his silence, Danny glanced over her shoulder, and her eyes narrowed on his position still in the doorway. "Something has happened."

He nodded, loving and hating how perceptive she was. "I need to go underground for a while." Possibly six feet under.

Her attention felt hot on his profile.

He didn't dare meet her gaze.

"This has to do with your ex-partner, doesn't it?"

Jesus, the woman was a mind reader. He nodded again, swearing he heard her brain connecting the story of his past with his vague statement.

"I see," she said at last, and he didn't doubt she did.

Good, he thought. Better to leave things unsaid. Now when they parted ways, there'd be no question she could take care of herself if the worst happened.

Crossing the room, she dropped to her knees to pull a large trunk out from under her bed and began throwing miscellaneous garments inside.

Percy watched, his brain unable to connect her actions to his words. "What are you doing?"

"Packing."

He blinked. "I can see that. Why?"

She quirked a brow at him, the arch taunting. "I'll need at least a few changes of clothes if we're to leave." She stopped and scrunched her nose. "Unless we're literally going underground." Scrutinizing the trunk, she pulled out a white nightgown and replaced it with a brown skirt.

Percy wouldn't entertain the warmth swirling inside his chest at her lack of trepidation. The chit was so fearless, he could say he was going to bunker down in a volcano, and she'd probably pack swimwear and a parasol.

Steeling himself, Percy left all feeling from his voice when he said, "You're not coming."

She paused, slippers dangling from her fingers. Intentions now clear, her jaw clenched as she set the slippers down and turned to face him fully. "I will not stay here without you. Where you go, I go. This man must be brought to justice."

"Justice?" The woman was impossible. "You can't right every wrong, Danny. This isn't some cat in a tree."

"No, it's a man who wants you dead, and I will not allow it."

God, how those three words—*not allow it*—soothed his soul. At least one person would mourn him if he didn't come back. It was more than a wretch like him deserved.

Percy swallowed, battering those welling feelings into submission. "I have men stationed on the grounds. You'll stay here, under guard, until my business is concluded."

"No."

"This isn't up for discussion."

When she went back to packing without a word, Percy felt his belly fill with fire.

"Did you hear what I said, Danny?"

"I heard." She folded a second set of breeches and placed them beside the first.

"Damn it!" He crossed the room and tore the blouse she'd picked up out of her hands. "You're not coming with me. You'll be safe here—"

"Under guard, yes, I heard."

Her calmness was maddening.

"Then we're in agreement?"

"Of course not."

"DAMN IT!" He grabbed her by the arms and shook. "He wants you. Wants to hurt you to get to me. I won't waltz you straight to him."

"You don't waltz, Your Grace."

Defiance sparked in her eyes, a flame Percy didn't doubt was smoking against her carefully built calm. Knowing he'd get nowhere if tempers flared, he said, "Stop this, please." He wasn't above begging. He released her and ran a hand through his hair. "I can't protect you and fight him at the same time."

"And who will protect *you*, Percy?"

He scoffed. The woman was impossible. "I don't need protection."

"Everyone needs protection from something."

Knowing what he must do, Percy's patience snapped.

"What do you know of anything, *my lady*? You with your privileged and happy family? Cosseted like a true aristocratic princess." He couldn't stop the words, even as they scalded. "How traumatic it must be to lose your favorite silver comb or scuff your new slippers. Alert the papers!" He drew the rage to him, shielded himself from the hurt and memories welling up. "Don't think I'm one of your precious servants, puppies, whatever weak creature you can rescue from fate's cruel grip. You know nothing about what it is to be alone. Go spout your nonsense about compassion and understanding to some eager pup who will listen, because all I hear is the incessant barking of a naive bitch. You *will* remain here!"

He turned away from her and the tears that would no doubt be in her eyes. What he'd said was unforgivable and he was the worst monster for voicing such blatant lies, but they were necessary. He'd known since parting ways with the Merry Men in St. Giles that Danny battled her own demons, but whatever trauma haunted her, she'd be all right.

She was too good to walk away. His duchess, the woman who'd risked her neck to climb a tree, who'd scraped her hands and knees to save that devil-spawned cat, she wouldn't hesitate to put herself in harm's way for a lost cause like him.

Let her hurt. Let her cry. She was better off without him. She'd *survive*, which meant everything. Marrying her had been the most selfish thing he'd ever done: selfish, cruel, dangerous. Someone as good and delicate as her would be crushed or worse, killed, when she learned she couldn't save him.

But when she responded, it was not delicacy in her voice.

"Don't you dare use my upbringing to put a wedge between us!"

Percy whirled around and watched her approach, her gaze blazing, a goddess's fury made flesh.

"This is about *your* insecurities and inability to let someone else in." She poked him with a finger right over the ache in his chest. "You don't get to walk away from me, understand? Spouting I couldn't understand because I was born wealthy and privileged. You're feeling sorry for yourself." She advanced, pushing him back, that inner fire searing his skin. "And don't you use such language at me. Ever. Again. Just because you didn't mean a word doesn't reason I will tolerate you, or *anyone else*, speaking to me as you just did. I am worth more than such abuse and so are you!"

Percy was frozen by her presence and her insight. He could look clear over her head—she was so slight—and yet he could see nothing aside from her face, fierce and beautiful and so full of honesty, it ripped his angry shield in two as if it were nothing but gauze.

She saw through him. She always had. But still she stood beside him, against him, whatever was right and good, even when it meant she risked her own happiness and more.

"Danny." Her name burned his throat. "There's no future with me."

She shook her head, her brown eyes fathomless. "There's no future without you."

Her words nearly brought him to his knees. He wasn't deserving, not of her loyalty or her regard. But he did deserve the lesson.

Danny knew her own mind and made her own decisions. She was a crack shot and an untapped talent for espionage. If he hadn't seen the red of her blood that day with Lord Pickles, he'd swear she wasn't human. But she was mortal, flesh and blood and even more glorious because she disregarded her fragile vessel for the sake of her steadfast morals. She was a fucking monster herself, and he'd been stricken with insanity to think he could stand against a warrior queen who'd give no quarter.

He admitted defeat and hung his head. "Apologies, my lady." When this was all over, if they survived, he'd fall at her feet and pledge his eternal fidelity.

She huffed. "*Now* I am angry."

Percy's head shot up to see her roll her eyes.

"You say you're sorry when you should be kissing me." She threw her hands in the air. "Men!"

She'd forgiven him just like that? Percy's heart squeezed. She was too good for him, always seeing the good *in him*. "I can't let you do this. If something happened to you—"

"Me?" Danny grasped his face in both hands. "Do you know what would happen to me if something happened to you? I'd be destroyed, in agony, a miserable pile of broken bones eaten by wild dogs."

Percy wouldn't read into her impassioned speech. She *would* be left in the uncomfortable position of leaving Grandfellow if he passed without an heir, but Lord Bromley would see to her care. She couldn't feel more than gratitude for him. "You'd fall out of that big oak tree?"

"Percy."

"When you say my name like that, all exasperated, it makes my heart flutter."

"I can help," she pressed. "I'm a good shot and I won't fall to pieces under pressure."

They both knew she was better than a good shot. "Nic won't succumb to your—while entirely delicious—charms. He won't hesitate to kill you."

"I've faced death before."

Percy shook his head, determined to make her see reason. She wanted to help, fine. But he'd find a task that would keep her as far away as possible. "Syd and Zans would never have really harmed you. Robbed you and sold off your pistol to the nearest arms' men at a criminally inflated price, yes, but even gang leaders must eat."

"I don't mean in St. Giles." Danny bit her lip, drawing his attention like a fly to a honey pot. Silence descended on them, as if the very air around them knew her next words would negate every preconceived notion he had. "I was kidnapped when I was a child."

Everything stopped. Lips forgotten, Percy's focus narrowed to the way her fingers curled into fists, a feeling of dread pooling in his gut.

"My father's wealth and public stance on women's suffrage made him enemies in the House of Lords." Her fingers turned purple from the force of her clenched fists. "One lord in particular wouldn't accept the audacity that his *property* would have rights and acted.

"It all happened so fast. One minute I was alone in the garden, the next..." Her fist went to her throat as if imagining hands there. "I remember trying to scream, but they held me too tight. I thought I'd faint from the lack of air. I think I did."

Percy watched the light in her eyes fade, knowing she'd gone back to the past.

"The warehouse where they kept me smelled of gunpowder and fish." She raised her shaking hands before her face, but her gaze wasn't focused. "The ropes around my wrists and ankles rubbed my skin raw, but I didn't cry because I knew the men wouldn't like it. I knew not to draw attention to myself, but it didn't matter in the end."

Danny hugged herself and went silent, not needing to voice the words, except for one last heartbreaking sentence. "I was ten."

It was those last three words that broke him.

Action. Abduction. *Assault.*

This was why she'd fallen apart in the alley. He'd thought she had cracked under the pressure of being accosted, but it was only after her reaction to the knife, her moan of pleasure, that the fierce warrior mask she'd worn had collapsed.

It didn't take a trained assassin to make the connection; her abductors had used knives—as a means of threatening or something unimaginable—and she had coped however she could. Instead of terror, her fear had turned to pleasure.

Ten. Percy knew intimately what abuse like that did to a child.

Predatory growls rumbled through his chest, and Percy offhandedly realized the sounds were coming from him. Whoever this lord was, he better pray whatever prison he had the good fortune to live out the rest of his scummy life in was unreachable by land.

When he responded, his voice sounded far away. "Were you harmed physically?" She'd been a virgin on their wedding night, he knew, but there were other ways to harm a woman. He wouldn't ask about the damage to her mental state. He knew the answer to that already.

Knew it and accepted it. Accepted *her* because there wasn't a single goddamn thing that wasn't beautiful about his wife. An inflated need for justice not only drove her, but it had also molded her, as it damn well should have. Knowing now what she'd gone through, there was no end to the justice *she* deserved. He'd line up a hundred monsters for her to slay if it took the shadows from her gaze.

"No, they never touched me. My papa paid the ransom, and I was left on the Yard's doorstep," she said, and Percy took his first easy breath.

Only to have her knock the wind out of him.

"We'll overcome our pasts, Percy. For our sake and for the sake of our future children."

At the thought of little dark-haired children, climbing trees and terrorizing that haunting creature, Mrs. Smith, Percy buried his face in her hair, those held-back feelings breaking free and leaving him lightheaded. Old hurts rose to the surface, screaming how the happy ending wasn't for the likes of him. But for her, he held on to hope. If she'd survived something so truly ugly and still found things to smile about, he'd learn to skip through foxglove meadows and recite poetry like a damn bard.

"I swear I'll try." His teeth clenched. "But I'm not a good man, Danny."

Hands brushed against his chin, her touch as soft as her words. "Good is for God to decide in the end. The only thing that matters is that you don't shut me out. We're in this together for better or worse, husband. And Lord above knows I'm no saint."

Percy shook his head. "I won't have you say such things. For all you do for everyone else—"

"You have it wrong." Danny's mouth turned down at the edges. "I'm not a savior or a saint. Everything I do is out of selfishness and fear. When I see someone in need, helping isn't my first response. My first thought is to run as fast and far away as I can. But I choose to stay and choose to face the danger for my own good." She pressed a fist to her chest, choking out words like they hurt to voice. "Don't you see? I *must* save them, Percy, because If I can save others . . ."

Percy's heart wrenched in understanding, understanding her and, through her, better understanding a piece of himself. "Saving others means you can save yourself."

When her gaze lifted to his, her eyes glistened with unshed tears. "I'm sorry I'm not perfect. I've always been scared. Ever since that night, I haven't known a moment without it. But with you . . ." She threw back her shoulders and determination turned her expression fierce. "You make me stronger. The fear is still there, but I no longer cower at my own response. You've shown me the beauty in my flaws. I don't need to be ashamed of who I am."

Percy stood stunned. There was no question she could handle the coming storm. Not only did she face those fears every day, but she had grown stronger despite them . . . Fear. He'd learned the word as a child. A word filled with dark worry. But through her eyes, from her mouth, Percy finally understood the courage that went hand in hand.

"You have so much good in you," she went on. "You may be a villain to yourself, the rest of the world can believe the lie, but you've been my savior. And I have every intention of staying and showing you the beauty you carry inside. I *can and will* be your partner, Percy. Someone you can trust."

Jesus, was that what she was worried about? He cupped her face in his hands. "I do trust you, Danny. And you are my partner. I'm an absolute ass for making you question that for a second."

She smiled. "Glad that's settled." She placed a kiss on his lips, leaving the lingering taste of honey scones behind. "But, Percy, my forgiveness isn't selfless, either."

He leaned forward, eager for another taste. "Meaning?"

Her nails on his cheek dug in. "Think to *handle* me again, and I will lock you in a closet with Lord Pickles."

God, he loved her. Fierce, flawed, perfect her.

He chuckled and brought her fingers to his mouth. "Clawed to death by a feline? My ghost would never live down the shame."

"Then you agree?"

"For the peace of my soul? I believe I must." For her, for what she'd just offered him—a future—he'd shred his nails dragging himself out of the deepest pits of hell.

CHAPTER TWENTY-ONE

PERCY EYED HIS companions, taking up half the carriage on the seat across from him. "Tell me again why you two tagged along?"

"Because your wife asked for our help." Hamish crossed his arms over his chest and leaned back into the cushions, his black sleeves straining against the muscles. "And to keep you from doing something stupid."

"Not me," Renard said from beside him, looking out the window at the dark streets, his light hair looking ridiculous with his new haircut sheared so close to his head.

The style made sense to differentiate him from Nic should the bastard show up—Percy had made the mistake himself before—but really. A man must draw the line at looking like a harvested sheep.

"I came to watch the spectacle," Renard explained.

Percy frowned. "I don't need an escort. It's not like I'll kill him."

Both men turned to him then, neither looking convinced.

Blowing hair from his eyes, Percy wished for the sixth time he hadn't left his bowler hat at home, if only to block the sight of his friends' meddling faces. "I'd never harm the crackpot. Tease mercilessly and set his latest contraption on fire out of spite, sure, but you must agree, it's for the man's own good?"

Percy wasn't even certain a blaze would be of note to the

inventor. Knowing Gregori, he'd work around the flames and use the heat to forge a new batch of glass until his skin blistered. His focus was a downright health risk.

"Those *contraptions* are what's flooding the rookeries with revenue and new jobs," Hamish said testily. "I'd rather they *and* my man stay intact."

Percy rolled his eyes. "Tell me, do you express the milk first, or do you let Gregori suck directly from your tit?"

Hamish didn't take the bait. "If you'd tell us what this is about, we wouldn't need to follow you around."

"Sorry, Your Grace. I'm not currently in need of a nurse-maid."

The carriage slowed to a halt and a distant horn blared from one of the ships coming into port through a thick blanket of fog over the harbor.

Percy exited the coach before the rest and made his way to the last warehouse on the wharf before giving the door a solid kick. "Wake up, Crackpot. I've a job for you."

The door opened a minute later, a disheveled Gregori complete with oil-stained breeches and a coat two sizes too big standing in the doorway. Upon seeing Percy, his gaze narrowed.

"We didn't make an appointment," Gregori said.

Percy made sure to show all his teeth when he smiled. "It's a surprise visit, friend."

Hamish and Renard came up on either side of him, like two enforcers standing guard . . . or two parents hovering over their willful child.

Percy's jaw clenched, but he kept smiling. "Won't you invite us in?"

Gregori glanced at Hamish. "Is he here to kill me?"

"Undetermined."

For fuck's sake! "I need to borrow one of those one-way mirror things you designed, okay? The product sample from the Prodding Pony." Percy shot Hamish a scathing glare. "Happy?"

"Depends on what the mirror is for."

"To show the optimal angle of your innards sliding out your body when I gut you."

"Wouldn't a regular mirror suffice?" Gregori asked, unalarmed and oblivious as always.

"Not for what I need. I'll be building a well-placed peephole in a tavern on the docks. About"—Percy made the rough dimensions with his hands—"this size. Six and six?"

"That's at least eight," Gregori said.

Percy dropped his hands, his ability to keep from throttling the whole group a credit to his endless humor. "Do you have it or not?"

"Precise measurements are important," Gregori said. "How you exaggerate your penile size to the ladies doesn't interest me."

"I see you've upped your insult game." If Percy weren't in such a hurry, he'd have offered the man a drink in commemoration. "Work on your bedside manner, genius. *Then* talk to me about playing nice with others. Now, the mirror, if you would?"

Gregori rolled his eyes and waved a hand to his left. "*Auf dem tisch.*"

Renard frowned. "What did he say?"

Percy smiled. "That your haircut reminds him of peach fuzz, and your vest is on backwards."

Hamish ran a hand over his face, lines of exasperation pulling the corners of his mouth down. "He said, 'on the table.'"

Percy eyed the Duke of Camine with new appreciation. "I didn't know you spoke German."

"I had to. It was the only way to negotiate Charlotte's release from foreign custody."

Percy laughed. How he wished he'd been a gnat on the sill listening to Hamish plead his wife's case in broken German.

Renard wasn't so amused. "Why is this the first time I'm hearing about my sister's incarceration?"

Percy, mournfully, interrupted what was shaping up to become a bloody battle of fisticuffs. "Gentlemen—and genius—I regret I have more important things to do than watch you . . . do anything." Like taking his wife against the wall and making her scream his name.

Hamish's call stopped him at the door. "Where to next?"

Percy looked to the rafters and sighed. He needed two dukes trailing his every step like he needed Danny to save another cat. Lord Pickles had already wormed her way into sharing his bed, slippers, and one particularly unfortunate bath neither of them would forget. He still couldn't look the stupid feline in the eye.

"Don't need a nursemaid," Percy reiterated. "Go home to your wives, enjoy married life, build a church."

"What if we agree to do everything you say?" Renard offered.

Percy rolled his eyes. He needed two *obsequious* dukes trailing him like he needed the cat rammed up his arse. "No need, duke. Wives," he reminded. "Pretty, feisty wives who no longer have a reason to throw shoes at your head, what with the babe out."

Renard—whipped man that he was—seemed to consider.

Hamish, reading the same expression on his brother-in-law's face, sighed and promised, "Fine. We'll stay out of it."

Finally.

Relieved, Percy forgot how close he stood to the genius when he mumbled, "Now if I could only get the Greens and the Merrys to play their roles."

"*Narren besorgung*," Gregori said.

Percy rubbed his temple. "Again with the German, genius? Really, you've lived in England for how long now?"

Gregori offered an uncharacteristic scolding. "It *is* a fool's errand. Encouraging gang activity is moronic and irresponsible."

Percy's gaze narrowed. "How do you know about that?" His machinations—a subtle bit of vandalism here, a false rumor there—none of the recent tensions on the streets could be traced back to him, especially by a man who only deigned to show his face in public for the rare tumble with the local pleasure girls. Decidedly open-mouthed pleasure girls.

Answering his own question, he glared at Gregori. "If we can get back to business?"

"I won't help you," he said. "Not if it means starting a war between the Greens and the Merrys."

Hamish jolted. "You're starting a gang war? Are you an idiot?"

Percy rolled his eyes. This was why he worked alone. "Not an actual war. Merely the illusion of one. I informed Markus of my actions before I expertly stepped on toes. No need to worry."

"What about the Greens?" Hamish said. "Did you get their cooperation?"

"Of course not. Any one of those ingrates could be in Nic's pocket." Seriously, *this* was why dukes made the worst partners.

"What about the locals?" Hamish's face resembled a rolling thundercloud. "I won't tolerate collateral damage. There must be another way."

"I took precautions," Percy said. He wasn't *that* irresponsible. "The port authorities were anonymously informed of the possible upcoming violence and additional agents were requested to patrol the docks. With all the grumbling over the recent sand theft on the incoming ships, even the captains are likely to throw in their support." He'd thought of everything.

Head popping up like a child's jack-in-the-box toy, Gregori asked, "Did you say sand?"

Percy gritted his teeth at the interruption. *Now* the man wanted to talk business? "I didn't say steel and timber."

"As in silica?"

Percy scoffed at the man's intensity. Only a scientist would get excited about dirt. "Is there any other kind?"

Gregori sent papers flying from his table in his search for a large, leather journal. "How much at a time?"

Percy sighed. There was no use teasing the automaton when he asked questions of measurement. "By the barrels." The lack of finesse in the next generation's criminal enterprise was sad. "Apparently, smuggling gunpowder and Scottish whiskey is too high an ask nowadays."

"This is bad," Gregori said, referencing his journal.

"I agree," Percy said. "So much harder to buy bootleg if there isn't any in stock."

The man quirked a brow at that. "Silica's versatility far outshines that of liquor."

Percy glanced at the other two men in the room. "Is he speaking German again? I could've sworn he just said something *un*-English."

Hamish looked down at where Gregori's finger held a place halfway down the page. "Are those ship inventories for the harbor?"

Gregori nodded. "I keep a record of a dozen ships, so if we ever 'borrow' supplies, we don't leave an easily led trail back to our operation."

"Not bad, genius," Percy said. No wonder the authorities weren't sticking a monocle up their bums. "I'll get you more sand, Greg. If that's what you're worried about?"

"You don't understand," Gregori said, turning the journal so the page was faced right-side up for the rest to see. "Silica is used in everything from glass making to art to weapons, particularly in crude counterweight mechanisms. And it's not the only supply regularly missing from manifests."

He'd need to carry a complete set of encyclopedias on his person to keep up with the man. "Get to the point, Gregori."

"Silica is used to make more than glasses. Add the missing metal and filaments taken in smaller batches and a mechanical picture emerges."

Maybe to a lunatic genius. "I'm sure those lovely little time turners *are* untapped profits—"

"Bombs," Gregori said.

"Okay, *bombs* of missed profits." Jesus, he'd sic Danny on the genius for all the word games. That was a bloodbath he'd pay to see.

Gregori shook his head. "Silica is used to delay triggers in bombs."

Percy's humor evaporated.

Renard choked. "You mean real bombs?" He pantomimed a falling shell and resulting explosion with his hand as if the man wouldn't understand his question.

Gregori ignored the idiot's antics and asked Percy, "Is there any way your ex-partner learned about bomb-making?"

Learned? The man had taught their regiment how to make makeshift explosives in the trenches when their guns had kept misfiring. They'd been fourteen.

"Fuck."

"It's Nic," Hamish said, face pale. "At the Leishires' ball, he aired our commandeering of sand barrels as one of his grievances. I hadn't thought a second more about it, the idea he was on a homicidal rampage over a bit of dirt." He ran a shaky hand through his hair. "He's making fucking bombs!"

His horror was mirrored in the other expressions around the room.

This changed everything.

"This is the importance of communication," Gregori said, the rat bastard.

Cornering Nic in the streets was pointless now, especially if he'd already chosen his target.

"How much damage could this kind of bomb reap?" Percy asked.

"Given the amount missing in the past months and the understanding my records are for only twelve of the thirty ships that make regular charters through the harbor . . ." Gregori took the graphite stick from behind his ear and jotted down a series of figures on a scrap of paper.

When he looked up from his math, his complexion had paled considerably.

The three men waited in silence, their tense postures all conveying they knew the answer before Gregori confirmed their worst fears.

"A crude bomb this size could take out Dockside in a single go."

The idea was unfathomable.

"What is to be done?"

"Call the authorities and evacuate the city?"

"There's no time. What if the plants are already in place? Unless we know—"

The three other men talked over each other, their emotions high—even the robot crackpot worried his lip and interjected when applicable—but they'd get nowhere without a point of origin.

Percy burrowed deep into his subconscious, where the men's conversation, the noise from the harbor traffic outside, the room itself faded away. He let his mind wander, processing the pieces of intel he knew of Nic's past as well as the information they'd gathered over the past years since Nic had reentered the picture.

Nic was gathering supplies.

He intended a large-scale attack.

He was using independent factions in the city. Mercenaries to buy him time and protection.

Personal vendettas had delayed his plans.

Ruled by emotions.

As the list continued, Percy reduced the man's complicated personality to the pinnacle of its driving principle.

Nic had always worked under the anger of what he'd per-ceived as past wrongs. The list of grievances had grown in length and mania as he'd aged, the ravages of war and exception to rules feeding an already warped sense of right and wrong.

Percy had to narrow down the list if there was any hope. But where to start?

He would hedge his bets Nic would go for a single grand spectacle instead of splitting the materials; he'd reveled in the flashier kill, the display of his prowess and genius.

Which left the damning question: Where would he strike? The Home Office? Fellow Hall? The Prodding Pony? The Harbor?

Whom would Nic see as his greatest foe? Where would he place the blame?

The person he deemed responsible for holding him back. The same person who'd taken away what fictitious future he thought he was owed.

"Me."

The three men fell silent.

Facing their expectant faces, Percy accepted their unflinching trust, his gut tight with the weight of his decision. "Nic will go after me at Fellow Hall."

If a bomb this size could take out entire blocks in the city, it could wipe the entirety of Fellow Hall off the map.

Nic had risen from the grave—a place far easier to manipulate his enemies while they'd dropped their guards—after learning of Percy's newfound wealth and power. Putting his plans in jeopardy because he couldn't stand the idea that Percy had acquired something unattainable without artifice: A play Nic had already used and lost when posing as the Marquess of Slasbury.

All because of him.

"That has to be the target," he thought out loud.

"We know where to go," Hamish said, his expression determined. "Which means we can anticipate him and stop this once and for all."

"It's not that easy," Percy said. Knowing the location turned all his plans sideways. He hadn't calculated a houseful of servants, or the disadvantage of an estate of blocked sightlines.

When he'd thought to lay out their line in St. Giles, the roof access and dozens of eyes would've kept their trap from springing prematurely.

But with hundreds of acres and an unknown number of associates on Nic's payroll, there was no way of pinpointing the direction of infiltration in the country. Any change of routine, any personnel not where they were supposed to be would tip Nic off.

Which left those whose presence wouldn't be thought of as suspicious.

Percy would rather shred his arm from a bear trap than involve his friends.

"Percy." Hamish's hand fell on his shoulder. "Talk to us. Tell us what you need."

Renard snorted. "Not even you believe *His Secretiveness* would ask for help."

No one would believe it.

The Home Office taught cooperation, obedience, but secrecy more than anything else. Percy had grown to rely only on himself, divulging plans on a need-to-know basis. If no one knew the full plan, a single setback wouldn't cripple a mission because contingency steps would be in place.

Percy gritted his teeth. He'd become as predictable as Nic with his actions.

And that was why Percy always lost.

If there was any hope of taking Nic down, there could be nothing held back.

Percy fought his gut reaction to keep his thoughts silent and chewed on the words before he finally said, "I need your help."

Renard startled. "Really?"

Gregori—the loveable scamp—blurted an out-of-character, "Bullshit!"

Hamish was the only one whose expression never changed. He leaned against the nearest table and inclined his head. "What's the plan?"

Percy returned his friend's composure with gratitude. They'd all need to keep their heads for the chaos to come. "Call in the troops," he said, stomach in knots. "We've a score to settle."

The gamble would decide all their fates: Hamish's, Charlotte's, Renard's, Camille's . . . Danny's.

Though slim at best, together, there was a chance.

Percy prayed he was right. The consequences of being wrong were too great to comprehend.

CHAPTER TWENTY-TWO

DANNY RUSHED INTO the Duchess of Camine's drawing room, certain she'd find Percy on the floor bleeding from multiple wounds.

The man had no decency. They'd been married less than a week and he was already running off. Now she got a message from her dear friend saying to come quickly as a matter of the utmost urgency. She should've known Percy wouldn't keep his word. He'd no doubt run headfirst into danger the second after he'd promised they'd face his enemies together.

Danny pressed a fist to her churning stomach. He'd better be all right because she was going to bash his stupid head in for making her worry.

But when she observed the room and its full occupants, it was to find her husband pale but whole, surrounded by not only the Duke and Duchess of Camine, but Charlotte's relatives, the Duke and Duchess of Lux, as well.

Directing her attention to the man who had the gall to not be prostrate on the floor, she said, "You're not dying."

Percy blinked. "I'm . . . sorry?"

Charlotte winced beside Percy on the settee. "My letter may have been a bit dramatic."

Yet Danny had never known her friend to exaggerate. "*Life and death,*" her note had implied. From the grave expressions all around, she didn't think her wording was far off. "Tell me what's happened."

She saw Percy take a deep breath, but the Duchess of Lux cut in. "Fellow Hall is now the target of a sadistic killer with explosives at his disposal. Care to help us eviscerate him?"

Danny's stomach twisted. Someone was going to attack Grandfellow? Not *someone*. Percy's ex-partner. Judging by her husband's gaunt face and colorless complexion, things were worse than before.

Forget evisceration, for making Percy worry, she'd take the man's head in penance.

Regarding the Duchess of Lux—turned towards the fire so her long, red hair looked alive in the reflection of the flames—Charlotte's sister-in-law, Danny knew immediately by her straightforward words and bloodthirsty nature they'd get along famously.

"How can I help, Duchess?"

"First, call me 'Camille.'" A slender brow rose taking her measure. "Word has it you're a good shot?"

Danny's brows lifted. "How did you know that?"

An enigmatic smile curled the woman's full lips. "It was in your brother's file. Any truth to the rumors?"

Danny had no idea what 'file' her brother had, but now wasn't a time for modesty. "Better than good."

Percy shook his head. "Whatever you're thinking, Camille, the answer is no."

Camille shifted to fully face the room, revealing a tiny infant nestled in her arms. "We're hunting a madman. Any successful ambush utilizes snipers and lookouts. You're supposed to be some great spy. Shouldn't you know that?"

Percy looked heavenward and cursed. "I hate that Renard lets you read."

The Duke of Lux chuckled. "Like I have a choice."

Danny didn't hesitate. "The western side of Grandfellow has a chapel. I'll have the best vantage in the bell tower, where I can survey most of the property without detection."

Charlotte and Camille shared a grin.

Percy groaned. "Where did you learn—"

"*The Art of War*, French translation." Danny explained.

A look of pure admiration crossed her husband's face before he let out a huff. "None of you women should be allowed to read."

"Get over it," the Duchess of Camine said. "What's our first step?"

"Round up his associates," Hamish said. "A man alone is a man undefended."

Percy shook his head. "We don't know how many people are working for him. Mercenaries, workmen—half the rookeries could be in his pocket. There'd be no way of knowing."

"Then plaster his face everywhere," said the Duchess of Lux. "Bond Street, Russell Street, nail it on the front of every fucking church door. Offer a king's ransom as a reward. Come Sunday morning, he won't be able to take a piss without someone recognizing him. He may have half the rookeries, but no man is rich enough to employ all of it."

Fully on board, Hamish piped in, "Charlotte could make the sketch." He laid a protective hand on his wife's belly. "She's as good as any professional artist. Better."

The duchess lit up at the praise, always ready to dive into action. "Camille could help fill in the gaps with anything I've forgotten. We'd have his likeness down exact."

Danny smirked, though the only humor present was from the young baby as the girl amused herself grasping at the front of the Duchess of Lux's gown.

"I don't doubt your skills, but throw his face on every lamp-post from here to Scotland, and he'll simply find a new one," Percy said.

Charlotte frowned. "I hate when the enemy is clever."

The Duchess of Lux agreed. "Much better when a man is awful *and* stupid."

Danny raised the glass Charlotte put in her hand. "Hear,

hear."

Percy huffed. "Why do I feel as if I've failed a test in some way?"

"Because you're awful?" Charlotte offered.

"As complimentary as ever, Your Grace." Percy looked at Danny. "Should you not defend me?"

Danny glanced at Charlotte and back and feigned innocence. "One doesn't like to question the insight of a duchess. She *has* known you longer."

Percy threw his hands in the air. "They've banded together now."

Hamish chuckled. "Finally realizing you're no longer head of anything, chap?"

"Not at all." Percy grinned. "I'm pitying Nic for the fool now that the ladies are prepared for battle. The war is all but won."

Charlotte gave a gruff sound of approval. "Not so awful after all."

"Back to the point." Percy cleared his throat. "I have a plan—"

"But we're not going to like it," Hamish finished, walking towards the bar. "I need a drink first before we break any more laws that could land us in the penitentiary."

"It requires some flexibility and a good bit of violence," Percy continued.

"I'm in," Camille said.

The Duke of Lux crossed himself. "Lord have mercy."

"First we need an instigator." Percy faced Danny. "When you said your family likes games, who holds the most wins."

Danny frowned. She'd told him what their 'games' consisted of. "Denise."

"Can she insult under pressure?"

Danny nodded. "With relish."

"What do insults have to do with anything?" Hamish asked.

Percy rolled his eyes. "I need someone who is infinitely creative at finding ways to needle someone for my plan to work."

"And who's Denise?"

"My younger sister," Danny explained.

"Ah."

The Duchess of Lux glared at Hamish. "What does that mean, *dear brother?*"

Hamish and Renard answered simultaneously, "Trouble."

Danny smiled at the duchess. "Denise *can* be a handful."

"Will she oppose our plan?"

"Conspiring to corner a killer?" Danny snorted. "She'll offer to be the bait."

"Sisters." The Duke of Lux sighed.

"Women," Hamish and Percy said together.

Charlotte smiled sweetly at her husband. "You're welcome."

"There will be danger involved." Percy's gaze stayed steady on Danny. "I can't vouch for anyone's safety."

She heard the fear he didn't voice, and her heart fluttered in her chest. He did this all for her, to keep her safe.

She *also* heard the censure in his voice and knew he'd prefer to take all this on himself if it meant saving his friends the risk. And he would shield everyone else as much as possible when that was no longer an option.

Hamish voiced the group's collective view. "We all know the chance of success." His gaze went to his wife across the room. "None of us is safe until he's dealt with."

Camille said, "We must play this smart. We all know that slimy crumb-pot can slip through a crack."

"He won't slip through anything," Percy said, his confidence filling Danny with hope and a suspicion he wasn't telling them everything. She wasn't the only one.

Hamish shook his head. "No, Percy. Not this time. Full disclosure or else."

Danny saw her husband's conflict to play out the threat with his usual humor or answer sincerely.

He chose the latter. "I'm going to ask the Merrys for help."

Danny wasn't the only one shocked.

Hamish froze filling his glass, the scotch decanter hovering above his glass. "The Merrys hate you."

Percy snorted. "Everyone needs to stop saying that. I'm quite charming."

A hand fisted on Danny's chest. "You can't go back to St. Giles. That Syd man said he'd kill you."

Everyone turned when both Renard and Camille fell into simultaneous fits of coughing that sounded strangely like laughter.

Danny caught Camille's guilty gaze, and a nagging sense of misplacement filled her mind.

Renard waved their questioning stares away and redirected the attention back to Percy. "What do you expect the Merry Men to do?"

"Run defense, blend in." Percy indicated the walls around them. "Nic will have a record of the servants who come and go through the grand estates. Grandfellow will be no different. A small addition to a staff won't be as suspicious if it is to a neighboring estate."

"Like Bromley Estate," Danny said, nodding. It wasn't out of the question for servants to visit houses of neighboring lords who were in good standing with their masters. And Danny's mother was known to go through entire batches of housemaids when in one of her tirades.

"It could work," she agreed.

"Then I'll go," Hamish said. "Markus will take the request seriously if I am the one to ask."

Percy shook his head. "It must be me. For this all to work, I need to make sure the knives by my side won't be the ones stabbing me in the back. I'll have Syd and Zans work in the background and utilize the other members Nic won't recognize on sight."

Hamish relented, though he didn't look pleased.

It was Camille who caboshed their new plan with the surprising insight, "Nic knows *all* the Merrys' faces. If you must use them, he'll sniff out the trap before it's sprung."

Percy's gaze narrowed. "How do you know that?"

She returned his gaze without flinching. "Renard and I had a run in with Nic at the Docks. The Merrys were there."

Percy cursed and ripped a hand through his hair. "Damn it, people, tell me these things!" He stood and considered the entire room. "Anything else I should know before I put all our lives at risk with half the details?"

They all exchanged expectant glances until Camille sighed. "If we're going for full transparency, you should know my darling nephew is hiding in the curtains."

A flurry of movement behind the curtains stopped them all in their tracks until they parted and the heir of Camine stepped into the firelight.

"Leopold!" Charlotte shot up from her seat. "What were you doing in the drapes?"

"Listening," the boy said without shame, his accusing gaze going to each person in turn. "No one tells me anything."

"Sweetheart." Charlotte crouched down to press a kiss to her son's head. "We're not leaving you out on purpose. There's a problem we're all trying to fix."

"I can fix things."

"This isn't for little boys to fix."

"I want to help Uncle Percy!"

Charlotte glanced helplessly at her husband, and the Duke of Camine walked over to take his son's other side. "Son—"

"No!" Leo pulled away, his determined gaze landing on Percy. He took out a child's slingshot from his pocket and brandished it like a sword. "I can help."

Danny's heart squeezed at the boy's courage. Love filled the room to bursting, but there was no place in this fight for him and everyone knew it, except one.

"Of course you'll help," Percy said.

Make that two.

Everyone turned to Percy.

He crossed the room and gave Leo's hair a good toss before

taking the slingshot from the boy's hand and tapping him on the nose. "Your mother was right, dear boy; you weren't left out of our planning . . . because you *are* the plan."

"Percy." Charlotte's warning tone was accompanied by a glare matched by her husband.

Leo looked up at Percy as if his uncle had told him he was the hero in his very own play. "I can do it," the boy said. "Whatever it is, I can."

Percy nodded and faced Charlotte. "He'll never be in any danger, I promise you."

Charlotte worried her bottom lip, clearly conflicted. Hamish placed a hand on her shoulder and looked down at his son, his expression serious.

"Uncle Percy is counting on you, Leopold. The very weight of your title and honor as a gentleman is on the line."

Leopold stuck out his chin, eyes shining with pride. "I won't let you down."

"There now!" Percy clapped his hands together. "With the addition of my godson, our army is formidable."

"Even with Pops and Leo on our side," the Duchess of Lux said, giving her nephew a warm smile, "it's not much of an army."

"That's because we're short a man," Percy said.

On cue, there was a knock on the door, and Mr. Frendstone popped his head inside to announce Percy's visitor had arrived.

Mr. Brinkley froze seeing the esteemed ensemble populating the room and after a moment remembered himself and bowed. "I came as you requested, Your Grace." He inclined his head to Percy and fussed with the hat in his hands. "I didn't mean to interrupt. I'll come back when you're not busy."

"That won't be necessary, Mr. Brinkley." Percy nodded to the room. "I will hand out everyone's assignments by tonight." With that ominous statement, he led his groundskeeper to a spot by the fire and spoke with him in confidence.

Danny made for the door, prepared to walk to her father's

estate immediately to request her sister's assistance.

Camille stopped her exit with a light touch to her arm. "Shall I accompany you?"

"There's no need, Duchess."

"'Camille,' please. I never use titles if I can help it and never with family."

Danny watched her snuggle the cooing baby in her arms, understanding for the first time what they were asking of these people. Charlotte and Hamish had become good friends, but their relations—while with a stake in the outcome of Nic's plots—had just had a child. There was no surety they'd come out of this unscathed, but still, they'd jumped on board Percy's plan without fail.

"Thank you," she said and she meant it.

"Family doesn't thank each other, either," Camille said with the perfect tone of an older sister. "Remember to use your head and trust your instincts. These creatures"—she jabbed her thumb in the men's direction—"will have you believe their superior *male* experience makes them infallible."

Danny smiled at her new friend's—*sister's*—concern. "No need for the reminder. I have a brother as well."

"Older?"

"Yes."

Camille nodded. "Enough said."

Danny laughed, and her attention fell on her husband across the room. He looked up from his conversation and their gazes snagged. Danny's chest warmed to the point of pain, a pain she no longer could deny.

She loved him.

The comfortable warmth between them had been spreading and growing for weeks now, until Danny couldn't pinpoint the exact moment gratitude and friendship had shifted into something deeper, something that felt like her life would shatter if anything happened to him.

He was a strong man, skilled. A lone hunter who couldn't see he was a born leader. There were still so many things she wanted to learn about his life and his past, but more than that, she needed to teach him about what their future could be, about the wonderful man he was deep down. There'd be laughter and children, sports and erotic exercises performed wherever their passions took them.

Whoever this Nic Brandt was and whatever his schemes, she'd fight for that future.

For the man she loved, she'd save him.

And herself.

CHAPTER TWENTY-THREE

PERCY'S VOICE STOPPED her in the hall.

"Danny, wait."

Danny closed her eyes, knowing if she looked over at him, in his dark moleskin coat and unruly, black curls, she'd never walk away.

"I must inform my sister of our need as soon as possible," she said, letting the draft from the front door clear the heat from his nearness. "I'll send a note when I arrive at Bromley, so you won't worry."

"All I do is bloody worry."

She turned then, unable to resist the frustration in his voice that called to her own tumultuous feelings raging inside.

Seeing his hands clenched into fists at his sides, his dark and piercing gaze searching her face with hot intensity, didn't help.

It took every ounce of willpower not to soothe the lines from his brow with her fingers and replace her fingers with her mouth, and then other parts of her, parts that ached for his rough touch.

Danny cleared her throat, forcing her desires away.

"You were wonderful in there," she said. "Authoritative, confident." *Handsome, arousing.* "All those team skills you learned as a boy paid off."

Percy rubbed the back of his neck self-consciously. "I felt like a damn fool with everyone all expectant." His expression shuddered. "One wrong move and we're all dead."

Danny clutched her warm belly, his overwhelming trust in dropping all pretense in her presence meaning everything. They were partners . . . and right now, she needed to be his.

"You can do this, Percy." She reached out and laid a gentle hand on his arm, forcing herself not to reach for more, not now with so much at stake. "Everyone in that room believes in you."

"And you?" he asked, his voice uncharacteristically reserved. "Do you believe in me?"

She'd do anything to wipe away that look of uncertainty in his gaze. But he wouldn't listen even if she admitted she trusted him with her very soul.

Forcing a pout, she ran a finger down his chest and over the hard span of his torso where her nail scraped the edge of his waistband, reminding herself it was to distract him and not to ease her craving to feel him against her skin. "I believe a man who can make me come six times in a single coupling can handle giving out simple instructions to his friends." She cocked a brow. "I, for one, find your *instruction* more than satisfactory."

Percy tracked her finger's progress across the wide brim of his trousers with a smile that was slow in coming and deliciously wicked and so much like his normal self, Danny felt her shoulders sag with relief.

"It *has* been a solid eight hours since your last lesson," he said, reaching out and twirling a loose curl from her coif around a finger. "I've been remiss in my husbandly duties, haven't I?" He tugged on her hair to elicit the slightest sting on her scalp, a sting he must have remembered she liked when he'd last taken her from behind and used her long mane as reins to pull them both over the edge of pleasure.

Danny's thighs clenched. There was a monster out there somewhere, bent on destroying those who had come to be precious to her, but even with the threat against their persons and home, even knowing Percy needed her strong and on point, her body had its priorities.

Her earlier revelation sizzled through her body and the resulting awareness left her feeling shy and awkward and horribly aroused despite the discomfort.

Percy stiffened. "What's wrong?"

She bit her lip, the ache between her legs stretching with desire. Even now he was attentive, all consuming, perfect.

It wasn't fair. She'd finally discovered the depth of her affection and now one madman could take it all away. They both needed to stay focused on their roles going forward. None of them could afford a distraction.

Percy's light touch on her cheek brought her back. "Danny?"

"I want you." She squeezed her eyes shut and pressed into his touch, not caring how selfish she sounded. "I want you here and now, against this wall, your cock inside me." *I want to know you'll always be close.* "But everyone is counting on you." On them both.

His responding chuckle had her eyes popping open.

His dark gaze fixed on her mouth. All the air was sucked from the hall as he growled and dragged her against him. "Everyone can fucking wait."

Danny didn't fight the sexual pull now. With the threat of violence and death, they both needed reassurance the other would make it out alive. They *would* because Danny refused to live in a world without him.

Percy's lips seared a line of kisses down her temple, along her jaw, playing at the corner of her mouth. "You look ravishing in that dress, Danny. I could barely focus on anything but dipping my tongue down your décolletage and taking a taste."

As his fingers mirrored his words, arousing her through touch, his voice aroused her with fantasy.

She hadn't thought of her outfit with its revealing lines and flattering vertical stripes, only that it was the nearest piece of dress within reach when she'd received Charlotte's missive. Now she wished she hadn't taken the extra seconds to tug on drawers and stockings.

His hands came to cup her breasts, lifting them high until her nipples skimmed the top of her bodice, the fabric teasing her sensitive skin.

"By all means, Your Grace," she rasped. "Feast away."

His chuckle of approval reverberated down her spine as his mouth dipped to tug a rosy bud into his mouth.

When she thought she'd go mad with ecstasy, his attention went to her other breast. "When this is all over, I'm going to take a solid week to taste every inch of you," he promised. He cupped her and flicked each breast with his tongue. "Starting with these."

Danny clutched his shoulder, doing her best to muffle her moans with the back of her hand.

Percy pulled away, his gaze fixed on her covered mouth. Hands falling from her chest, he *tsked*. "This will never do."

Before Danny could protest, Percy opened a nearby closet, barely big enough for the two brooms and bucket it held. Removing the supplies, Percy inclined his head, his gaze wild.

"After you, my lady."

Danny's arousal didn't allow for questions. Entering, her body pressed up against the back of the closet as Percy stepped in behind her and closed the door.

The space was cramped, difficult to maneuver. Danny hadn't even the room to turn around and was about to voice her misgivings when fingers bunched in her skirts and lifted.

Both still standing upright, Percy nudged her legs apart with his foot and worked his fingers through the slit in her drawers to find that coil of nerves at her core.

Danny gasped at the touch and the position, resting her forehead against the cold, wooden paneling and marveling at her husband's ingenuity. Unable to keep the excitement from her voice she asked, "Here, Percy? With everyone next door?"

"Here," he whispered in her ear. "Now."

His barely restrained growls were followed by a snap of buttons popping open and his hard length pressing hot against her backside through the thin knit of her drawers.

Yes, here and now. It was all they could guarantee.

His fingers parted her slit and he pushed upwards in one nail-scraping, core-clenching thrust while his other hand turned her face for better access to the delicate skin between her ear and her shoulder.

"Danny," he murmured against her skin. Massaging her hips, he guided her bottom flush against his pelvis and grinded into her with every shallow buck; urgent thrusts that came faster and faster, giving her no time to think or breathe.

The tension, the limited space, he was everywhere, touching, kissing, drawing her higher and higher towards that bright spot where Earth met the heavens.

He cupped both breasts in his hands and rolled her nipples.

"Percy!"

The orgasm hit hard and brutal, much like the man who gave her such pleasure. There was no need for gentleness or holding back. She wanted all of him: the rough-and-tumble man, the spy, the unbeknownst leader. He was different things to different people, but in this moment, the only thing that mattered was he was hers.

She found his hand that had moved to her thigh and laced their fingers, urging him faster, harder, anything to prolong their connection.

If she could have frozen time and kept him to herself forever, she'd have done so without guilt.

But she had no such power, and when he found his own release with a roar that sounded like the final screams of a tolling bell, Danny's heart crumbled knowing they were all out of time.

⇛⇚

PERCY SLUNK THROUGH the alleys of St. Giles, toeing the new territory lines between the Greens and the Merrys, knowing he'd eventually find one of the lower gang members if he walked far enough.

It was rotten luck the Merrys' blasted dimber-damber had

found Percy first.

Syd slid out of a darkened doorway, the knife in his hand needle thin and gleaming wickedly. "Looks like Christmas came early this year. How I hoped I'd be the one on patrol when you stuck your filthy head out of your hole."

Percy eyed the man's ever-hidden face, the inability to read his enemy's expression another obstacle he must overcome if he was to gain the Merrys' cooperation. Unfortunately, Percy never stopped to think before he spoke. "You scarred under that hood, Syd? Or just ugly?"

Syd twirled the blade in his hand, showing a level of deftness and skill that had Percy swallowing audibly. "Too damn handsome is the problem. Couldn't get anywhere without a mob forming."

The humor took a moment to register. Percy felt his jaw slacken. The Merry leader had left the stick up his ass home today.

He licked his lips to moisten them and prayed the rare show of humor meant the bastard would hear out his proposal before the stabbing started. "I need your help."

Syd snorted. "Your duke friend told Pops you were coming. You here for an update?"

"Something like that."

Syd sighed. Probably disappointed he must stall his plans to use Percy as a pin cushion. "The Greens' raids started two days ago." He shook his head. "I don't know how you got them riled up, but they're encroaching on our territory as planned."

Ah, so victory had assuaged Syd's normal *kill first and cooperate later* mentality.

"And your response?" Percy asked.

A flash of teeth in the dark hood and then, "Have them holed up in a warehouse by the docks they think they won from us last night."

The warehouse Percy had instructed Markus to 'lose' in a brawl with the rival gang, the same warehouse that secretly sat on top of a network of underground tunnels that connected to the Merrys' den.

"Say the word," Syd said, voice laced with violence. "We'll crawl up through the sewers like rats to the feast."

Percy flinched. This was where the stabbing would start if he weren't careful. "About that . . . Plans have changed. I no longer need the docks out of commission."

Syd was too smart not to read between the lines. Knife rising, he leveled the tip at Percy's chest and accused, "You promised us the Greens' territory."

"And you'll have it, I swear." Percy inhaled a steadying breath and took a bigger risk stepping close, his hands upraised. "But the distraction was for a bigger catch, the destruction of a mutual enemy. An enemy that needs a tighter net to snare."

Syd snorted. "Backpedaling now, Percy? Can't deliver on your promise and now you're making excuses—"

"Nic Brandt is back on the streets, alive and unfortunately *alive*."

Syd's growl was rough and followed by a string of curses that left Percy wishing to cover his manhood.

Syd turned sharply back to him, knife angled at his throat. "No more games, Percy. If this is another ploy—"

Percy pressed his neck into the knife tip and felt the sting as the metal bit into his skin. "I'm dead serious, Syd." And because Percy had no hope of winning favor without offering everything, he said, "The bastard is after the woman I love."

Percy had to have heard wrong. The man—heartless bastard and leader of the most ruthless gang in Dockside—couldn't have sighed.

"The woman from the alley?" Syd asked.

Percy nodded, his head spinning from the man's out-of-character outburst. "Help me stop him, and Nic Brandt is yours."

Voice going back to its usual bland hatred, Syd asked, "How?"

"I know where he'll be three days from now."

Syd's hand shook, anger at the man they all had a score to

settle with or the anticipation of exacting revenge, Percy didn't know.

After a tense moment where Percy had real concerns he'd lose his head and a rather underappreciated singing voice, Syd retracted the knife and hid it in his waistband.

"Talk fast, Percy," he said. "I already sent word to my men there was a hare in the streets, and my wolves like to come in teeth snapping."

Percy swallowed again and stepped into the dark doorway and out of sight of anyone passing by.

This was going to work. The fact he hadn't been skewered was a good sign.

Gaining the Merrys' cooperation was imperative for his plan to succeed, especially now when every position of defense counted. The Merrys' identities may have been compromised, but that didn't mean they couldn't be useful, a lesson good old Ridley had reminded him of.

Old hurts and grudges meant nothing if it kept Danny out of harm's way. He'd get Syd on his side if he had to dispose of every Green within the rookeries.

Either that, or he was wolf food.

He extracted the plans from his coat and passed them to Syd, knowing this gamble was bigger than the rest. One didn't like to hand over the exact layout of one's mansion to known criminals without a bit of trepidation. But for Danny, he'd invite his second-worst enemy into his home. He'd serve the whole lot of bastards from his own plate if that was what it took. "Take a look at these and tell me what you think."

Syd glanced at Fellow Hall's architectural prints and frowned. "What does an old house have to do with Nic?"

Percy pointed to a spot on the drawing, the perfect place on the estate to trap a monster. "Everything."

CHAPTER TWENTY-FOUR

NOT ONLY HAD Denise agreed to her ridiculous role as instigator, she'd roped Don into playing second fiddle. Whomever Percy unleashed the Deime siblings on, they didn't stand a chance at composure with those two needling like it was a personal mission from the Home Office.

Which, in fact, it was.

When Percy had informed her of his visit to the Home Secretary after their *instruction* in the broom cupboard, she'd been angry, knowing the man responsible for manipulating Percy since childhood currently held the title. But if the man offered to look the other way as three of the most prestigious aristocratic families played war, she'd hold her tongue, especially if pardons would be in order.

There'd been no time last night for one last embrace or talk. Danny and her sister received their missions via Charlotte and each of them had spent the remainder of the hours in seclusion to memorize their instructions and prepare for the next day.

And there'd been no sign of Percy all day. Not at breakfast when the three women—and Don—had joined the Duke of Lux and his wife staying at Fellow Hall. Not after lunch as they sat on the veranda overlooking the parks visible on the northwestern side of the estate. And not as the afternoon sun sunk low when the group of individuals dispersed to their designated posts without a word. Small talk had been far from anyone's mind.

Percy's instructions to the whole group had arrived just after tea: *At half past four, move to your positions. Keep focused and alert at all times.*

Danny checked and rechecked her rifle in the old bell tower, the *clicking* sound of the gun's reload like a shot in the prolonged silence of the day.

Danny knew the gun was for her protection. Percy never expected her to pull the trigger on another person.

She was the lookout, and her instructions were clear. Danny picked up Percy's note to her and read the contents again, loving the tight but beautiful lines he used to write it, so different from what anyone would expect.

> *Raise the flag if you spot the enemy. Green from the west, red for the south, blue for the north, yellow for the east.*
> *Watch for movement at the treeline. The enemy will wear dark clothes to blend into the vegetation. Pay attention to the wildlife.*
> *Be safe.*

Upon making her way up the stairs and into the tower, the flags, the rifle, and ammunition had been skillfully placed at each corresponding gap in the wall as if left by a corporeal ghost.

Percy had thought of everything.

Danny couldn't stop her gaze from straying to the maze, knowing instinctively Percy would be there.

Those last two words in his note ripped at her.

"Be safe."

He'd be safe. He had to be. His boasting of skill and experience hadn't been falsehoods.

But every minute watching the treeline was a minute for doubt to creep its way in.

What if this Nic was just as skilled? What if the enemy came on two fronts? What if the Merrys didn't see her signal? What if they'd overlooked something crucial?

A sharp breeze whistled through the openings in the walls.

Flash.

Danny squinted at the woods.

Flash.

Stomach twisting, Danny let out a strangled cry as the setting sun flashed over metal in the woods to the west.

Snatching the red flag, Danny raced to the southern wall break, seeing the flash again from a different angle. She stopped.

The flash came again.

Danny hesitated. No trained gunmen would shift his weapon to catch the light.

Minding her gut, Danny used precious seconds to press her gun's scope tight to her eye and traced the outline of something big and weighted swaying in the fading sweep of wind.

A weapon much worse than a group of armed men.

Danny's heart stopped. "My God."

She scrambled down from the tower, her toes skidding on the stairs and her shins screaming for a reprieve that wouldn't come. Not now.

Not when her husband had forgotten to give her a signal for this.

Not when they *had* overlooked something crucial.

Not before she got to Percy and told him she'd located Nic Brandt's bomb.

⋙⋘

AVOIDING DANNY ALL day had done nothing to ease the dread in Percy's stomach.

He'd been so busy running around, finalizing plans, and laying the final trap, there hadn't *been* time. But now, sitting in the maze's courtyard, standing under the very fountain that had reunited him and Danny after all those years apart, he'd been an idiot not to look on her face one last time, touch her skin, breathe in her scent, tell her how much he bloody loved her!

Nic better appreciate how quickly he planned to slit open his throat. For how much grief he'd put Danny through, Percy felt the uncommon desire to exact punishment at a glacial pace.

The sound of racing steps had Percy's mind switching off and his body notching his first knife into place behind his head for a throw that would take his enemy in the ear. A move he'd made countless times and with fatal results.

He slowed his breathing and cleared his mind, counting, listening until the person was just beyond the opening in the wall.

Step . . . step, step.

Now!

The person rushed into the courtyard, and Percy's knife clattered to the flagstones along with his stomach.

"Danny?" *God damn it!* "I could have killed you!"

At his outburst, she beelined for him, her eyes wild and her hair a mess. "Percy, thank God, I found you in time." She stopped and looked around, her attention waning in apparent confusion. "Where are the Merrys?"

Percy shrugged noncommittally. "Around."

Her gaze narrowed. "Why did no one stop me? I could've been anyone running through the maze."

Percy sidestepped. "They're well trained and know when to come out in the open."

Unlike a certain duchess who was a damned beacon in that riding habit. Good God, what color was she wearing? Easy-to-spot, easier-to-kill blue?

Anger returning, he set his jaw and growled. "You were supposed to wait in the bell tower and *out of sight*. I made those flags so you wouldn't have to come out in the open."

"*You* should've waited for backup."

"There wasn't time!"

"*Make* the time."

"Go back—"

"Be quiet and *listen*," she said.

Danny shook her head, muttering something about men being pigheaded, and Percy's anger leached out at the picture she made.

She was gorgeous with her tight trousers that showed off her generous backside and her hair plaited down her back in one long, practical, but feminine braid. And while the ridiculous light-blue color of her outfit was *im*-practical for remaining unseen, the tones of sky and sea did set off the golden flecks in her dark eyes.

Done muttering, Danny pointed to the south side of the property. "I found something. It's near the treeline, half-hidden in a bundle of birch trees."

Percy whirled in the direction of her finger and took to the maze wall, finding prickly hand holds in the heath that bit through his thick gloves.

Peering over the top, he surveyed the trees to the south, looking once, twice, making out lines of white trunks in the fading light that didn't look quite right on his third pass. He squinted and saw the faint outline of a pulley system and a heavy bag.

She'd found the bomb.

"Shit and fire," he whispered. The bastard had somehow circumvented all his traps.

No one without a hawk's gaze would be able to see it unless they knew it was there. No one except his exceptional wife.

Heart thudding the inside of his chest, Percy dropped back to the flagstones and planted a kiss on Danny's lips. "You're a marvel, wife."

Give the woman simple instructions to locate the enemy and she found the ultimate weapon. He feared what would happen if she needed her rifle.

If Danny could stomach the bloodshed, she could pick off the first of the mercenaries entering the clearing around the mansion. Or cover him while he made his way to the site.

But as soon as an enemy got too close, the rifle would be useless.

"Here, take this." He handed her a knife from inside his coat, one of two that had been with him since his first mission for the

Home Office, a set that had never failed him. He still mourned the loss of the mate, lost forever in the thorny vines of Lady Leishire's courtyard garden. "I assume you know how to use it?" He made light.

Danny smirked. "I do." She pushed away the offered handle and extracted a different knife from the waistband of her trousers. "But I prefer this one."

Percy blinked down at the familiar ivory handle, the silver design twinging through the white like streaks of lightning. He hadn't lost it that night at the Leishires' ball at all. The swelling of emotion wasn't just for seeing the set reunited. "You kept it?"

Her mouth quirked in a teasing smile. "Once I knew how dangerous it was to confront villains in the dark, how could I not?"

Percy saw through her lie, saw it and felt his heart swell to bursting. "You kept it as a reminder of me."

"Yes," she said, something deep and warm and too much resembling affection in her eyes. "I kept it as a promise to myself that I would see you again."

The pain in his chest tipped over the edge and into a place Percy couldn't describe. How this perfect woman—lovely, brave, and loyal—had known their fates from the start was of no consequence. What mattered now was that he would make that same promise to himself now.

Grasping the blade of her knife, Percy let the edge slice into his palm and vowed with every beat of his heart, every drop of blood in his veins—hell, every drop dyeing the stones at their feet. "I will see you again, Daniella Cole."

She paled at the blood, but her reply was steady. "I'll be waiting."

Percy stepped back, her strength and resolve rejuvenating his own, and wrapped his hand with the edge of his coat. "Go now, Danny."

She went without a word, turning into the maze with confident steps.

Percy knew a moment of true pride watching her walk away, not once looking back.

That was the woman he'd married, the woman he'd asked to be his partner.

Fuck, who was he kidding? He was lucky enough that she'd chosen him, trusted him. He hadn't pursued her. She'd deigned to accept what meager offerings he'd foolishly taken ages to give. She'd found him much like she'd found that knife and waited, not knowing if he'd come back or that he'd come up to snuff. Thank God she'd had patience. Thank God she'd seen worthiness in him when he couldn't see it in himself.

Whatever sins he carried, the past he'd survived, he would do what he must to be a better man, starting with keeping his promise. Because Danny deserved his everything and a lifetime was a perfect start.

He hadn't meant to survive this reckoning, not really. Deep down, he'd resigned himself that this would be the end of him, the end of all the ugly he'd wrought on the world.

But there was more growing inside him than death and destruction. It had been growing now for some time. A seed of hope had been planted in the bowels of his darkness by a young, defiant lady who didn't let her fears define her.

If it were possible, Percy's love grew, until that seedling inside burst through the cracks in his armor and overtook everything else.

He felt reborn, alive, like the darkness once dominating his entire life flinched away in decimated defeat.

All because of her.

Settling his mind, Percy wove his way through the maze and out onto the clearing. Heading for the southern forest, Percy shoved away his former training. An agent didn't cling to attachments or let emotions hamper his mission. But that wasn't him anymore.

Percy let his emotions rise to the surface, filling him to the brim and then some: love, fear, happiness, hope. What he'd once taken as a liability became an infinite source of strength. Though the time for rash decisions and heavy promises was over.

Now the delicate work began.

PERCY'S PROMISE WEIGHED on Danny's chest like an elephant on an ant hill.

Keep walking, she told herself. *Don't stop*. If she did, that pressure would crush her into dust.

That glimmer in his eye, Danny wouldn't delude herself into believing Percy had finally realized his worth. A man berated all his life, his proposed inadequacies thrust in his face by people without compassion, wouldn't magically come to his senses. But he had seemed grounded, as if understanding the true devastation his death would reap with risky maneuvers.

He'd take his time now, assess and reassess before jumping headfirst into something foolish.

A good thing too because Danny had just told the greatest lie of her life.

She made for the woods on the opposite side of the clearing from the bomb, having made a secondary discovery during her early perfunctory survey of the area.

Sensing her intent, the person hiding in the towering oaks uncurled from their crouched position and waved from the upper branches, unrecognizable except for a familiar dark hood.

Danny gritted her teeth, not allowing her fear to take control.

Percy had shouldered most of the risk and all the planning, leaving himself a too-easy target. He may have been skilled, but even Danny saw half a dozen ways he'd be caught in the web of his own making, even with his newfound caution.

Danny trudged ahead, her gaze fixed on the trees where the Merry Men's gang leader had spotted her progress and jumped down from the branches to intercept her.

Heart galloping, Danny didn't retreat. There was no time for hesitation. She was not some obedient wife or damsel in need of protection. She was a woman with a mind and a hundred-yard center shot, and a duke who'd offered her a partnership in life. And right now, her partner was letting his fear for her safety leave a blind spot.

Danny kept walking. Because she was that strong woman, because she had her own skills, and because she was sick and tired of playing it safe while everyone else took turns playing a not-so-innocent game of assassin roulette.

Danny didn't stop at the respectable distance when she should have. Didn't bow to her nerves and let her confidence slip. Her gaze fixed on the face hidden in shadows, she walked up to stand toe to toe with the leader of the most ruthless gang in Dockside.

And struck a deal to set her own haphazard plan in motion. She prayed her instincts weren't wrong.

CHAPTER TWENTY-FIVE

PERCY KNEW NOTHING but the swiftness of his legs and the surety he was heading straight for a bomb constructed with more than one safeguard and a probable secondary ignition.

Risking a straight path to the bomb, Percy ran with confidence, knowing Danny would be watching his six and twelve and all his sides . . . which was why he was surprised when a man in a silk vest and familiar greying hair snuck up behind him without gaining a new hole to breathe out of.

He wheeled around, hand going for his knife.

Percy dropped his hand and cursed. "Ridley?"

What the hell was the old man doing here? Had something fallen apart on his end?

"Did the pardons not come through?" he asked.

"Pardons are safe." Ridley patted his breast pocket. "No need to worry." His usual grin looked seething. "The names of the Duke of Lux and the Duke of Camine were interesting additions. It's unlike you to involve other people."

"Is that why you're here?" Percy huffed. He didn't have time to deal with the other man's vanity right now. He could see the bomb in the trees from here, the weighted bag more than half-empty with the slit in the bottom for the sand to fall through.

Percy mumbled something compliant and completely hogwash to the other man about trust and remembering the chain of command.

His attention flicked back to the trees.

Why weren't there guards posted? Did Nic not trust anyone too close for fear of setting the thing off? Or were reinforcements waiting out of sight, given orders to ambush the first person who stumbled upon the device?

"I have a pressing matter, Ridley. If you'll excuse me?" Percy didn't wait for an answer. He aimed for a spot farther back to come at the bomb from an angle through the trees, hoping to displace any unsuspecting sentinels with a good blade to the spine before they became a problem.

Guess he'd have to do a solid pass through the entire surrounding area first before he'd get his chance at defusing anything. A delay he wouldn't have to make if those insipid Merry fuckers had been doing their jobs.

It would take time—time they lost with every moment—but he'd walk the whole estate if that was what it took to do this right.

He made it all of ten steps.

Percy stopped cold at the sound of a hammer cocking.

His mind raced, his muscles went rigid at the immediate danger, but it was the lump of muscle in his chest that had him frozen in place with the first realization of betrayal.

He glanced back at Ridley and the gun the other man had pulled from somewhere on his person.

For all his boasts of skill, Percy hadn't suspected once. The ploy of official orders, the offer to assist in hopes of learning the shortfalls, this ridiculous production. "It was *you?*"

Ridley smiled. "Surprise, old friend."

Percy ran a hand through his hair, cursing, reeling, at a loss of composure. He'd known Ridley for half his life. "Are there even mercenaries, or was that all twaddle too?"

"Oh, my men are very real *and* well paid," Ridley said. "And with no connection to HO, there's no chance of help coming."

Jesus, he'd told Ridley everything about the Merry Men and his friendship with Gregori. Percy could only pray now his missive to Ridley's office detailing the discovery of explosives and change of trap from the docks to Fellow Hall had come after the rat bastard had set out to blindside him.

If Ridley was the one pulling Nic's strings, the entire play had changed. Ridley would never set off a bomb in London where the lack of forewarning would cast the Home Office in a poor light, especially over the man who ran it. *Unless* the real target was too unpredictable to track down.

Until a dukedom had rooted him in place.

Percy was a threat, had been since leaving the Home Office with all its secrets. But he'd never given any reason for a man like Ridley to question the looseness of Percy's tongue.

Something else was driving Ridley to take him out now. Percy's newfound status and pull in society? Didn't matter the reason. Because if the old goat was involved, there was a chance everyone could still walk away without bloodshed. Percy would take negotiating with a grasping bureaucrat over a homicidal maniac.

If he played his cards right, gave Ridley the inkling Percy knew more than he did, he could bluff a way out of this mess. He had to. The bag was emptying.

"Whatever you're scheming," Ridley said, "don't. You have no play here. This face-to-face was but a courtesy. I could have shot you in the back and been done with this headache at any time."

Percy shifted his weight for a more solid footing, waiting for any tears in Ridley's defense. "Gone soft for me after all these years, Ridley? I'm touched."

Focus, he told himself. *Play the cards.* "If you wanted an intimate kill, why the bomb, old friend?"

Ridley's brows rose, giving Percy hope. "Know about that, do you? You never cease to amaze." The gun twitched in his grip with the slightest hand tremble. "What else do you know, *old friend?*"

Was that fear in his voice? Percy latched on to his opponent's weakness and went all in.

"I know you've been working the system for a long time now."

Ridley flinched.

Percy was on the right track.

"I know you've opened doors for personal gain," he continued.

If the man got any paler, he'd be transparent.

Now the real gamble. Which card to push? Money? Power? Both.

"I did some digging after our little reunion the other day, purely for selfish reasons, you understand?" Percy shrugged with as much swagger as he could muster. "Didn't want you changing your mind about those official orders once I held up my end." Percy shook his head, careful to watch the other man's smallest ticks. "What a naughty boy you've been, Ridley. Skimming funds, misuse of resources . . ." He put every ounce of confidence into his final draw. "I'm sure the prime minister will enjoy the report I sent this morning about your activities. Should arrive, oh"—he checked his timepiece—"before the good ol' boy wakes up for his usual midnight snack, I'd think."

For a moment, Percy thought he had him. Ridley certainly looked horrified, but that wide-eyed expression slowly twisted into one of confusion.

And then it cleared entirely.

Ridley's sight on the gun firmed, and the smile he offered was like a slash of a sharp blade across his face. "Nice try, Percy. Marks for creativity and superb guesswork. I have, indeed, been stealing money *and* using agents for my betterment for years." His eyes glinted with malice and cunning. "But if you discovered all my sins, you'd have uncovered your own active role in my machinations."

Percy recoiled. "I've never stolen from the department."

"That's not what the reports say."

Fucking hell! "You planted false evidence to incriminate me?"

Percy gritted his teeth. The bastard didn't get to win like this. "Doesn't matter. I'll get free of this somehow and I *will* confess everything to the prime minister, reveal what you've done. Incarceration and torture have never frightened me."

Ridley slapped his leg with his free hand, a crude version of applause. "An unforgiving speech, old friend. Top marks again. I would have believed you too. The man cruel and cold enough to stab his closest friend in the back." Ridley's chuckle sounded like a devil's laugh. "But that was before *you'd* gone soft."

There was nothing but cold steel in Percy's veins now. Given the chance, he felt confident he could shred the worthless git with his bare hands. "Try me, old man. I'll show you my resolve and guard are as strong as ever."

But Ridley had one last trick to play. "Your guard. But what about *hers?*"

Ridley's smile had icy dread sinking low in Percy's belly, especially when he followed Ridley's gaze to a figure emerging from the treeline, a figure in a familiar blue riding coat.

Danny.

And the man following her out of the woods wasn't any of the Merrys, not with the gun he held to the back of her head.

"No." Forget the prime minister, forget the maggot posing as his friend and mentor. This couldn't be happening. Danny was back up in the tower, safe.

His feet moved forward of their own accord, needing to see for himself that his eyes were wrong.

Ridley's *tsk* froze him in place.

Smug smile pulling his stubbled facial whiskers to one side, Ridley shook his head. "Should have disarmed me when you had the chance."

"Should have taken your knife and stabbed you through the eye in your office," Percy said, though his thoughts were far from the past, far from his present. What mattered was Danny's future. A future that was seconds from being blown away by the orders of a man he'd considered his friend.

For what purpose? There wasn't a purpose good enough for what Ridley meant to take from him.

Desperation seeped into his words just as they strangled any attempt at a plan. "Why, damn you? You wanted a legacy." Percy pointed to the south side of Grandfellow, where his quick calculations indicated they had less than twenty minutes before they'd all be blown to hell, Ridley along with them. "How will killing us all leave you with more than a roasted corpse and a short obituary?"

"Simple." With his one hand holding the gun steady, Ridley's other lifted to draw the wig from his head to reveal a patchwork of alopecia and a telltale line of powdered makeup where concealed skin at his forehead met a harsh contrast of yellowed scalp.

Percy's attention went to the older man's eyes—the discoloration he'd thought from tiredness—where now evidence of an aggravated state of jaundice was present.

"I'm dying." Ridley's laugh was hoarse and disbelieving. "After all the work, all the politics and backstabbing to finally be in my position. Liver failure, the physicians say."

That accounted for the abrupt reappearance of Nic. His partner was out of time.

"You couldn't wait any longer to 'tie up loose ends,'" Percy said. But the old blackguard had meant he couldn't afford any skeletons coming to light. Which meant . . . "You were covering up our involvement in the French ambassador's assassination." Fucking hell, his treachery went back that far. "We weren't sanctioned to be there at all."

"One quick slit of a throat, an anonymous finger pointing at the figures in office, and I had all the political backing I needed to propel myself up to Home Secretary. All thanks to you." Ridley smiled. "The only ones connected to my treachery that day in France were you and Nic.

"I was certain when you escaped and didn't come back, you'd figured it all out." He sneered. "Imagine my distaste when it was that cur Nic who showed up at my door, demanding to know who'd set him up. A damned nuisance spinning everything and getting him back on a leash, so focused on his revenge and distractions in the slums. The boy never could say 'no' to a riddle and a fine piece of skirt. Went mad somewhere along the way. Poor bastard."

Percy's insides coiled, the truth too twisted to imagine. "You told him I was the one behind his death warrant. That I had lied about the mission." He clutched his roiling stomach, feeling he might truly be sick. "Just like you told me he was killing people out of turn."

"And you believed every word without question." Ridley's glee was acid in Percy's chest. "When Nic was following *my* orders the entire time."

Orders based on lies.

He and Nic hadn't been enemies. They'd been pawns to advance a grasping man's career.

"You'll be happy to know I ended his suffering quickly," Ridley said.

Percy didn't see the blow of his words coming and was unprepared for the ramifications and violence on his person. Something akin to regret slammed into his chest, followed by a knockout kick of betrayal to the stomach. Air refused to fill his lungs, so all that came out was a whisper. "You killed him?"

Ridley shrugged. "The man was more than half-dead already when he dragged himself into my office, wounds festering and dripping with disease from the Thames. Didn't even fight back when I drew the knife across his throat."

A night bird called faintly across the field, happy and clear, but Percy's distracted mind couldn't focus.

Grief echoed through him like a distant rumble of thunder.

Nic was dead. Had been for more than three years.

Which meant the stealing of cargo from the harbor, Percy's re-conscription to the army, the thugs in the alley—all of it had been Ridley's doing.

The rumble of grief faded, leaving behind a charged silence. A loss, but, with it, came relief.

Truth was, Percy had mourned his lost friendship a long time ago. Nic had suffered as a child, had suffered all his miserable life: abandoned by desperate parents, raised on the streets, shaped by the coldness of humanity long into adulthood. His bloody end was inevitable for all the charlatans like them. The same fate Percy would have suffered if he hadn't found his odd but loyal family.

A family currently doing their part to take this sadistic bastard down behind the scenes. The cooling paperwork trail from the Birmingham East Office fire he'd put Hamish and Renard on would no doubt have already led them to the Home Office. If they were creative and patient, a few inquiries and they'd find the man on top.

Trust didn't come naturally to Percy, not for a man seasoned in the lies and betrayal of those he'd once seen as comrades. He had living, festering proof of the evils of human nature not five feet away. But he'd force his trust to take root now. He'd leave the mercenaries to the Merrys—wherever the fuck they were— and Ridley's exposure to obnoxious dukes.

The threat in front of him took priority.

As if sensing his resurgence in resilience, Ridley invited Percy with a raised hand to watch the two figures make their way across the park, still too far to discern faces.

Percy's inner balance shattered.

He scrambled for where he'd miscalculated. It *had* to have been an illusion. Danny would never have been caught. Not his clever girl.

But there was no mistaking that blue color.

That damn bird called again, having the audacity to chirp like nothing was out of place.

Everything was out of place with Danny in harm's way.

Percy could only imagine her state. How the hired man pointing a weapon at her, promising death, would raise all sorts of dark memories of her childhood abduction to the surface. Memories of a past Ridley would know about working closely with the House of Lords. Torture within torture.

Percy's hands trembled at his sides, his rage tempered by growing hopelessness. The heartless bastard would kill Danny in front of him, all because he couldn't accept his mortality.

That was *his* plan, anyway.

A plan Percy would see bleeding out at his feet, along with the man who'd dared threaten his wife.

Percy took his faithful knife from his coat, the familiar weight and knowledge its mate was close grounding him. Tightening his grip, the blade thrummed in his hand as if it knew too.

He'd trust in Danny to keep her head. She hadn't wavered in the alley with the Greens, and she wouldn't now, no matter how many guns were pointed at her. Though that didn't stop him from sending up a silent prayer to the Woman Upstairs. Something eloquent and pious:

> *Keep Danny from harm. Give the maggot holding her hostage a bout of cramping or diarrhea or sudden bleeding from the eyes and rectum so she may escape.*
>
> *. . . and if your magnanimousness has time, make the two-faced, mangle faced rat hoarder facing me drop dead.*
>
> *Ah . . . ahem.*

Percy waited a second, two. When Ridley didn't clutch his chest and turn into a lifeless bag of flesh, Percy shrugged. That was what he got for never attending church.

Ridley chuckled at Percy's defense and lifted his gun. "A bullet is still faster than a knife, Percy, my boy. Certainly, I taught you that?"

"You taught me many things, old man, except how to survive." Percy enjoyed how Ridley stiffened. The man may have twenty years more experience and a lifetime of insanity over him, but Percy had *her*. The gap between them could swallow oceans.

"If the French couldn't kill me with an army, you can't possibly believe you'll have better luck?" he said.

"You did always exceed expectations," Ridley acknowledged. "But you've never bested me, not once."

Percy flipped the knife, catching the tip between his thumb and pointer. "Guess it's time to change that."

He'd see this done. He had a promise to keep and a wife waiting.

That was all the motivation he needed to charge.

Getting on with age or his disease taking its toll, Ridley didn't pull the trigger fast enough. Pushing the muzzle down, the gun fell from his grip without going off.

They lunged at the same time to recover the weapon, but Percy rolled at the exact right moment, lifting the gun and standing in one fluid motion.

Catching Ridley on his knees, Percy trained the gun in the center of the man's forehead and tasted his first sip of victory. "It's over, Ridley. You're done."

But Ridley had one last hand to play. "We both are."

Too late, Percy pulled the trigger. But Ridley had already given his man the signal.

A second gunshot rent the air.

Percy whirled, heart shattering. "DANNY!"

She crumpled to the grass on her stomach, her arms flung out as if to break her fall.

Percy ceased existing. For a suspended moment, there was nothing but silence and blue against a bed of green.

The ringing in his ears cut off and the sound of the breeze through the trees was deafeningly loud.

He glanced around to find his bearings. The details of the night's mission were coming back piece by piece.

Ridley's man had already reached the treeline, fleeing after witnessing his benefactor shot between the eyes.

Percy didn't give chase, didn't signal the Merrys to throw the net. He couldn't move. Couldn't breathe. He may have returned to the world around him physically, but his mind remained far,

far away.

Danny lay so still.

Why was she so still? His fearless woman wouldn't fall so easily. Not by anything short of her favored goddess's smiting.

And Athena would never fell such a devout woman of justice.

"Get up," he whispered.

He laughed at how eerie his voice sounded. Then laughed more at Danny lying in the grass.

How ridiculous this was. To make such a spectacle at the end.

They'd won. Ridley was gone. Nic was gone. Their life would be peaceful.

How could she just lie there when they could finally begin the rest of forever together?

"Danny—" His step forward met with a complete lack of strength. His kneecaps hit the dirt, an impact that should've hurt, but the only thing Percy felt was numb.

Not just numb—hollowed.

And the truth of the lifeless figure before him filled the space like nails to the eye.

"No." To any goddess listening, he added, "God damn you, NO!"

He stared down at his hands and the gun clutched tightly in his right one. He'd made a promise to come back to her. It had been the most important promise he'd ever made. She'd known that.

But he couldn't fulfill that promise, not if she was . . .

His Danny, his heart, his soul, the very meaning to his treacherous life, was dead.

With her gone, there was nothing left for him.

As if sensing his utter defeat, Ridley's man reemerged from the treeline, his frame small, but his hood dark and forbidding. The man's face didn't matter. The approaching figure could be Satan's own malformed henchman with milky-white glazed eyes and blood-dripped claws for hands, and Percy wouldn't have fled.

Hell already held him, but not his soul.

That was lost with her, and with her gone, the Devil himself had no bargaining tool.

He watched the slow trek of the hooded figure, his broken mind seeking out any lingering threads of *her*. Her spiced smell still lingering in the air, her soft breathing, even his approaching executioner had a similar way of lengthening his strides when in a hurry.

Percy's mind fought for focus, narrowing in on the man's lean legs and subtle gait. The figure didn't walk just 'similarly.' He walked exactly like Danny.

Percy found his feet, the pins and needles sensation a welcome pain as he propelled himself forward.

The hood fell, revealing the figure's face, and Percy let out a strangled cry.

He closed the distance and pulled her tightly to his chest, not caring if this was real.

"Danny." He didn't brush the tears from his cheeks, wouldn't break the contact long enough to do anything that would keep her from filling his arms. "Danny." He murmured her name again and again. A prayer or a chant, her name on his lips slowly brought his consciousness back to his mind and life back to his body.

He pressed his face into her hair. "You're alive."

Her fingers wound in his curls and held tightly. "We both are."

"But I saw you fall." *I saw you die.*

"Not me." She leaned back to give him a smug smile. "You saw my double."

"Double?" His eyes widened. He glanced back at the body lying on the ground and then back with understanding. "You pulled a 'Frenchman's Switch'?"

Danny grinned. "More like an 'Englishwoman's Switch.'" She planted her hands on her hips. "I gave you the signal. Twice."

The bird calls.

Jesus, Joseph, and Mary, she was a miracle.

"But who played the fake?" Camille was too tall, Charlotte's features were too light, and none of the women servants at Grandfellow were under the age of ancient. "Who's left?"

Percy turned to the slumped person in blue, the body now rising to its feet in a nightmare of seamless movements, as if the clothes on its back were too big and slid along a smaller figure. His mind less frenzied, he now saw the woman's hair was not the shade of almond and chocolate, nor her eyes the warm and honeyed gaze of his one and only love.

And when the woman finished brushing the grass and dirt from wrinkled trousers and looked up with a smug smile, Percy had no recollection of the dark-haired woman or such blue eyes that brightened with humor.

No recollection at all, until the woman spoke.

"After all we've been through, Your Grace, call me 'Sydney.'"

Percy stared at the woman's face—fair skinned, rosy cheeked, decidedly *feminine*—sure his eyes were out of their sockets. "You're a woman?"

Syd—*Sydney*—Laundry smiled wolfishly. "Not as clever as you thought you were, ehh?" She nodded to Danny. "Not like your wife here."

He'd known Syd for years, and Percy had never suspected anything but a grumpy phallus under that hooded ensemble. He adopted Syd's favorite curse. "Fucking quims."

Syd smiled. "Exactly."

Somehow, Danny had uncovered the Merry leader's secret and gotten her to agree to play dress up and risk her life on a charlatan's con. Miracles of miracles, he rounded on his wife. "When did you find out?"

Danny ducked her head. "I had my suspicions in Charlotte's drawing room when Camille and Renard reacted to me mentioning Syd as a 'he.'" She shrugged. "After that, it was following my hunch and asking Syd directly in the woods."

Syd winked. "Bold *and* effective. You'd make a fine Merry."

"She will not be involved in any gang activity." Percy

growled, still reeling. For fuck's sake, what else had he overlooked over the years?

Syd rolled her eyes. "Not like there's much activity anymore." She scrunched her nose, looking reluctant to admit, "Guess we all have you to thank for the Greens falling, anyway. The Merry Men now control everything north of the Thames as far as Charing Cross."

They'd hit the Greens at the warehouse, then. Percy gritted his teeth to keep from cursing. "That's why you were late?" They'd risked the entire operation!

Syd showed no remorse. "Good thing, too. We stumbled upon the outer guards and took them out so that bastard couldn't box us in or call for backup." She eyed him like a roach under her shoe, but her expression turned to admiration as they settled again on Danny. "That's where your lady love found me too."

Percy's irritation ebbed. Secrecy, tardiness, and botched positions: The only reasons none of them were currently cooling in a coroner's office was because nothing had gone to plan. And he was an arse not to kiss the slimy wench's feet for her role in protecting Danny.

Extending his gratitude along with his hand, Percy said, "Thank you, Syd."

Eyeing his hand like a serpent ready to strike, Syd took it and said as rudely as ever, "You owe me, killer, and I still don't like you."

Percy laughed. "Noted. And the feeling is mutual."

Danny eyed *them* with a frown. "Strangest friendship I've ever seen."

"We're not friends," they said together.

"Ri-ight," Danny said. "You'd think a few kind words would set the world into chaos the way you two carry on."

Percy didn't deny the charge. Chaos wouldn't be the worst of it. The rest of his mind switched back on as his stomach bottomed out. "The bomb—"

"Someone called 'Pops' went to disarm the bomb," Danny

said. "The man appeared confident."

Percy relaxed and nodded. "Markus was a captain for the Dragoons. The man knows his way around all kinds of nasty things. Good thing too. I'm not sure I could muster the strength and brain power to dispose of a three-ton incendiary device."

He frowned, his mind working backwards. "But the 'French—Englishwoman's Switch,'" he amended at both women's clearing throats, "is an illusion ploy. Why did you fire the gun?"

Danny and Syd shared a glance. "We'd only meant to reassure your captor that he held the upper hand until you made your move."

"Then how did the gun go off?"

"I was hit." Danny pulled out a rock from her pocket, small and rounded and with a drop of blood.

Percy's gaze cut to the scrape on Danny's wrist and his mind made the connection. "Oh." *Fucking hell!*

"Where do you think it came—" Danny's question cut off as her gaze flicked up to someone on the hill.

"Your Grace!" Everyone turned as Mr. Brinkley raced down to meet them, the old groundskeeper breathing heavily from the exertion, but his face bright with young adventure. He stopped and caught his breath before he addressed Danny. "Thank heavens you're all right, Your Grace. We were all in an uproar when that shot rang out."

"And that's my cue to leave," Syd said, doing just that with a quick farewell to Danny and an invitation to come visit when Her Grace got sick of her "pain in the ass, can't tell a ruse from a rooster" duke.

"I like her," Danny said when it was the three of them.

"What a surprise." Not minding Mr. Brinkley, Percy pulled her into his arms and pressed a kiss to her temple. After his scare, he may commission the very leash he'd admonished so she could clasp it around his neck and keep him at her side for always. "You like anything that's unlovable."

"*You're* not unlovable."

God, he hoped that was true. Since he'd be keeping his spleen, innards, and his reason for existence for the foreseeable future, his most pressing mission now was to make his lovely duchess fall madly in love with him.

Her loveliness looked about the grounds. Aside from the cooling body the Merrys dragged in the direction of a waiting coach, there was nothing amiss.

"How did you manage all this?" she asked, awe evident in her tone. "How did you know the mastermind would show in person?"

PERCY SIGHED. "I knew whoever was in charge would never leave research of the grounds and staff to someone else. Every agent knows to pay attention to discrepancies between architectural plans and any additions before infiltrating enemy territory. Luckily for us, the very man who taught me such basics conducted himself in the same manner."

His fingers curled into white-knuckled fists, and Danny felt Percy's betrayal, imagining it was one more ache in a lengthy line of painful regrets.

Percy's fingers relaxed. "That traitorous bastard lost by his own teachings."

Thinking over his plan, Danny stared at him in disbelief, having heard or seen nothing as much as a mallet outside the kitchens. "You planted false prints of Fellow Hall?"

Percy chuckled. "Good God, no. That would take far too much time. I'd have had to find a decent draftsman and register the updates through the county committee."

"Then how did you make it look like Grandfellow was under improvements?"

Percy clapped Brinkley on the back. "We changed the names

of all the parks, officially."

With all her previous research helping her brother turn a good portion of Bromley Estate into a protected nature reserve, Danny knew name changes went through the same office in the archives as new construction. Anyone taking note of the files coming through would see the name of the estate, but none of the details since the committee seat dealt with the landowners personally.

The plan was perfect in its simplicity.

Percy offered Brinkley his hand and pumped with vigor. "Those bastards were taken down by the greatest name-giving groundskeeper in England."

Brinkley's ears went red at the praise. "It was all brilliant, Your Grace."

Danny shook her head, heartily in agreement.

"Now that I know Her Grace is all right, I should get to the others to ease their concerns," Mr. Brinkley said.

Percy glanced towards the house and rubbed the back of his neck. "Start with the main house, would you?" He couldn't seem to meet either of their gazes. "Call off the duchess's family and send them home."

Mr. Brinkley frowned but obeyed with a farewell bow. "Yes, Your Grace."

When he'd gone, Danny laced her fingers with his, needing contact. "You *were* holding something back."

Percy ducked his head, his expression contrite. "Hard habits. How about I spend the rest of my life making up for it?"

"Then it's over?" Danny asked, hardly believing.

He wrapped her in his arms, pressing her close so she felt the steady beat of his heart.

"Yes, my love. It's over."

She sighed and relaxed against his chest. "Thank God for that. But don't think I'm done with you, sir. You have much to answer for."

Percy chuckled. "I'm ready to face any forms of torture you

design. What would you have me do, my lady?"

"What you promised." Danny's fingers worked inside his coat and trailed down his stomach to the growing ridge in his trousers. "Take me to bed, husband," she commanded.

Percy's lips curled upwards. "Yes, my love."

CHAPTER TWENTY-SIX

DAYS LATER, DANNY lay in Percy's arms, panting, sweaty, and completely satisfied after three rounds of vigorous sex: first on the bed, then on the rug by the fire, and then the chaise in the corner. Finally able to make coherent thoughts, she propped her chin on his chest.

"So, what *was* Denise's role?" she asked. Now that she thought back to that night, she hadn't seen or heard anything of her siblings once they'd taken up their posts. "Waylaying constables? Causing a crush of carriages in the street?"

Percy's connections may have won them a pardon for inserting another breathing hole in the previous Home Secretary's face—an easy decision by Her Majesty when verified evidence of Ridley's treason had become known—but traffic accidents and purposeful blockades wouldn't be on the list of forgiven crimes.

Danny groaned, imagining. "Tell me my siblings weren't involved in anything illegal?"

"Oh, that." Percy's ears turned a most guilty shade of red. "I may have bent the truth a bit when I asked for your sister's assistance."

That *sounded* criminal. "What exactly were she and Don doing?"

"Needling my butler and housekeeper."

Danny's eyes widened. He couldn't mean . . . "Percival Cole, you did not sick my siblings on the staff to make them resign?"

No wonder she hadn't seen hide nor hair of Mr. Lancaster or Mrs. Smith in days. She rubbed her temples. "I can already see the written complaints from the trade union." Denise and Don would've been vicious. "The poor dears."

"No one should be that composed all the time," Percy defended. "I took you four different ways our wedding night with the *door open* and not even a glare of disapproval. If those two can withstand a frontal assault from both your siblings, they can withstand my horrible personality. But at least this way, *I'll know* they're deranged but good-natured psychopaths and not neglectfully unconcerned automatons. I'll have you know, both of them remain in their positions, with a large number of pounds added to their yearly salaries."

Danny shook her head, afraid to ask. "And what was little Leo up to? Scaring cats from the barns?" *Please let him have been scaring cats in the barn.*

If Percy had looked guilty before, Danny braced herself for what followed his newest expression.

"Actually . . ." Percy leaned over and took a grey object out of his discarded coat's pocket. He grinned. "The lad was supposed to hit a tree or something, cause a distraction if things got dicey." He ran a hand through his hair and nodded towards the rock he placed in her hand. "I had no idea he was as good a shot as you."

Frowning at his nonsensical words, Danny turned the rock towards the firelight: round and smooth, with the faintest smudge of brownish red that might have been blood.

Upon closer inspection, Danny recognized it was the same rock that had knocked the gun from her hand when she'd been posing as one of Ridley's agents. The same rock that had set the gun off when it had been flung from her hand.

"The most important role."

Danny's stomach dropped and she found herself wishing for the days when Percy had done nothing but lie. He *had* given Leo a job. A job Percy would think the most important of all: Cause a distraction in order to protect *her.* Which meant that little boy had been in the thick of things, close enough to use a child's sling shot and well within range of any of Ridley's men who managed to slip through the Merrys' net.

Thank God no one had gotten past.

"Where did Charlotte think Leo was?" Danny asked.

"In the kitchens, overseeing the preparations for our victory dinner with cook."

How would she ever look Charlotte in the eye the next time she faced her friend? "If you ever try anything half so dangerous with our children, you'll lose more than digits, my love."

He winced. "I see my head mounted on the wall and the taxidermy is not flattering." Gaze steady, he vowed, "Never again."

She blew out her breath, satisfied with his answer while her relief at the favorable outcome to this battle doubled, tripled. "Pray," she said, sending up her own. "Pray Charlotte and Hamish never find out how close their son came to harm." She'd have no legs to stand on if her friends took more than that from her husband.

Percy nodded gravely. "I do believe I owe my godson a horse, or gold, or a castle, or . . . what is better than a castle?"

"His first woman?" Danny offered.

Percy chuckled and plucked the rock from her hand to place it back in his coat's pocket. "I have thoroughly corrupted you, haven't I?"

Danny glanced at the knife on the nearby table, the handle still wet from their last coupling, and her body grew hot remembering. "I do believe I was corrupted long before you, dear husband."

Shame snuck through the cracks, sending threads of cold through her body.

Shaking the strands loose, Danny said, "I wonder if those negative feelings will ever fade completely? Someday, when I won't be ashamed to speak of them aloud."

Percy played with the end of a curl. "You shouldn't fear telling your friends."

Danny shook her head, the idea mortifying. "Could you imagine the conversation over tea? *Lovely biscuits, Your Grace, and did I mention I get wet when a knife slides across my skin?*" She buried her face in his chest. "They'd be appalled."

Percy laughed. "You've not spent enough time with the Duchess of Camine. She'd ask for details while hosting a royal dinner party. And besides, you fret for no reason. No one need know," he said. "It is, after all, not anyone's business."

She rolled her face to the side to be heard. "You're right." And he was. But she couldn't release the tension in her chest. In her heart, she knew she wouldn't breathe easy until she'd shared the words out loud. "It feels like a lie, hiding as I do. What I like, how I feel, is who I am. *You* accepted me." Was it so inconceivable to think others would too?

He leaned down and kissed her on the nose. "There is nothing wrong with you."

She frowned, disbelieving. "Just everyone else?"

"Exactly!"

She rolled her eyes. "Arrogant as always, believing your opinion is the only one that matters?"

His smiling expression sobered. Taking her hand in his, all trace of humor was gone from his voice when he said, "No, my love. The only opinion that should count is yours. How you feel and what you like is who you are." She smiled at the reference as he continued. "You must learn to accept yourself, and if you need to confide in someone—other than your fabulous husband—then do what you must, for you and no one else. I would never presume to get in the way of what you need to be happy."

Danny felt the tears running down her cheeks before she acknowledged the overflow of gratitude. Not just gratitude. She sat up and pressed a soft kiss to his mouth, letting her actions speak of the feelings she had yet to voice. There was no need to state her love; Percy was a man of action, and actions always spoke volumes louder than mere words.

Percy ran his palms down her arms until both their hands were twined together, feeling the same warmth of emotion. "I love you." His voice was quiet, but his expression brooked no denial.

Danny's legs had fallen asleep during their awkward positioning minutes ago and the chill from the banked hearth had seeped into her bones, but her husband's nearness now flooded her body with warmth . . . and wicked heat all over again. They hadn't yet coupled on the window seat, an oversight to be rectified as she regained feeling in her toes.

"I know you don't share my feelings yet," Percy said, interrupting her fantasies of ruining the window seat stuffing with a brutal pounding of their bodies.

"I mean to change that," he continued. "For now, I'll love enough for the both of us until you find a way to open your heart to me."

Blinking, Danny drew back, sure the cleverest man she'd ever known had said the stupidest thing she'd ever heard. "Since when don't I love you?"

He smiled. "I meant as more than friends and partners."

"So did I."

He stilled. "You love me?" His expression pinched. "Since when?"

She shrugged. "Since you kissed me at the Leishires' ball or thereabouts."

For whatever reason, her answer seemed to anger him. "You mean you've loved me for *three years*? Why didn't you tell me?"

Danny scoffed. "I spoke through my actions."

"That's not how this works," he said. "You. Never. Said. A. Word."

"I didn't see a need."

"Of course there was a need!" He ran a hand through his hair. "How else am I supposed to know?"

Danny rolled her eyes. "Men." Really, the creatures were impossible. "Then let me be perfectly clear, sir. I, Daniella Cole,

Duchess of Grandfellow, friend to hopeless criminals and winner of archery wagers, love you." And then for good measure . . . "I love you, Percy." She shook her head. "Frankly, if being willing to strip naked and pass myself off as a hired mercenary for you isn't enough of a statement, there's nothing else I can do."

⟫⟩⟨⟪

PERCY BLINKED, DUMBFOUNDED. She loved him. "Why?" He was ornery and a liar. Yes, they'd shared a heightened emotional situation surviving a near splatting of their persons all over Fellow Hall by a sadistic madman, but that had been days ago.

"I don't understand," he said in all seriousness. "I won't dance and refuse to eat anything resembling a potato." Aside from keeping the male population from offering for her hand every other minute, his only redeemable quality was an encyclopedia of erotic positions and the stamina of a racehorse. "Why on Earth would you fall in love with me?"

Idiot! Why was he probing for reasons when he should be kissing her senselessly before she changed her mind?

Expression bland, she must have garnered his disbelief and unwillingness to listen to insipid nothings because she said in all seriousness, "Why else? You fuck like a tiger."

Laughter burst between his teeth, great bellows he hadn't realized he could produce. Composing himself with effort he said, "A tiger?"

"They are cited to be quite relentless maters."

He was reading the wrong articles. Resignation gave way to amusement and then unalloyed joy. "You love me."

"I *did* say it this time."

She did. And her declaration had dripped with sarcasm too.

"I love you." He repeated the words over and over, punctuating each with a kiss to her forehead, her cheeks, her nose, her ear.

Afterwards, she asked breathlessly, "Then you approve of my

affections?"

"Approve?" He gathered her into his arms and pressed his face into her clove-scented shoulder, finally knowing where he belonged.

"I approve," he said, his heart and life full. "I am the luckiest of men."

CHAPTER TWENTY-SEVEN

TURNED OUT BEING the luckiest of men didn't mean the luckiest man's wife wasn't still angry he'd used her family to terrorize the staff.

Percy should've known he'd been called to task when his wife had met him at the top of the stairs and escorted him to dinner in the most distractingly low-cut gown in carnal red.

So distracting, it had taken him a matter of thirty whole seconds to register the vile smell wafting from the covered platters lining the sideboard, like earthy roots steeped in bog water.

Danny personally uncovered each dish and proceeded to stack mounds on his plate, each more rancid than the next: baked potatoes, mashed potatoes, fried potatoes . . . Percy swallowed as a footman placed a tureen filled with white broth in front of him.

"Soup?" he asked, not bothering to hope.

Danny's smile confirmed his most unappetizing fear. "Potato vichyssoise."

"Ah," he said. Because what was worse than a steaming pile of shit? A cold puddle of it.

The very Devil had made this evening's menu, and that Devil happened to share his name. He'd admit his stance to keep Danny out of harm's way had nearly cost them all their lives. And perhaps siccing his in-laws on their devoted staff had been unnecessarily cruel. He'd even admit he deserved punishment, but this was maniacal.

Frankly, he'd have preferred to eat the actual crow.

Danny took her seat beside him and sipped at her wine, a wicked smile on her lips. "Something the matter, dearest?"

The Goddess of Justice is a twisted beauty.

"Not at all." He managed his first bite with little gagging, a copious amount of wine chasing the dry taste of wet cotton down his throat. By the second bite, he'd have given his three favorite fingers for another pardon.

"Had enough?" Danny asked.

Wiping his mouth with his linen napkin, he threw his white flag down in surrender. "Yes."

"Good. Then I'll tell Cook to hold off on the frittata and shepherd's pie."

Di-a-bol-i-cal.

"Thank you," he said.

"If you have any other mortal enemies, tell me now," Danny said, smugness gone in seriousness. "I never want to fear for your safety like that again."

He stood and wrapped his arms around her when she stood to meet him halfway. "You have my word. No more life-and-death situations unless you vet them first."

She chuckled and shook her head. "That's all I ask."

"You ask too little." He smiled, remembering he had a surprise of his own. "Speaking of vetting dangerous activities, an old connection mentioned he needed assistance with his business. I thought now that we're lacking enemies, we might put those superior conning skills of yours to use."

"I can't see you sitting at a desk." She scrunched her nose, her eyes narrowing. "What kind of business requires conning people?"

He winked. "The fun kind."

She laughed. "Tell me."

"In good time." He captured her mouth and tasted the sweet notes of cherries from the wine. His growing arousal strained against his stays, wishing to feed its own hunger. Her gasp when his teeth nipped her ear set his blood to boil.

"I'm famished, sweetheart," he growled.

"I can imagine." Her arms wrapped around his neck, her smile coy. "Might I interest you in a *titillating* spot of 'chicken'?"

His cock jumped at 'titillating.' "God, I love that word."

Lifting her to sit on the edge of the table, he pressed between her skirts and kissed her soundly, forgetting all about the appalling scene of vegetable carnage until he stuck his hand directly into a scalding plate of mash.

"Ahh!" Percy broke their kiss and flung chunks of potato across the tablecloth, his stomach rolling in revulsion.

Danny's giggles gave way to a most unladylike—and supremely enticing—snort.

He smiled despite the need to amputate his hand.

"I'm never crossing you again." Not when he had a horrible suspicion if the classic potato dishes didn't suffice, she'd have concocted her own.

The sideboard strained under the weight of thirteen varieties of potato preparation, a veritable line of fodder for the bin. Not even his aversion to wasting food could make the awful setting appetizing.

He sighed. "Perhaps the pigs are hungry."

"No need for that."

Percy raised a brow in question when he heard voices in the hall.

The doors to the dining hall opened and two sets of ducal couples stepped inside.

Fussing with the skirts of her blush dress, the Duchess of Lux said, "Apologies for our tardiness." She shot a dirty look at the man standing next to her. "*Someone* decided it was a good idea to cram four normal-sized people into a dollhouse coach."

The Duke of Camine smirked at his sister.

The Duchess of Camine, on her husband's arm, looked radiant in fitted trousers and an open golden jacket over a red blouse that offered a full view of her increasing belly. "I found it quite cozy."

Camille rolled her eyes at her sister-in-law. "Pregnancy has addled your brain."

Danny smiled at the group. "You're right on time, actually." She inclined her head towards the dishes. "Help yourself. There's no use standing on ceremony."

The Duke of Lux grew animated at the back of the group, his coattails flapping behind him in his haste to fill a plate. "Don't mind if I do."

Percy could've kissed his wife's feet when a footman brought out a separate dish of roasted lamb and mixed greens, not a chip in sight.

When they'd all filled their plates and taken their seats, Danny lifted her glass.

"To friends."

"Bah," the Duchess of Camine said, lifting her own glass of water. "To family."

"To family!"

Toasted harmony settled over the group in a beautiful cacophony of clinking crystal, and Percy gazed at the faces of his friends, an alarming sensation of gratitude leaving his chest tight.

Family.

Reformed dukes and revolutionary duchesses: What a bunch of misfits made up theirs. *His.*

Percy laced his fingers with Danny's under the table, unable to keep the emotion from his voice for the woman who'd given him everything. "I don't deserve you."

Her fingers tightened as if she were preparing to argue.

"But," he said, raising their hands and kissing each of her fingertips until they relaxed, "I'm honored to have the rest of my life to prove I'm worth the trouble."

Her eyes were glassy when her gaze lifted to his.

"I love you," she said.

"And I love you."

She offered a smile worth every bite of putrid potato in the room and glanced at their friends and family across the table. Gaze straying to Charlotte, she squeezed his hand and said quietly, "I'll be right back."

Percy squeezed back and offered encouragement for his own sake. "She'll understand."

Danny nodded, her expression radiant and confident. "I know."

⟫⟫⟫⟩⟨⟪⟪⟪

CHARLOTTE POUNCED THE moment the library door closed. "Are you pregnant already?"

Danny laughed. "Not as far as I know."

Pouting, Charlotte dropped a hand to her swollen stomach. "A shame. I was hoping little Ella would have a playmate close to her age."

Danny smiled. "How do you know it's a girl?"

"The same way I know you have something hard to say to me or else you would have spoken in front of the rest of our party."

Fighting nerves, Danny indicated the settee. "Perhaps we should sit."

"Good gracious, that sounds ominous." Charlotte arranged herself on the cushions and let out a long sigh. "This is beyond comfortable. Everything at home is either hard enough to break my back or soft enough I can't roll to my feet without assistance from every maid, footman, and cook in the house."

Danny could only imagine. Her friend, while as beautiful as always, did resemble a salmon roe. "I'll have Percy send the settee in our carriage after dinner so you may have someplace to sit until the end of your confinement."

Charlotte's grateful expression slid into a narrow-eyed perfunctory sweep of her person. "This must be dire if you've sunk to bribery. Out with it, then."

Danny dragged the breath into her lungs, held it for one last second of inner peace, and said, "I like knives."

A moment passed.

"And?"

Danny's mouth made a series of syllable shapes, but no sound came out.

Charlotte didn't wait long to admit, "I prefer guns myself. Rifles are preferable but pushback isn't good for the baby. But recently, I found double barrel pistols with a short trigger are just as satisfying."

Danny blinked. Somehow, in all her acquaintance with her brazen, wild friend, she hadn't quite expected *that*. She envisioned Charlotte brandishing dueling pistols in each hand, her blonde hair flung behind her, belly round and heavy, her very essence screaming of a fertile and fierce goddess. The most hardened general would waive the white flag against Charlotte's unconquerable spirit.

Danny sat tall and trusted that very spirit to accept her secret. "I like blades," she tried again, swallowing. "Smoothed across my . . . person."

A second passed. Two. Charlotte tilted her head. "Sexually?"

Danny coughed, then couldn't stop. Leaning forward, it was all she could do to breathe. She felt Charlotte rub soothing circles on her back until the coughs subsided.

"Forgive me," Charlotte said. "I forget how people react when I state things so bluntly." She smiled at what Danny imagined had to be cheeks the color of wild primrose and leaned forward. "Any particular place on your *person*?"

Danny's shock didn't leave room for embarrassment. "You're not offended?"

Charlotte sat back, voice incredulous. "Whatever for? Because you like metal against your skin? I've tried it myself before—not a blade, mind you—but chains, shields, a particularly large plaque in Parliament." The last she said with a touch of a smile. "The texture was not unpleasant. I assume you enjoy blades for the added danger?"

Danny nodded and stared. She'd thought she'd known most everything there was to know about the Duchess of Camine, but the lady was more than fierce and kind—she was shameless.

Danny threw her arms around her friend and squeezed. "I'm so glad. I thought no one would understand, but of course you would. You are wonderful!"

Charlotte laughed as she returned the embrace awkwardly around her belly. "Go on."

Danny pulled back, her heart light enough to float out of her chest. "I mean it. I've hidden my"—she cleared her throat—"*preferences* for so long, knowing if someone found out, I'd be ruined."

Charlotte snorted. "Don't get me started on society's prudishness and the very large stick shoved up its arse." She froze. "Wait! Did someone scold you? Was it Percy?" Her gaze went dark. "If he so much as flinched at your desire, I'll use a blade on *him*, the pointy end."

"No." Danny bit her lip, her heated cheeks having nothing to do with embarrassment this time. "He is more than willing to . . . accommodate me."

Charlotte cocked a brow. "Guess he's good for something, then." Her gaze softened. "This has weighed on you, hasn't it?"

"Deeply." Nerves sparking again, she told herself, in for a penny . . . "There's more to my preference, and it isn't nearly as easy to digest."

Charlotte reached out and squeezed her hand. "Then tell me, my friend. I am here to listen."

Danny swallowed the emotion clogging her throat and told her friend everything about her father, the abduction, and her past. With every detail that passed through her lips, Danny felt each sliver of shame and regret burn away into smoke.

When she'd finished her story, Danny knew a moment of peace. Whatever Charlotte's reaction, kind and compassionate or loyal and angry—Danny expected the latter—the wounds inside continued their journey of healing, until only the faintest of scars was left.

Scars she'd accept because they were now a part of her.

And by her husband's words, there wasn't a piece of her that wasn't beautiful.

EPILOGUE

Eight Years Later

"I HAVE AN announcement to make," Hamish said from his spot by the mantel, the same spot he claimed every Saturday after their weekly family dinner.

Camille snorted and gave her sister-in-law a pitying expression. "Charlotte, you poor dear." Her gaze cut to her brother. "Four children wasn't enough?"

Percy chuckled from the window seat where he currently held the Duchess of Lux's latest of six children. "The heir, the spare, the pair . . ." He winked at Hamish. "Have a care."

"Still no Byron," Don Deime mumbled beside him.

Percy gave his brother-in-law a grin. "But it rhymed."

Danny rolled her eyes at their antics and took her usual role of peacekeeper—a full-time job with this family. "You have an announcement, you say?"

Hamish raised his scotch and beamed at his wife. "Charlotte is to be published."

When the exclamations and congratulations died down, Renard asked, "How did this come about?"

Hamish took Charlotte's hand and smiled. "Cambridge academics finally came to their senses. Her research on the comingling insect species of the Egyptian desert will take front page on the next edition of *Entomological Journal*."

Charlotte scowled. "Under a male pseudonym." Her face softened into a smile that didn't bode well for the stuffed shirts. "But that is temporary, I assure you."

"I happen to like 'Charlie.' He has fire," Hamish said.

Charlotte giggled. "You like the trousers that come with the name."

Hamish's voice went low. "I like when you take them off, anyway."

Camille gagged. "Go back home if you're going to be gross."

Hamish arched a brow. "You're one to talk, sister." He made a pointed look at her stomach and the swell of baby growing inside. "What did you say about *poor dear?*"

Renard came to stand behind his wife and rested a hand on her shoulder. "We *also* have an announcement."

"Not much of an announcement." Hamish chuckled. "We see the evidence clear enough."

Camille made a vulgar gesture with both hands that left the women occupants of the room grinning.

"*Our news,*" Renard said. "Miss Forthright's Home for Female Companions is now franchised."

"We break construction in Southwark by month's end." Camille's smug tone did nothing to detract from the pride in her voice. "Not only that, after providing proof of the rise in job productivity in the local area since our founding, we received word from the local parish at Greenwich they'd like a consultation to improve their existing Home for Women, possibly converting into our system of education and relocation."

Charlotte applauded. "Brava!"

Danny and Don raised their glasses.

Hamish swelled with brotherly pride. "Well done."

Percy caught his wife's eye and watched her tip her chin in a small nod. Chest light, he stood and addressed the room. "Well, since we're sharing." Percy gazed at his lovely wife, who laid a hand on her midriff. Happiness bubbled up until his smile could no longer be contained. "We're—"

"Pregnant!" Charlotte squealed, launched herself at her friend, and tugged her into a tight embrace. "I'm so happy for you both."

Don offered Percy his hand. "Congratulations, Byron."

Percy had no illusions he grinned like a fool. "Thank you."

They'd waited a long time for children, to the exasperation of Danny's mama and the quiet concern of Lord Bromley. But Percy and Danny shared no regret for how they'd chosen to spend their nights working for a private inspector—Percy's old contact—an inspector who'd decided to retire this year and leave the business to a less-than-proper duke and his duchess.

No one knew of their sleuthing or Danny's growing skill range from pinpoint shots of a *moving* target to lockpicking to identifying counterfeit sculptures on sight.

Using his experience to save women from abusive relationships, locate stolen funds for the local shelters, find loving homes in the country for six of Lord Pickles's seven kittens—all at the behest of his knowing wife—the past eight years had been the happiest and fullest of Percy's life. Gazing down at his beautiful wife, glowing with the early signs of pregnancy, he had a quiet suspicion his happiness was to double in the coming months.

Don finished hugging his sister, his smile genuine. "Make sure to remind Denise not to tell Mama until you are eight months and no longer able to hide your condition. We'll all be happier for it."

Danny winced. "Actually, I have yet to tell Denise *or* Mama." She shook her head at her brother's sour expression. "I meant to tell you all together after she returned from her outing since you know how troublesome Denise is when she's the last to know—"

A commotion outside cut her off and then the doors to the drawing room burst open, and the troublesome woman herself stood in the doorway, hair askew, eyes wild.

"I was here the entire morning!" Denise squeaked before she dashed to the open seat on the divan, smoothing her lavender skirts and snatching an embroidery hoop from the basket on the floor—a leftover from the staff, no doubt, since none of the women in this room so much as touched a needle that wasn't attached to a doctor's kit or torture device.

Percy shared a knowing look with his wife, expecting to see the Countess of Bromley track through their home any second, Bible in hand. After eight seasons and no proposals, everyone knew from experience to run and hide when Lady Bromley was within lecturing distance of the youngest Deime sibling.

Danny shook her head at her sister. "What did you do now?"

"Nothing!"

"Denise—"

"DENISE DEIME!"

The scandalous shriek had everyone in the room turning to the drawing room doors, where Lady Kendra appeared, red faced and breathing as if she'd given chase up the two flights of stairs at a cheetah's pace, in skirts.

Percy spared a glance at his sister-in-law and enjoyed a rare vision of the spirited woman blushing fiercely.

"You can't run away after that," Lady Kendra said.

Denise swallowed and failed miserably at sounding composed. "Lady Kendra, what a pleasant surprise. You know my sister, the duchess—"

"Don't give me those insipid pleasantries. I demand to know what you meant by kissing me the way you did!"

All attention went to Denise, whose face was now the color of boiled beets. "I—I . . ."

"You said you loved me," Kendra continued, eyes fixed on Denise. "Did you mean it?"

The room held its breath. Percy saw the fear in Denise's face, fear of reprisals for admitting what everyone else could plainly see.

Denise bit her lip, her eyes pleading.

Kendra would give no quarter. "Did you?"

They all waited. Denise glanced at her sister, then brother, seeing their shocked expressions widen into grins of approval.

After eight seasons, they'd all shared suspicions that Denise Deime preferred hens to cocks.

Frankly, this was long overdue.

Denise's sigh of relief was short-lived as she answered the other woman. "Yes, I meant what I said."

Kendra nodded. "Good."

She crossed the room, and in full view of the three couples—and Don—the heartless wench they'd all known as an envious-flirt-turned-spinster took Denise's face in her hands and kissed her, soundly.

Camille hooted.

Charlotte applauded.

Danny laughed.

Percy gazed in awe at the assembled band of lunatics he was honored to call his family, feeling his wife's hand slide into his.

He wrapped an arm around her shoulders and cushioned her head. "Well, I'm properly scandalized."

She smiled. "That *was* unexpected."

"You know what this means?" he whispered.

"We need to up our game?"

"Absolutely." Percy regarded Denise and Kendra as they shared shy glances next to each other on the divan, the unmistakable warmth of love in the air. "We can't allow your sister's grand spectacle to stand. What we need is a bold counter."

"Fireworks over the Thames? Knife-throwing at St. James? Pinching the new bear sculpture from Pleasure Park?"

"I was thinking of a walk through Hyde Park stark naked."

She laughed. "Your competitive spirit may very well end up in the pen, dear husband."

Percy tipped her chin up and caught his breath at the glint of mischief in her eye. Eight years after their wedding, and he still found himself at a loss for words—and a desire for a loss of clothes—when she touched him. "Any objections?"

She shook her head. "None at all. I've plenty more suggestions."

His body shivered at the innuendo in her voice. "Tell me."

Running a finger down his arm, she raised up on tiptoes to whisper a wicked image of a circus tent by the river's edge and something unimaginable with high wires.

His own trousers tenting at the erotic scene she conjured, he nipped at the sensitive lobe of her ear. "When did you concoct such a naughty fantasy?"

"After I read a *History of the Barnum and Bailey Greatest Show on Earth*."

Percy sighed. "Have I mentioned how I adore how much you read?"

She chuckled. "Glad you agree."

"Shall we begin practicing now?" he asked. "There's a narrow ledge in the maze that would do nicely."

She smiled knowingly. "This ledge wouldn't be part of a fountain, would it?"

"Perhaps."

"Hmm." She wrapped her arms around his neck and glanced at the beckoning terrace doors. "We must be careful. People have been known to spend hours lost in the maze."

"Hours, you say?" Percy ran a hand down her back, maneuvering them around furniture and away from the others still lost in the joy and distraction of Denise's budding romance. "My darling, we have a lifetime of avoiding the authorities to look forward to."

Danny grinned. "Why does that sound more appealing than it should?"

Percy rubbed his nose against hers and tickled her side with deft fingers. "Because you married a dangerous man."

Danny shook her head and laughed. "You are up to no good, sir."

He caressed her cheek and stared down into the eyes of his goddess. "Does the idea make you happy?"

"Exceedingly."

Entwining their fingers, they stepped out onto the terrace

that overlooked a greenhouse of coconut trees—a successful batch of a small variety that had survived when three other varieties had never made it past a year. Remembering those first three years of failures and his wife's endless teasing, Percy sighed.

Laughing, as if she too remembered, Danny led him down the stairs and into the hedge maze, where they lost themselves for a lifetime.

And never considered finding their way free.

Note to Readers

I admit to giving myself over to writer's prerogative, seeing as how the grand spectacle of the English football finals in 1895 was not actually played inside the Crystal Palace, but in the arena close by that shared its name. While unrealistic that the 110,000 recorded spectators would fit neatly inside a structure made of glass, it does make for a captivating setting, one I dreamed of capturing after I read Ruth Goodman's account of the sport's history in *How to Be a Victorian*.

About the Author

An educated artist, J. M. Diedrich previously worked as a freelance columnist for the Independent Observer. When she's not writing steamy kissing scenes or driving her characters into life-threatening situations, she's binge-watching anime. She lives in Minnesota with her husband and two boys.